The Way *of* Love

Books by Tracie Peterson

WILLAMETTE BRIDES
Secrets of My Heart
The Way of Love

THE TREASURES OF NOME*
Forever Hidden

BROOKSTONE BRIDES
When You Are Near
Wherever You Go
What Comes My Way

GOLDEN GATE SECRETS
In Places Hidden
In Dreams Forgotten
In Times Gone By

HEART OF THE FRONTIER
Treasured Grace
Beloved Hope
Cherished Mercy

THE HEART OF ALASKA*
In the Shadow of Denali
Out of the Ashes
Under the Midnight Sun

SAPPHIRE BRIDES
A Treasure Concealed

A Beauty Refined
A Love Transformed

BRIDES OF SEATTLE
Steadfast Heart
Refining Fire
Love Everlasting

LONE STAR BRIDES
A Sensible Arrangement
A Moment in Time
A Matter of Heart

LAND OF SHINING WATER
The Icecutter's Daughter
The Quarryman's Bride
The Miner's Lady

LAND OF THE LONE STAR
Chasing the Sun
Touching the Sky
Taming the Wind

All Things Hidden*
Beyond the Silence*
House of Secrets
Serving Up Love**

*with Kimberley Woodhouse
**with Karen Witemeyer, Regina Jennings, and Jen Turano

For a complete list of Tracie's books, visit her website
www.traciepeterson.com

The Way *of* Love

WILLAMETTE BRIDES · 2

TRACIE
PETERSON

BETHANYHOUSE

a division of Baker Publishing Group
Minneapolis, Minnesota

© 2020 by Peterson Ink, Inc.

Published by Bethany House Publishers
11400 Hampshire Avenue South
Bloomington, Minnesota 55438
www.bethanyhouse.com

Bethany House Publishers is a division of
Baker Publishing Group, Grand Rapids, Michigan

Printed in the United States of America

Library of Congress Cataloging-in-Publication Data
Names: Peterson, Tracie, author.
Title: The way of love / Tracie Peterson.
Description: Minneapolis, Minnesota: Bethany House Publishers, [2020] | Series: Willamette brides ; 2
Identifiers: LCCN 2019055493 | ISBN 9780764232282 (trade paperback) | ISBN 9780764232299 (cloth) | ISBN 9780764232305 (large print) | ISBN 9781493425112 (ebook)
Subjects: GSAFD: Love stories.
Classification: LCC PS3566.E7717 W39 2020 | DDC 813/.54—dc23
LC record available at https://lccn.loc.gov/2019055493

Unless otherwise indicated, Scripture quotations are from the King James Version of the Bible.

Scripture quotations labeled NIV are from THE HOLY BIBLE, NEW INTERNATIONAL VERSION®, NIV® Copyright © 1973, 1978, 1984, 2011 by Biblica, Inc.® Used by permission. All rights reserved worldwide.

Cover design by LOOK Design Studio
Cover photography by Aimee Christenson

20   21   22   23   24   25   26   7   6   5   4   3   2   1

For all who are suffering.
For those who feel less than worthy.
For anyone who needs to know they aren't alone.
You are loved.

"I have loved you with an everlasting love; I have drawn
you with unfailing kindness." —Jeremiah 31:3 (NIV)

CHAPTER 1

Faith Kenner looked around the room and nodded. "It's perfect. I believe I'll be very happy here."

Her cousin Nancy Carpenter went to the window and pulled up the shade. "It should be quiet here for your studies. Although the house is never all that noisy, even for a boarding-house. Except for ours, everyone else's bedrooms are upstairs. We hope to convert more downstairs rooms into bedrooms eventually, but for now, it should be peaceful."

"I can usually study without fearing disruption. My mind is like that." Faith began unpacking her trunk. "It always has been. Just give me a space to spread out my books, and I'm quite content."

"I think it's wonderful that the university has brought the medical college to Portland. It'll be nice to have you close. And the trolley is nearby and will take you right downtown to classes." Nancy ran her hand over the large armoire. She looked at her fingers as if inspecting for dust. Appearing satisfied, she turned back to Faith. "What can I do to help?"

"Nothing. I don't have all that much to unpack except for books. Father has always kept track of the number of book crates. He swears they double each time I move." Faith went to the corner where those crates had been stacked. "And, frankly, he might be right. But I need all of them. There's so much to learn." She frowned. "I don't think I have a pry bar. If you have one, I'll be able to get these open and the books put away. By the way, the shelves you provided are perfect." Faith glanced across the room at the two large mahogany bookcases against the wall.

"David, the young man who delivered your things, arranged for his father to make them. The man is positively a genius with woodworking. He's made several other pieces for the house. As for a pry bar, I'll ask David if he has one. He's out tending our horse at the moment."

"That's fine." Faith went back to the trunk and began pulling out stacks of folded clothes.

At thirty years of age, Faith was determined to be happy in life, and as long as she was practicing as a doctor, she was. She had loved helping her aunt and mother whenever they were called upon to deliver a baby, but most of all she loved going with her aunt Grace to tend the sick. Faith found it fascinating to mix various herbs and procure a remedy for whatever ailed their patient. Nancy's mother, Grace Armistead, had an uncanny knack for healing. It was a gift that her mother and grandmother also had, and now Grace proclaimed that gift had passed to Faith.

"I find it so impressive that you even want to attend college," Nancy said. "I was glad to be done with school, and much to my mother's regret, I have no interest in the healing arts."

"I was glad to be out of school too, but in this day and age, a degree and certificate from a college means a great deal to people. At least some people. Honestly, I know far more than some of

8

the younger students graduating with their certificates—and that's not just me bragging. I've been helping your mother since I was fifteen. When she called on patients, I always tried to tag along. She trained me, and I'm quite proficient, if I do say so myself." Faith laughed. "Although my professors say it too. They're always surprised when I come up with a diagnosis before testing, or a cure or treatment that they're unfamiliar with. They sometimes debate me on the usefulness of said treatment, but it usually proves right. And if for any reason it doesn't, I'm not too prideful to change my methods."

"If Mother taught it to you, I've no doubt it proves right. She has a gift, just as you said."

Faith pulled another stack of gowns from her trunk and placed them on the bed. "I'll need to press these."

"There's a laundry room just off the kitchen by the pantry. You'll find everything you need there. Or, if you want me to tend to them, I charge three cents a dress." Nancy grinned. "After all, I can't play favorites."

"Thank you, but I can manage. You've been so generous and kind. I feel at home already." Faith returned to the trunk and took out a stack of white pinafore aprons. "This is my self-designed uniform. I wear the dark dress and white apron, and I have a nicely tailored jacket to go over it all. I look very professional." She grinned at Nancy and placed the aprons beside the dresses. "Well, that's one trunk down and two to go. Plus the books. I should have plenty to keep me busy."

"Are you sure the room suits you?"

Faith glanced at the flowery wallpaper and matching drapes. "Well, it's a little more frilly than I would normally choose, but I honestly believe it will be cheerful and perhaps even inspiring. When times are difficult, it might even help me to press on."

Nancy gave her a sad look. "And are you happy, Faith?"

"What a strange question." Faith stopped and looked at her cousin. "Of course I'm happy. I'm doing what I've always wanted. You know they haven't always allowed women to attend medical school. Letting women become doctors is the stuff of my dreams. Why would you ask?"

"I just think it's a pity you don't feel you can marry and settle down with a family."

Faith shrugged. This was a matter that had been discussed at length with her parents. "God calls some to remain single. I've always figured, given my heritage, that He's planned that for me. Of course, I suppose something could happen to change the laws. Or maybe I'll find a handsome man like Uncle Adam who is part Indian, and he won't mind that I'm half Cayuse."

"Do you think about it a lot?"

"Being half Native?"

Nancy nodded. "I mean that . . . and how your mother was held hostage when the Indians massacred the men at the Whitman Mission. When I finally heard the truth of what happened there, it was all I could think about for a long time. I still think about it sometimes. How awful it would be to be forced to . . . be intimate against your will."

Faith sat down on the end of the bed. "I know. I think about it from time to time. I can't imagine my poor mother learning that she was with child. It would have been terrible for others to find out, and I can't believe she was the only one who ended up in that condition."

"You truly think there were others?"

"As I understand it, every woman and girl over the age of twelve was imposed upon during that month of captivity. My mother couldn't have been the only one to conceive. The women involved just don't dare to talk about it. Not even among themselves. It would have been, and still is, considered the height of disgrace to bear a child who is even part Indian. And those who did no doubt freed themselves of that baby as soon as possible.

"I think Mother did the only sensible thing by going to live with Isaac and Eletta Browning far from Oregon City and all of their friends. It saved my mother and her family the embarrassment of having to explain. The Brownings became my first parents, and I loved them dearly. I love too that they were missionaries and that I grew up with the Native people along the Rogue River. It was a wonderful thing for me—especially since I'm half Native. Although the tribes are vastly different."

"Do you ever feel concerned about passing yourself as white?" Nancy asked, then looked mortified. "I'm sorry. Of course you're white too."

"Don't be upset. I think about that all the time. Am I living a lie to call myself white? After all, I am half of each, so I don't think it's wrong to choose one over the other. Although I know I am living the life that is easier, given all the government has done to the Indians." Faith lowered her head. "Some of my happiest days were living with the Indians, but I know that life is gone forever. I talked to Aunt Mercy about working with them on the reservation, but she said it wouldn't be the life I used to know and that if I was going to do it only for that reason, I shouldn't come."

"But you still talk about being a doctor on the reservation."

"Yes." Faith looked up and smiled. "I want to help the people there. I don't want them thinking everyone is against them. They get so little care, and while they do have their own healers, I could offer something different. So I wouldn't be going there just to reclaim my childhood memories."

"Would you tell them you're half Indian?"

Faith often asked herself that same question. Half-breeds

weren't very well received by either race. "I don't know. If I had to choose today, then I'd say no. I want to do as much good as I can, and I don't think I can accomplish it being Indian. Neither side would be inclined to accept me into their circles if they knew the truth."

"Well, I suppose you're right on that account." Nancy moved toward the door. "You have a few hours before supper. I'll let David know you need a pry bar. I think he's still here, tending the horse." She paused and smiled. "I'm really glad you've come to live with us, Faith."

"I am too."

Nancy had just finished setting the table when her sister-in-law, Clementine Carpenter, entered the dining room followed by Nancy's brother, Gabe. Nancy had shared a friendship with Clementine since childhood, and Nancy's husband had been best friends with Gabe.

"One more for supper?" Gabe asked with a devilish grin.

"Of course. I didn't know you were in town. I'll fetch another place setting. What have you two been up to?"

Gabe moved toward her. "We'll tell you all about it at supper." He kissed the top of her head.

Clementine followed Nancy into the kitchen. "I'll help you finish up. Is Mimi home?"

Mimi Bryant and Clementine worked at the small private school just a few blocks away. Mimi was the perfect boarder, a Christian widow who was just approaching the one-year mark of having lost her husband. She was outgoing despite her season of mourning and always helpful.

"She returned nearly an hour ago. I figured you had probably gone shopping. Little did I think my brother would be in town." Nancy gave her friend a teasing look.

"He just got in this afternoon. He said he wanted to surprise us. He showed up at the school and took me for a little drive." They gathered the food Nancy had prepared and took it into the dining room. "Mmm, this smells so good. Fish stew?"

"Yes. I thought for this cold day it would be just the thing."

"Did your cousin arrive?"

Nancy placed a platter of sourdough bread on the table. "She did. She's in the downstairs bedroom just beyond the sewing room." She headed back to the kitchen to pick up a bowl of peas and potatoes, as well as the butter crock.

Clementine glanced around the kitchen. "Do you want me to bring the cake?"

"No. We'll get it after everyone's eaten. I don't think there will be room on the table otherwise. But if you don't mind, please bring the coffeepot."

"Got it."

They stepped into the dining room just as Mimi and Faith were taking their seats on the far side of the table by the sideboard. Gabe was chatting with Faith about the farm, but Nancy didn't hear what was being said because Seth chose that moment to make his entrance.

Nancy put the food on the table and went to her husband for a kiss. "I've missed you."

"Not nearly as much as I missed you." Seth embraced her and kissed her tenderly. "Handling legal cases isn't half as much fun as being here in your arms."

"Handling me, eh?" Nancy raised her brow and grinned.

Her brother tossed a linen napkin at them. "Knock it off, you two. I'm starved."

"Gabe, you haven't missed a meal since you were born." Nancy sighed and separated herself from her husband. "But I agree. Let's eat while it's still hot."

"Is Mrs. Weaver coming down to join us?" Clementine asked.

Mimi shook her head. "No, Nancy already took her a tray. I stopped to check on her, and she said she was just fine."

Clementine placed the pot of coffee beside Gabe. "She's such a sweet old woman. I wish she felt more open to joining us."

"She's made great progress since she first arrived last summer." Nancy allowed Seth to help her into her chair. "In time I'm sure she'll be dining with us more and more."

Seth took his seat. "I'll bless the food, and we can begin."

Gabe helped Clementine with her chair. "The aroma's so grand, it's almost as good as eating."

Nancy glanced heavenward. "Then I won't serve you any food, and you can just sit and sniff all you like."

"Hardly, sister dear." Gabe threw her a wink. "I happen to know you're an amazing cook."

"The sooner I pray, the sooner we eat." Seth bowed his head, not waiting to see if Gabe heeded his comment. "Father, we thank you for this abundance and for the hands that prepared our meal. Bless all who live here and those who visit. Amen."

"Amen," the others murmured in unison.

Nancy handed her bowl to Seth. "If you pass your bowls around the table, I think it will be easier than trying to pass the stew. As you can see, I used my very largest tureen. Seth can fill each bowl and pass them on. Meanwhile, we can pass around the bread and butter and peas and potatoes."

It wasn't long before everyone was amply served. Nancy couldn't help but sigh. She loved managing the boardinghouse. It gave her a sense of satisfaction that she couldn't explain.

Everyone dug into the meal with gusto and complimented her as they ate. She knew she was a good cook but appreciated hearing it from her guests. Seeing that everyone was content, she picked up her spoon and began to eat.

"How's everyone back home?" Seth asked.

"Doing good." Gabe picked up a knife and buttered his bread. "They're doing a lot of fence repair before winter sets in fully. Pa wanted everything done well before Christmas so that Mama would relax. But you know her."

Seth nodded. "Well enough. I don't think any of the women in your family sit still for long."

"Except for Meg. She would sit and read all day long if she could."

Nancy smiled at this. Their little sister was always borrowing books from the library, even though the selection was limited. She didn't care if it was a novel or a studious text.

"Are you all planning to come home for Christmas?" Gabe asked before stuffing a good portion of the bread in his mouth.

Seth shook his head. "I'm not sure. It's hard to get away from work. A lot of folks want to straighten out legal matters at the end of the year, and this year has been no exception. Nevertheless, we hope to be there."

"Well, I know they'd love to see you. Clementine and I are both planning to go back." Gabe turned and grinned at the redheaded woman beside him. "Especially now."

Nancy looked up. "Why especially now?"

Clementine's cheeks flushed as she turned to Gabe and grinned. "Because we're engaged."

"You are?" Seth looked at Nancy. "Did you know about this?"

She shook her head. "Not at all."

"I stopped by your folks' place before coming to Portland.

I asked your father's permission to marry Clementine, and he eagerly agreed. He was so quick about it," Gabe said, giving his bride-to-be an endearing glance, "that I feared perhaps something was wrong with her that I hadn't yet learned."

Seth shook his head, smiling. "No, I'm sure it was their desire to have another Armistead in the family. No one has a better name in the community than your family. Your folks' reputation alone would be enough reason to want her to marry you."

Gabe's brows came together. "Hey, I was kind of hoping it was because they wanted me as a son-in-law."

Seth laughed. "I'm sure it was. I know I'm delighted. Brother and sister married to brother and sister. That will simplify things. Our children will be double cousins."

Nancy sipped her soup and listened to them go on about the future. She was thrilled by the news and could clearly see how happy Gabe was about the situation.

"Where will you live?" Seth asked.

"I talked to the family about that. Pa wants me to take charge of the sawmill here in Portland, so I guess we'll be living here."

Nancy was delighted at this prospect. Over the last few months, she and Clementine had renewed their childhood friendship, and Nancy hated the idea of losing her so soon. "How wonderful! I'm so happy to hear that. I will enjoy having you close by. Perhaps we can attend events together."

"When will this wedding take place?" Seth's question caused all gazes to turn toward the happy couple.

"We neither one feel the need for a long engagement," Gabe replied, looking to Clementine for her confirmation.

She nodded. "We thought maybe in the spring. Perhaps May. We just figured a small collection of family in Oregon City would suffice."

"Once all of our family gathers in one place, it won't be small by any means," Gabe teased.

"That sounds wonderful." Nancy calculated quickly. "That should give us plenty of time to create a beautiful wedding dress and veil."

Clementine seemed surprised. "Are you offering to help do that?"

"I am." Nancy smiled and passed the platter of bread around again. "It's the least I can do for my dear friend. We'll start planning out what you want immediately. I'm sure Mrs. Weaver would be happy to help as well. She's quite talented with a needle."

"I'd like to help too," Faith said. Until now she'd been rather quiet. "I'm not that gifted at sewing, but I'm sure I can help in some way."

"Of course." Clementine couldn't seem to stop smiling. "The more, the merrier."

That night as Faith took inventory of her new room, she sighed in satisfaction to find her things were in order. Seth had just removed the last of the trunks and crates, and the room looked even larger than before. It was certainly larger than the room she had shared with three other girls down in Salem.

Faith went to the desk that stood beneath one of two windows. Atop it sat the black doctor's bag her parents had given her. She ran her hand over the soft leather and smiled. She was doing what she wanted to do. She was studying to become a doctor so she could truly help people. Perhaps one day she would work on or near the reservation and offer her services to the Native people. But as much as this appealed to her, she couldn't help feeling a little envious of her cousin Gabe and his engagement.

All of her life, she had longed for someone to love that way. But from the time she'd been old enough to share such thoughts with her mother, Faith had had to face the very real situation of her circumstances. It was illegal for her to marry a white man. She was half Indian, and such marriages were forbidden.

"But what if I just break the law?" she'd once asked her mother.

"Would you want to put the person you love at risk with the law? Would you sacrifice their well-being because of your selfish desires? If so, that isn't love."

Faith had carried that conversation close to her heart. She knew her birth—her very existence—had come from cruel circumstances. It wasn't her fault that it had happened, but it was a part of who she was. She couldn't change it and was just fortunate that she could pass for white, or the entirety of her world would be different.

She looked again at the black bag and thought about her previous conversation with Nancy. God did call many people to remain single. If that was His calling for her, then Faith would accept it and move forward.

Running her hand along the side of the bag, she smiled again. "This is where my future will be. This is who I am and who I will continue to be. It will be enough. It must be enough."

CHAPTER 2

I'm so glad you decided to travel to Oregon City with us," Clementine told Faith. "Gabe always finds someone to go off and talk to. I swear he's never met a stranger."

Faith laughed. "I remember that about him and his brother. In fact, I think most of the family was that way except Nancy. She always kept to herself. Especially after their youngest brother died."

"I know. We were good friends, but she changed after that." Clementine looked over the boat's railing at the Willamette River below. "I missed her joy so much. I'm glad to see it's returned."

"Your brother did that." Before Faith could say more, she heard a scuffle. It seemed to be coming from the deck above them. "Sounds like a fight." She tucked her black bag under one arm and moved toward the stairs. Where there were fights, there were usually injuries.

"Faith, wait. Maybe you shouldn't go without Gabe."

"I don't have time to chase down Gabe. Someone could be hurt."

When she stepped onto the upper deck, she could see that

she was right. A bearded, dark-haired man clutched his forearm while two other men held back a big, burly man. A bloody knife lay at the feet of the large man, and an old Indian man sat on a straight-backed chair just outside the wheelhouse.

"A man shouldn't have to work on the same boat as a dirty Injun," the large man said.

"You knew I had people of color working for me when you hired on," the bearded man replied.

"Yes, but not Injuns."

"I'm the captain, and I decide who works for me and who doesn't. As it happens, this man has more right to be here than you do. He's worked for me for many years." The bearded man glanced down at his wound, then back up at the men who held the big man. "Take him below until he cools off."

"Yes, Captain. Should we lock him up?"

"No. He'll settle down once he thinks about what he's done. I'll put you off at the next town. Whether or not I summon the police, I'll consider this your resignation." The captain held up his wounded arm.

The big man grumbled but calmed as they led him away. Apparently the thought of jail time was sobering.

Faith raised a brow and looked at the bleeding man. "You're the captain?"

He grimaced. "I am. Do you have a problem, Miss . . . Missus . . . ?"

"Miss." Faith nodded toward his arm. "I do have a problem with that. I need to get you somewhere so I can examine your arm. It's probably going to need stitches, from the looks of it."

"Are you a doctor?" he asked, his voice skeptical.

"I am." Faith gave him a smile. "And I'll soon be fully certi-fied for surgery. I've been helping healers and midwives since I was fifteen and have sewn up more than my fair share of cuts." She held up her bag. "I even have all my tools with me. Now, where can we go?"

He hesitated a moment. "I've never been tended by a woman doctor."

"And I've never watched a man bleed to death." Faith smiled as though they were discussing nothing more critical than the weather. "Well, I take that back. One time when I was sixteen, Mr. Petey cut his leg with an ax. We almost lost him because of his stubborn attitude. Later, that leg festered something awful, and I thought we'd have to cut it off—"

"Fine!" the captain interrupted. "Come into the wheelhouse, and I'll let you take a look." He looked a little green.

"Faith, what's going on?" Gabe asked as he and Clementine reached the top of the stairs.

"There was a fight, and the captain is injured. I'm just going to treat his arm. Nothing to concern yourselves with. I'll meet you in the saloon when I'm finished."

She followed the captain into the wheelhouse. He was already seated on a high stool. He had shed his coat and was rolling up his bloody sleeve.

He turned to the young man at the wheel. "You've got the helm a little longer, Denny. It would seem I need some medical attention." Turning back to Faith, he frowned. "Close the door. It's cold enough in here."

"You're cold from loss of blood. There's quite a pool of it out there." Faith opened her bag. "I need hot water, a basin, and some towels and washcloths. Do you have them?"

"I do." His tone was pained as he grabbed his arm to stem the flow of blood. "You saw the old man sitting outside the door?"

"I did."

"You can ask him for those things."

Faith nodded and opened the door once again. She spied the old Indian man on his knees, already cleaning up the blood. "Excuse me. I wonder if you could help me."

He smiled up at her. "I can help. What you need?"

"Hot water, a clean basin. Make sure it's clean. And a couple of towels and several washcloths. I need them rather quickly."

The old man nodded and jumped up as if he were decades younger than his gray hair suggested. He hurried away without another word.

Faith returned to the captain. He looked pale, and she feared he was going into shock. "Is there somewhere you can lie down? I don't want you fainting off that chair."

"I won't faint," he growled. "Just do what you have to do."

The wheelhouse door opened moments later, and the Indian held up a pot of water that he'd placed inside an enamel basin. Beneath this, he had a stack of towels.

Faith motioned him inside. "Just set it here." She pushed aside several navigation charts.

The old man did as she instructed, being careful to deposit the towels first. Once the hot water was secured, he pulled several folded washcloths from inside his shirt. "These clean. Towels clean too."

"Thank you so much."

"He gonna be all right?" He looked to the captain.

"I think so, but I haven't had a chance to examine him. Could you please step out of the room? We're a bit crowded in here."

The old man nodded and left.

She turned back to the captain, who watched her with great interest. "Now, let's get you cleaned up." She took one of the towels and spread it out on the countertop. "Place your arm on this but keep pinching the wound closed as you are doing until I get the water and washcloths ready." She reached into her bag and pulled out a large bottle of the solution her aunt Grace had taught her to make. The infusion contained vinegar and herbs.

"What's that?" the captain asked.

She smiled. "It's better than soap for cleaning out a wound. I carry it everywhere."

Once her things were gathered and placed where she could get to them easily, Faith cleaned her needles and silk and then started cleaning the long gash in the captain's arm. The cut was about four inches long and deeper at the point of entry.

"What was the fight about?" she asked, hoping to keep the captain's mind on something other than the sewing she was about to begin.

"You've probably already figured that out."

"I heard the part about the man not wanting to work on the same boat as an Indian. He ought to be grateful he has a job. Nevertheless, his opinion seems to match up with most folks'. Sad though that may be." She put some gauze on part of the wound to absorb the steady flow of blood.

"So you don't mind being on the same boat with a 'dirty Injun'?"

Faith smiled. If he only knew. "I didn't think the man was particularly dirty, and a person can hardly be blamed for their heritage, although others would disagree with me on that account." She picked up her needle and paused over the open end of the wound. "I'm going to start sewing."

"Then get to it." His impatience was clear. "Denny will have us all the way to Milwaukie before you finish."

Faith stuck the needle into his arm. He jumped, and she smiled. "Sorry. I tried to warn you."

"You are an aggravating woman," he said between clenched teeth.

"I've heard that before. Usually from ill-tempered men." She tied off the first stitch and continued to the second. "We haven't been formally introduced. I'm Faith Kenner. And you are?"

"Andrew Gratton. Captain of the *Morning Star*." He was a little calmer.

"I'm pleased to meet you. Honored, really."

"Why?"

"Because few men would stand up for an Indian. I find that admirable."

"You do?" He looked surprised.

She tied off another stitch. "I do. I believe all people have value."

"Most whites don't see Indians as people."

Faith shrugged. "That's their mistake." She moved the gauze and continued her stitching. "I have to have compassion on them as well. Perhaps the man who cut you lost family to Indians. I have no way of knowing, but I do know that hate is a powerful adversary. It poses as a friend, or at least a sympathizer, but it always leads to destruction. I'm always glad when I meet a man or woman who thinks otherwise."

"As a Christian man, I am called upon to love others as Christ loved them." He raised his gaze to hers.

Faith momentarily lost herself in his dark brown eyes. The anger that was there earlier had been replaced with something else. She realized she was forgetting herself and got back to work. "My faith in God is important to me as well. I was raised with folks who shared the gospel with the Tututni people on the Rogue River. I grew up with them and had many friends there, and I believe God has given me a gift of healing. I would like to work with the Indians again one day."

"So you think you're gifted?"

"I do. I have cared for a great many patients."

"Ever lost one?"

"Yes." She thought of the dozen or so she'd attended at death. "Usually they were old, but there were a few who went well before they should have. Most of those were accidents, but there was a case or two of disease that was just too far gone." She pushed those sad thoughts aside. "But overall, when my patients are obedient and do as I direct, they heal quite nicely."

"I suppose only time will tell if that's the case." The gruffness in his voice had returned.

Faith smiled. The captain was so easy to tease. "I generally get few complaints."

He grunted at the next stitch. "Tell me more about your upbringing. It sounds unusual."

"It was. We lived along the Rogue River in the south coastal region of the state. The Tututni were a peaceful people and lived in these wonderful houses they dug halfway down into the earth. I thought them such great fun. You had to crawl down a little ladder to go into the house." She told him about the school they had for the children and the games she learned to play. "Then the Rogue River Indian wars began, and many of my friends were killed. We had to leave the area. The government moved the people to Grand Ronde Reservation, and I never saw most of them again."

"Why was that?"

"They died. Some said it was from diseases brought about by living so close together. Others said the white man had poisoned them. But I think it was mostly heartbreak. Their hearts had broken and couldn't be mended." The memories made her sad, and Faith had to fight to hold back tears.

"I'm sorry. That must be difficult for you."

"Yes, but I know those who've passed on went to a better place. Many of the Tututni had accepted Jesus as Savior and put their hope in Him for the future. I know I'll see them again."

She worked in silence for several minutes, then tied off the final stitch.

"There. You'll have to be careful for a while." She pulled a roll of bandages from her bag. "I'll wrap the arm, but try to keep it dry, and in a couple of weeks, get someone to take out the stitches. If you have to take them out yourself, get a pair of tweezers and pull up on the knot, clip one side, and pull the thread through. But leave them in for at least ten days." She made short work of wrapping the arm, then tore the bandage strip down the middle and tied it off in a knot. "Oh, and keep it clean."

"I'll do just that, but how can I wash it off and keep it dry at the same time?"

She smiled. "Well, you can wipe it down with this." She handed him the bottle containing the vinegar solution. "Then dry it thoroughly. Even let it air out for a short time before re-wrapping it. But only do this if it's dirty. If you keep it wrapped and dry, you should be just fine. You should probably buy some bandages or make some."

"We have plenty here on board. I'll see to it."

Faith gathered her things and put them back in her bag. "There. You can go back to barking out orders, but you might want to get something to eat and drink first. It will help with the blood loss." She headed for the door, avoiding the chance to look into his eyes again.

"Miss Kenner."

She turned back and met his gaze despite herself. "Yes?"

"I guess in time we shall know if you're truly gifted or just full of yourself."

Nodding, Faith turned away with a grin. "You're welcome."

"I wasn't expecting to see you and Uncle Adam." Faith embraced her aunt Mercy Browning. "What a wonderful surprise."

"We just finished meetings with the state Indian officials yesterday in Portland," Mercy replied, brushing back loose strands of hair that fell across Faith's face. "We intended to stop by and see if Nancy had room to put us up at the boardinghouse, but Adam found out a boat was leaving immediately for Oregon City, and we hurried to catch it instead. We figured we could see Nancy on our way home."

"I'm living at her boardinghouse now. The medical college transferred its classes to Portland."

"That's wonderful. You'll be much closer to home."

"A fact that we are very pleased with," Faith's mother, Hope Kenner, declared.

Mercy nodded. "I can well imagine. How we've missed you. It seems like just yesterday we were all together with the Tututni."

"I know. I was just telling the captain of our boat about the Tututni and my time there."

"Whatever prompted that?" Faith's mother asked.

"He was injured defending an old Indian man. I was sewing up his arm and wanted to keep his mind occupied, so I started talking about my life on the Rogue River."

Aunt Grace entered the front sitting room with a huge tray of refreshments. "I thought you all might need to warm up with a little mint tea. I've also made muffins."

Faith noted the orange tint to the muffins. "Ooh, are these the muffins with orange, pineapple, and carrots and coconut?"

"Along with a few other ingredients," Grace said.

Faith reached for one as soon as the tray was on the table. "I love these. Oh my, they're still warm."

Grace smiled. "You said you had to stitch the captain's arm. Was he surprised to have a female doctor?"

"I think he was. But even more surprised that I don't hate Indians." Faith sampled the frosted muffin and smiled. "This is so good, Aunt Grace. I'd forgotten just how good. I love all the nuts you've put in. Does Nancy have this recipe?"

"I'm not sure, since I didn't start making these until about ten years ago." Grace poured tea into each of the china cups she'd brought. "Since we can so readily get pineapple and coconut from the Hawaiian Islands, I've experimented by putting all sorts of things in the batter. It's a different kind of fruitcake."

"Well, Nancy needs to make these for the boardinghouse ladies."

"She might have the recipe, but in case she doesn't, I'll write it down for you to take back. Nancy's so creative with recipes that she may have already come up with one of her own. She's really a much better cook than I am."

"I don't know that I would say that, but she is a very good cook. The boarders love her." Faith took another bite of the muffin.

"I can understand why. Goodness, getting three delicious meals a day and having a wonderful house like Nancy's to live in would be such a comfort," Mercy replied. "I'm sure you enjoy not having to cook for yourself, Faith."

"I do. Cooking is not my strong suit. Mama tried her best to teach me, but it just didn't take." Faith gave her mother a grin. "I'm better at cooking up medicinal concoctions."

"Everyone has their talents," Aunt Mercy declared.

"Your uncanny understanding of the body and illness more than makes up for that," Mother declared. "Don't worry that you can't cook. You are a great healer, and people will appreciate you for that. You can always hire a cook."

They chuckled at this.

"But a husband will expect a good wife to cook," Meg, Nancy's younger sister, said as she came into the room to join the ladies.

The laughter and smiles faded. Faith hid her frown by pretending to sip from her teacup. Meg hadn't yet been told about Faith and Hope's past.

"Meg, why don't you play us a song on the piano?" Grace suggested.

The girl all but danced to the instrument and sat down. "Do you want me to play hymns or classical? I just learned a Schubert piece."

"That will do nicely," her mother replied.

Meg threw herself into playing the song. Faith closed her eyes for a moment and imagined herself sailing on the ocean. When she'd come to Oregon City with Adam and Mercy after being evacuated from the Rogue River area, she had voyaged on a ship up the coast. It had been the most difficult time of her life. She had just lost the man and woman she knew as her parents. She hadn't even been given time to grieve. Everything she knew and loved had been stripped away. This song's haunting strains along with her conversation with Captain Gratton made her memories surface.

"When will Gabe be here?" Mercy asked, bringing Faith back around to the moment.

"He told me to tell Aunt Grace he'd be here for supper, along with Clementine," Faith answered.

"I'm so happy for those two. They are a perfect fit." Aunt Grace reached for the teapot. "More?" She glanced at each woman, but everyone seemed satisfied. "I remember once when Gabe was helping Clementine out of a tree. They were very young, and she and Nancy had gotten themselves stuck. Alex and I watched helplessly while Gabe climbed up to them. As he was bringing Clementine down, Alex said, 'Wouldn't it be something if those two married? We might get redheaded grandchildren.' Now here we are with them engaged."

The ladies chuckled and continued talking about their family for quite a while. Faith enjoyed hearing about her cousins and what they were doing, especially when it came to Mercy and Adam's daughter, Constance. Faith hadn't seen Constance in some time. She'd left the area to attend Mount Vernon Seminary in Washington, D.C.

"Connie will be coming home to us after her graduation in late May," Mercy shared. "I will be so happy to see her. We haven't seen her in all these years, and while she has been faithful to write, I miss her more than I can say."

"Of course you do. She's your only daughter," Hope said, reaching over to give her sister's hand a squeeze. "Is she coming back to live at the reservation?"

"I hope so. She told me about some program in Washington, D.C., that has to do with cataloging Indian life on the reservations. She's hoping to get involved because of her close ties. Her desire is to be assigned to the cataloging group coming to Oregon."

"I'm sure that would be perfect for your family. Speaking of which—how is Isaac?" Faith had last seen her cousin Isaac several years ago when the Brownings came to the farm for a respite from their work. He was nearly eighteen at the time and planned to go to college back east. Otherwise she knew very little about what he was doing.

"Isaac is doing great. College didn't appeal to him, so he's back with us. He's at the reservation right now, helping Mr. Singleton manage in our absence. I think the simpler life agrees with him. He's actually considering sheep farming. The land there is perfect for it."

"Well, we can certainly help him with that," Hope declared. "We're expecting quite a few lambs come spring, and we have several rams we were planning to sell. I'm sure we could set him up with a small herd of his own."

Mercy smiled. "That would be wonderful."

"I'd love to see him again. I hate that we've all grown up and never see one another." Faith stretched as the clock chimed four.

"Goodness, where has the time gone?" Grace got to her feet. "Meg, that's enough music for now. We need to get dinner on. Your father will be home soon."

"Your father too," Hope said, glancing at Faith. "And I imagine your brother Brandon is already home from school and through with his chores, which means he's going through the house looking for food. Let's go stop him before he gets into the cake I prepared for supper."

Most of their evening meals were shared, so Faith knew it wouldn't be difficult to put together a grand feast in no time at all. She smiled as the women launched themselves into action. This was the homelife she missed and loved. There was such a sense of unity and harmony—of family. The only family she would ever have.

CHAPTER 3

Faith gathered with some of her fellow students in the small medical library to discuss their last class. The trip home to Oregon City had refreshed her, but now she felt eager to get back to her studies.

"I believe this class on infectious diseases is going to be one of my favorites," Malcom Digby announced. "I'm intrigued by the causes and cures, aren't you?" He fixed a smile on Faith. "Is it not absolutely fascinating that starting with a simple sore throat, the infection can become scarlet fever and then rheumatic fever if not treated early?"

"It is." Faith returned his smile. "If we can figure out what causes such things, then perhaps we can develop a cure or preventative measure, as they have done with smallpox."

Violet Caprice planted a large bag on top of the study table. She rubbed her upper arms. "I've developed new strength from carrying all this stuff around, if nothing else."

Faith smiled at the very plain young lady. "I've often thought the same thing. Juggling books and a bag, as well as anything else that comes my way, has strengthened my arms in ways that remind me of when I helped my folks with the sheep."

Two additional young men joined them. "I hope someone will explain the reading we had for chemistry. It's my worst subject," George Zufelt said in such a dejected manner that Faith couldn't help feeling sorry for him.

"We can have a study session on it at three today, if you like," she said.

He perked up. "I'd like that very much."

"I would too," Violet declared. "I just want to make sure I'm understanding it correctly."

"I wouldn't mind being there," Lewis Kent said, taking a seat at the table.

"Let's meet after dissection class. We'll be frozen after spending time over the livery stables," Faith suggested. "We could see about getting the back room at Mrs. Madison's café. It has that big stove that she always keeps full of coal."

They all nodded in agreement.

"Oh, and I wanted to let you know that our discussion about hosting fundraisers to provide medication for the Indian reservation was met with wholehearted approval by my aunt and uncle."

"I'm excited to be a part of it," Malcolm declared. "If the government can't or won't provide the needed medicines, then the public must step up with charitable contributions."

"I agree," Lewis Kent added. "I like the idea of hosting informative events where people can learn about helping. With donations of money and goods, life on the reservation is certain to improve."

Dr. Harvey, the man who taught classes on the diseases of women and children—the very one whose lecture they had just come from—entered the library. "Students, I'd like you to meet some of your supporters," he announced with a smile.

Faith had claimed a seat at the table but rose to greet their guests. Two men accompanied her professor. One was dark-haired and quite handsome, while the other was older and looked more distinguished.

"Gentlemen, this is a portion of our 1880 graduating class. Students, this gentleman is Samuel Lakewood." Dr. Harvey motioned to the older man. "And this is Gerome Berkshire." The men gave a slight nod. "I was just giving them a tour."

Faith had heard of Berkshire from Nancy. She'd been told more than once that he was not to be trusted. Not only that, but he made no secret of his hatred for people of color.

"I'm pleased to meet you all," Mr. Lakewood declared. "I have long been an avid supporter of our medical college." He smiled at Violet and Faith. "And its inclusion of women."

"These are the best of this year's class," Dr. Harvey continued. "Faith Kenner in particular has shown the greatest promise."

"That is merely due to my experience," Faith demurred. "My aunt and to some degree my mother were practicing healers, and I learned a great deal by their side."

"There is nothing quite so fine as seeing families pass knowledge down to their young. Still, I'm sure you have been challenged by your academic work here with the university," Mr. Lakewood said.

Faith nodded. "Indeed, I have. I am most grateful for this education and have learned so much. The professors here are quite learned and equally gifted in teaching."

"Well, that is good to hear," Lakewood replied, smiling. "After all, my donations to this society would seem ill-used otherwise."

"Then, fear not," Malcolm declared, getting into the conversation. "This school is the best in the land. I believe it would rival any back east." He extended his hand. "Malcolm Digby."

"Have you personal knowledge of the schools back east?" Mr. Lakewood asked, shaking the younger man's hand.

Malcolm's chest puffed out a bit. "I do. I began my studies there and moved west with my family."

"So you're married?"

"No." He flushed a bit. "I moved here with my mother and father and three brothers. My siblings are much younger, and my parents had need of me."

"Admirable indeed, sir." Lakewood nodded.

Dr. Harvey interrupted. "If you'll excuse us, we were about to have tea in my office."

"Oh, do invite the students to join us," Lakewood more commanded than requested. "I'd like to hear more about their studies."

Harvey seemed surprised by the request but wasn't going to refuse the request of a donor. "Do join us, students. If you have the time."

"I can come," Malcolm said, grinning from ear to ear.

Faith considered her schedule. "I suppose I can join you for a short time as well."

The others declined, having projects that required their attention. They seemed as disinterested as Faith felt. Only Malcolm remained enthusiastic.

"You may leave your things here," Dr. Harvey instructed. "We shall be just across the hall in my office."

Dr. Harvey led the way, stopping only long enough to ask his secretary to bring refreshments for two more.

"I must say, this is quite fortuitous, getting to meet you," Gerome Berkshire said, coming alongside Faith and stopping her just inside the office door. "I believe you are related to my friend Nancy Pritchard. Oh dear. I should correct myself.

Nancy Carpenter. I believe she remarried very shortly after her husband's death."

Faith heard the disapproval in his tone. "Yes, Nancy is my cousin. We're quite close." She hoped her tone made it clear that she wouldn't brook any insult to Nancy.

"Of course," he said, smiling. "It seems that your family are all very close. I have enjoyed my own special relationship with your cousin."

"From what I've been told, your relationship was with her first husband. You were business partners—at least from time to time."

Berkshire sobered. "Yes, Albert Pritchard was a dear friend. He was like a brother, really."

"I'm sure his loss was difficult for you, Mr. Berkshire."

"Call me Gerome, as Nancy does." He smiled. "I should like for us to be very close friends. Perhaps even more. Perhaps you would allow me to accompany you to the opera on Friday."

Faith was surprised at how quickly he'd maneuvered the conversation into an unwelcome personal invitation. She glanced across the room to where Malcolm was doing his best to juggle a cup and saucer and entertain Dr. Harvey and Mr. Lakewood. For once she envied her friend.

"I'm afraid, Mr. Berkshire, that I am rather devoted to my work."

"But surely a beautiful woman such as yourself longs for other things as well."

"What I long for is far too personal a matter to be discussed with a stranger."

"But that is my point, Miss Kenner. I'd like for us to be friends and no longer strangers."

Faith knew from Nancy that Berkshire possessed a persistence that edged well into inappropriateness. Still, she didn't wish to make a scene.

"I believe my God-given calling is to be a doctor," she said after a moment of silence. "I've felt that way since I was young. To be called by God to such an important matter means a great deal to me and must remain my heart and driving focus. I am sorry to disappoint you, Mr. Berkshire."

"I would love for you to join us, Miss Kenner," Mr. Lakewood called, casting a knowing look at Berkshire. "You too, Gerome."

She smiled and sighed in relief. Berkshire was every bit as obnoxious and pushy as Nancy had described.

"Miss Kenner," Mr. Lakewood said as she joined them and accepted a cup of tea, "I was just telling these gentlemen that my wife is hosting a tea next Wednesday. I believe she and her friends would love to hear about your endeavors to become a surgeon. Would you consider coming to speak to them? It would be at three in the afternoon."

Faith smiled. Lakewood struck her as quite the gentleman. "I would be honored, sir."

She looked at Dr. Harvey, who nodded with a wide smile. "I told you she would be delighted," he said, sounding quite excited.

Faith hid her smile in her teacup. Anything to please a donor.

Later, after supper, Faith sat in the front parlor with the others at the boardinghouse. She had shared her adventures and the honor of being asked to the Lakewoods' home. Nancy said very little until everyone else had gone to bed.

"I'm sorry Seth was tied up this evening," Faith said. "Would you like me to keep you company until he returns?"

Nancy shook her head. "No, but there is something I need to say."

"Then speak. You know we needn't have secrets between us."

The look on her cousin's face suggested otherwise. "Gerome Berkshire is bad news. He's a dangerous man who hates the Indians and anyone of color. I know I've told you this before, but you should avoid him at all costs. Lakewood is no better when it comes to prejudices."

Faith could hear hesitation in her cousin's voice. "But this is about something more, isn't it?"

Nancy lowered her head and appeared to stare at the sewing in her lap. "There is something else. I told you about Seth originally coming to Portland to investigate my husband. And you know that Gerome was occasionally involved with my husband's affairs. I don't know all of the details, but he and Albert worked with others to supply guns and liquor to the Indians. Lakewood is also involved."

"I just had a conversation on this very subject with Aunt Mercy when I was back at the farm. At least regarding guns and liquor. She said she and Uncle Adam are very frustrated by the amount of whiskey being consumed by the tribes on their reservation. They have no idea who is bringing the stuff in. They're out in the middle of nowhere, and it would take great effort to carry in those goods."

Nancy raised her head. "I think it was probably my late husband who aided this tragedy. You can't tell anyone, however. The investigation is continuing, although Seth is no longer involved. Gerome learned of his participation and became suspicious of Seth. When it was clear Seth's involvement wasn't as useful, the authorities removed him from the investigation. They have, in turn, encouraged Gerome to spy for them. I'm sure he isn't loyal to the army or the government, but he gives the pretense of serving their cause, and that in turn allows them to keep an eye on Gerome."

Someone opened the front door. Nancy stiffened, and Faith saw momentary fear in her expression.

"Hello?" It was Seth, and Nancy relaxed.

"We're in the front parlor," she announced.

He came from the foyer, absent his hat. "Good evening, wife." He kissed the top of Nancy's head, then smiled at Faith. "And cousin."

Nancy didn't smile, and Faith found herself frowning. "Good evening."

"What's going on with you two?" he asked. Neither spoke, which only prompted a rewording of his question. "Someone better tell me what you have been discussing."

"I'm afraid I caused a bit of a problem," Faith declared. "I was just telling Nancy about being introduced to Gerome Berkshire and Samuel Lakewood today at school. Mr. Berkshire was rather persistent that I share an evening out with him. The conversation led us back to a warning Nancy once gave me about Berkshire."

"How much do you know?" Seth met Faith's gaze, then looked at his wife. "What has been shared?"

"She knows that you were once investigating him and why, and that he is now playing agent with the army and government," Nancy said matter-of-factly. "Faith knows how to keep a secret, and I wanted her to fully comprehend the danger that Gerome and Mr. Lakewood represent."

Seth sank onto the settee. "I wish you'd said nothing."

"I'm sorry, Seth. I pushed her." Faith tried not to sound overly concerned. "But you needn't fear. I won't say anything about Mr. Berkshire. I made it clear to him that I wasn't interested in going out with him—that I'm devoted to my duties as a student and a healer. Mr. Lakewood, on the other hand, asked me to speak at his wife's tea party."

Seth straightened and shook his head. "Speak about what?"

His concern surprised Faith. "About females being accepted into the medical college and about my passion for medicine."

"Lakewood is dangerous. He isn't the man in charge of all of this, but he's running things in Portland for someone. He certainly makes no secret that he stands against people of color, and Nancy and my sister overheard him talking about the guns and whiskey at a party he held for Berkshire."

Faith shook her head. "Well, when it comes to me, I am certain all he cares about is me entertaining and educating his wife and her friends. He's a strong supporter of the medical college."

"Faith mentioned talking with Aunt Mercy. She and Uncle Adam are very concerned about the whiskey that is flooding the reservation," Nancy said, changing the subject.

Seth's brows drew together. "What else did she say?"

Faith shrugged. "Just that there have been a lot of internal fights because of drunkenness. They have no idea who is supplying the alcohol, but it's a growing problem that Aunt Mercy fears may lead to large-scale problems."

"You need to say nothing more about this, Faith," Seth said sternly. "You too, Nancy. This is dangerous for both of you, and you need to leave the matter well alone."

"What's the problem with talking to our aunt about something she was openly discussing with the family?" Faith countered.

"Because the evidence points to their involvement." Seth raised his hands. "You didn't hear that from me. In fact, I wish I'd kept quiet, but now that I've said it, you must know that you cannot share this information with your aunt and uncle. They are at the very center of this investigation, and it doesn't look good for them."

Instead of being afraid or even angry, Faith couldn't keep from laughing out loud. The look of surprise on Seth's and Nancy's faces only amused her more. "Honestly, you can't be serious."

"Very serious." Seth looked at his wife, who nodded.

Faith stood up and shook her head. "Then neither of you know Mercy and Adam Browning as I do. They would no more corrupt the Indians under their care—or any Indian, for that matter—than they would their own children. Their love for the Native people runs deep, and they would never allow anything that might bring them harm." She sobered. "No matter what your evidence says, it's wrong. They have nothing to do with this, and if you have proof otherwise, then it has been planted to deceive you from catching the true culprits."

She turned and left the room, unwilling to hear more.

CHAPTER 4

Andrew Gratton tidied his quarters, including the dirty bandages he'd just changed. He'd have them washed to use again. He glanced at the wound on his arm. It had healed nicely, thanks to the very interesting and beautiful Faith Kenner.

He smiled at the memory of her taking him to task. She was witty and charming but also decisive and forthright. The latter traits were more positive than negative.

"Captain?" Denny stood at the door.

"Come in, Denny. Did you bring the log?"

"I did, and a report. The cargo has been offloaded, and the return shipment is being taken on as we speak."

"Very good. Thank you." Andrew took the log. "After you see to that, you and the boys are free to take the afternoon off. Just make sure you're back in plenty of time for our departure for Oregon City."

"Will do, Captain." The tall, skinny man, hardly more than a boy, whistled as he walked away.

Andrew got back to the work of checking his log entries, but his thoughts kept returning to Faith. He wished he could see her again, even if just to thank her for her kindness. But even more, he'd like to confirm her claim that she was gifted as a healer and get to know what other gifts she might have.

"Captain?" It was Denny again.

Andrew frowned. "Is there a problem?"

"No, sir. I found a lady on the dock. She said she needed to see you."

Andrew closed the log and got to his feet. "Take me to her."

Denny led the way, and much to his delight, Andrew found himself face to face with the very woman who had been on his mind.

"Miss Kenner." He tried his best not to sound overly enthusiastic. "What brings you here?"

"I heard the *Morning Star* was in port. Or dock. Whatever it is you say." She smiled. "I felt it my duty to come check your arm. It has been nearly two weeks since I set the stitches."

"Yes, I suppose it has."

"Have you had them removed?"

"No. I haven't had the time, to be honest. I was delivering up around Astoria."

"Might I examine your arm and remove them now?" She held up her black bag. "I have all that I need to do the job."

"I suppose there's no harm in that. Come to the wheelhouse." He led the way. Once they reached the wheelhouse, however, he paused and held the door open. "After you."

Miss Kenner stepped past him and placed her bag on the counter. She then pulled off her gloves and began unbuttoning her coat. Andrew watched, almost mesmerized. What was it about this woman that so captivated him?

"I think you'll find it quite cold in here," he said. "You might want that coat."

44

She shrugged out of it just the same. "I find it easier to work when I'm unencumbered. Now, please sit and roll up your sleeve."

Andrew removed his wool coat and did as instructed. "I just stopped using the bandages. The wound has completely closed and no longer seemed at risk of oozing or taking in dirt."

She nodded as she considered it. "It looks perfect. I'll remove the stitches for you."

She opened her bag and rummaged around until she produced a bottle of her family's special cleaning tonic. Andrew's nervous energy left him unable to remain silent.

"Say, that stuff is rather remarkable. I wonder if you might sell me several bottles. We often have wounds onboard, and I believe it would be a good thing to keep in stock."

"I can do that," Miss Kenner replied, returning to the bag for something else. She finally brought out a pair of tweezers and scissors, as well as a small piece of cloth. "There, now we can proceed. Do you have a clean towel?"

"Ah . . . yes." He reached into the cupboard behind him. "It's not very large."

"That's all right. I just need it so I can clean up." She spread the towel over the counter, then carefully poured a little of the fluid over her scissors and tweezers. She finished by doing the same with her hands. When she seemed satisfied, she looked up and smiled. "I'm ready if you are."

He nodded and watched as her delicate fingers made easy work of removing the sutures. He couldn't help but wonder at this stranger. Why wasn't she married with a family of her own?

"What does your beau think of you working as a physician and helping strange men?" he asked.

Miss Kenner laughed, something Andrew hadn't anticipated. "You don't seem all that strange to me," she replied.

He smiled. "I meant that in the sense of us being strangers."

"But we're not. You're the captain of the *Morning Star*, and I'm the woman who nearly painlessly stitched your arm."

"Painless? You thought that was painless?"

She laughed again. "See there? I'm learning more about you by the minute. And to reciprocate, I am not married."

"Might I ask why not? I mean, you're still in your youth and not hard on the eyes."

"I'm thirty. Quite the spinster, I'll have you know." She cleaned her instruments again, then put them back in her bag. Her intense blue eyes seemed to flash with amusement as she met his gaze.

"Yes, I can see that." He smiled. She did have the most remarkable way of putting him at ease.

Just then the door opened. "Sorry. I didn't see you had a visitor."

"That's all right." Andrew motioned the old Indian man into the room. "Come and formally meet the woman who stitched me up. Miss Kenner, this is Benjamin Littlefoot, but most folks call him Ben. He's from the Nez Perce tribe."

"Ben." She nodded and extended her hand. "I'm pleased to meet you." To both men's surprise, she spoke in Nez Perce.

The old man's face lit up, and he replied in kind. "You speak my tongue. How can this be?"

"I can speak numerous dialects. I learned as a girl. My uncle Alex has a dear friend who is Nez Perce, and when he visited, I'd ask him to give me lessons."

"I'm very glad to meet you," Ben replied, still smiling. "I seldom hear my tongue spoken anymore, and never so beautifully."

Andrew couldn't help but pipe up at this. "I speak to you all the time." He saw the surprise on Faith's face. "I, too, speak several languages, including French, Spanish, and Chinook Wawa, or Jargon, if you'd rather." The latter was the trade language among the Indian nations.

Miss Kenner nodded. "That's marvelous. I speak those as well. We three can tell many secrets, in multiple languages."

Andrew frowned but raised a hand to scratch his beard and hide his reaction. Hopefully Miss Kenner hadn't noticed. Secrets were always dangerous to tell, and he knew far too many to be comfortable with such an idea.

"It is best to guard the secrets," the old man said, sounding a bit sad. "There is much trouble in this land." He slipped from the wheelhouse without another word.

"He's right, of course," Miss Kenner agreed.

"He usually is."

Miss Kenner seemed deep in thought. "The newspaper this morning referenced the trouble with the Utes and Shoshone last year while expanding on the current problems with Victorio and his Apaches in the Southwest. But while Victorio is a fierce leader, he is mainly trying to keep his people from being forced onto the reservation, where they will have to live with their enemies. No one wants to live with their enemies."

"The same could be said for the whites with the Indians."

"But the Indians don't have to be the enemy of the whites," Miss Kenner protested.

"But that's the way it's been seen for decades, even centuries." Andrew knew his thoughts weren't lost on her.

"True, but that doesn't make it right. Doing the wrong thing over and over will never turn it into the right thing. We need to find a way to make it so that the whites and Indians can live together."

He smiled. "You think you and I could just sit down and figure that out, do you?"

"I meant a collective *we*. If this government and all the peoples, no matter the color of their skin, would work together, we could resolve this warring mentality. My fellow students at the medical college feel the same. We want to help in whatever way we can. I've even written to my folks about the desire to hold lectures to educate people. I think education is key. Just imagine if we could get everyone working together."

He shook his head. "I'd like that more than you can imagine, but it's never going to happen. No matter how hard we try."

"Why not?" Miss Kenner seemed genuinely confused.

"Because each side cherishes their differences enough to refuse to yield them. The whites don't want to get along with the Indians. They want to eliminate them. Whether that means kill them or force their assimilation, they don't want Indians, with their cultural ways and different languages and dress. They want replicas of themselves."

Miss Kenner considered this a moment and nodded. "I hadn't thought of it that way, but you are right for the vast majority."

"Sadly, I know I am. I've heard the talk up this river and down. I've heard it from Oregon's ports to California's."

"Then we must seek a higher power to resolve it. I believe God would have us live together in peace. The New Testament speaks about there no longer being Jew and Gentile, so why not have it no longer be an issue of white or Native?"

Andrew appreciated her unwillingness to give up. "I'm not sure God is listening anymore."

"Then we must pray all the harder. Like nagging children seeking their father's attention." She straightened and gathered her things. "We must pray without ceasing and come to

48

Him all the more humbled and yielded in obedience. But we must never stop seeking His help, because I know He hears us. I know He cares."

Faith was glad to have followed up on her stitching job. She told herself it was that alone that made her feel so happy. She tried not to remember the way her heart beat a little faster when Captain Gratton smiled or how he seemed to respect her opinions and thoughts. How different he'd been during this encounter! He was unlike some men, who treated her as if she were too stupid to reason. He reminded her of her father and the logical process he used to think through his circumstances.

"I must say, it's quite a surprise to run into you in this part of town."

Faith looked up to find Gerome Berkshire standing in front of her. She forced a smile. "If you follow me now, you'll be even more surprised by my destination."

"And why would that be? Going to a dress fitting? A tea?"

"A dissection."

He choked back whatever witty statement he had planned to deliver. "A dissection?"

"Yes. I'm making my way to the livery at the corner of Southwest Park and Jefferson Street. You're welcome to come along. As a benefactor of the school, I'm sure you'd be welcome to join us. We rent rooms above the livery. Have you ever seen the dissection of a human body?"

"Human?" His face paled even more.

Faith smiled. "I do love application. It's one thing to discuss cancerous growths, all black and oozing, but to see them for yourself—to feel them and smell them—well, there is nothing more beneficial. The same is true for broken bones or defective hearts. I want to see these things and better know what to look for in the future."

Berkshire wiped his mouth with a folded handkerchief before dabbing his sweat-dotted forehead. "Your topic is most unusual for a beautiful young woman such as yourself. But no, I can't accompany you, as interesting as it sounds. I'm on my way to a board meeting."

"I understand. Perhaps another time. I'm sure, if you spoke with the medical college president, he would be happy to set it up." She smiled and bid him farewell. "Now, if you'll excuse me, I must catch that trolley."

She all but ran for the car and, once aboard, turned back to find Berkshire hadn't moved an inch. She wanted to roar in laughter but knew it wasn't compassionate to make fun of someone about to lose the contents of his stomach.

Perhaps her love of medicine and all its idiosyncrasies would be enough to drive him away from her without Faith having to be forceful and harsh. She thought of Nancy and Seth's concerns about Berkshire acting as a spy for the government. It was clear even to her that people like Berkshire served only themselves. Men like him never had any other loyalty. Faith had known a lot of Berkshires in her thirty years of life. So many people pretended interest in one thing while truly seeking to benefit their own desires. She was thankful she'd learned early on about the games people played and the falsehoods of fools.

Her first mama, as she used to call Eletta Browning, had taught her to give everyone a chance but to guard her heart and mind at the same time. If what others said or did lined up with God's Word, then that was the first test. The second was in motives. Watching a person's actions and seeing what was most important to them and their desired end result would help her judge their motives. People who were truly determined to give of themselves and be servants of God would always do so in such a way that was never to their own glory.

Her second mama, who was in truth the woman who gave her life, reflected that same thought. When Eletta died, Faith had found her journal. Eletta had detailed Faith's violent conception and birth. Her mother, Hope Flanagan, had been raped and impregnated by the Cayuse brave who'd held her hostage. Hope was only one of many other women. Aunt Mercy had been there too, but she was so small that Hope convinced everyone that Mercy was years younger than her true age. It worked, by some miracle, and Mercy never had to endure the horrors that Faith's mother had gone through.

Even thinking of such things now made Faith sad. She hated to see her mother pained and thus seldom brought up her many questions about that time in Hope's life. She definitely never asked about her biological father.

Faith had never blamed Hope for giving her to the Brownings. In fact, she seemed to have an innate understanding of it, as well as a great sympathy for her mother. As Faith grew up with Hope and Lance Kenner after the Brownings died, she came to love them both and felt blessed to have had two sets of parents who cared for her. They were the best of people, and she had learned so much from them.

But there were times she would have liked to know more about her biological father, although the word *father* seemed like the wrong word entirely. She knew he had been hanged after a trial in Oregon City. She'd later read in the archives of the newspaper that the trial hadn't really been fair. The government had chosen the Indians to stand trial based on the assurance of some of the women who'd been at the mission. Most felt the men chosen were guilty—after all, they were Indians and in the area at the time of the attack. Some were less convinced. Nevertheless, they were found guilty and hanged. After this event, however, nothing more was mentioned about the guilty, and Faith had no way to learn anything about her history. At first she was frustrated by this, but as time went on, she found God had given her a sense of peace. Isaac Browning had been a blessing in her life. And the only father who really mattered was the one who had taken her in as his own, and Lance Kenner was a wonderful man.

Faith smiled as the trolley neared her stop. Lance had always encouraged her, even in her endeavor to become a certified doctor and surgeon. There had never been the slightest bit of condemnation in his demeanor that she wasn't seeking a more feminine path. He knew what she was up against with the laws and her heritage, but Faith knew that if she sought to become a wife and mother, her father and family would support those efforts as well. They would always encourage her, no matter the path, as long as it was one that honored God first.

As Captain Gratton's smile flashed through her mind yet again, she reminded herself that the love and support of her parents was all the family she needed.

CHAPTER 5

Mrs. Weaver joined the boardinghouse residents for breakfast the next morning. It was Faith's first real opportunity to meet the older woman, and she found her quite charming. Virginia Weaver's appearance suggested frailty and shyness, but once she joined the conversation, Faith quickly saw that she was neither frail nor shy.

"I do love your fried potatoes and gravy," the older woman declared in her Southern drawl. "It reminds me of home. Mother loved fried potatoes."

"I thought Southerners were more given to grits and hominy," Clementine said, scooping out a portion of sausage gravy.

"Oh, there is a love for those foods as well," Mrs. Weaver said, smiling. "As a small child, I used to sneak out to the slave quarters to sample grits and gravy. They were a favorite of mine, but my mother refused to serve them, declaring grits to be slave food."

"How sad." Faith thought of her own upbringing, which encouraged sampling all types of foods. "I mean, if something is good to eat, should it matter where it's from or who has suggested it?"

"I've dealt with people like that as well," Nancy joined in.

"We once had a summer picnic at church. Quite a few wealthy people attend our church, and when I revealed that I had brought corn bread, you would have thought I'd committed a crime."

"Corn bread is a staple for most homes," Mimi said, shaking her head. "Why be offended?"

"It's my experience that the wealthy, more snobbish folk are always offended by something. My corn bread was a success, however, and I had no reason to hold their thoughts against them. If they wanted only white bread, then that just left more corn bread for those who preferred it."

Clementine laughed. "Those people only deny themselves. I've seen such behavior in their children as well, but I've always tried to broaden their experiences. We've studied various cultures this year. Nancy got me thinking about it when we went to the Fourth of July celebration last summer. I now keep track of my children's cultural backgrounds, and we have a special unit on each one. Their mothers often make food for us or even bring in traditional clothing."

"Good for you." Faith speared another piece of sausage. "Education is the way to lessen prejudice. Let folks see that just because we have differences doesn't mean we are bad or unacceptable. The sooner people put aside prejudices, the sooner we'll have peace in our country."

"It makes me sad to suggest that will never come," Mrs. Weaver murmured.

"It is hard to imagine the possibility," Nancy agreed, "but it must surely be what we strive for in our daily living. If we ignore the problem, it's not going to diminish."

"Truer words were never spoken," Clementine agreed. "It's amazing to me how much the small children in my classes hate some races or even genders. I have heard young boys deny the value of their female counterparts until I suggest that without them, humankind would be incomplete."

Faith shook her head. "I imagine that was not what those children wanted to hear."

"No," Clementine continued, "but it is easy, as a teacher, to quickly discern what parents believe by what comes out of their children's mouths." She glanced up at the clock. "Oh goodness, look at the time. We're going to be late, Mimi, if we don't hurry."

That declaration sped up the meal for everyone, even though Nancy, Faith, and Mrs. Weaver had nowhere in particular to be. Faith's first class wasn't until ten o'clock, so she eased back in her seat and sipped her coffee in leisure.

"I understand you're attending college to become a doctor," Mrs. Weaver said as Mimi and Clementine bid them good-bye.

Faith gave the ladies a wave, then turned her full attention to Mrs. Weaver. "I am. I've considered myself a physician since I was twenty, but this way I'll have the paperwork behind me to back my claim."

"I cannot imagine enjoying such . . . intimate work."

Faith nodded. "It certainly isn't for everyone. The very thought of doing what a physician must do is overwhelming to most. But it's my calling. I felt from a young age that God wanted me to work one-on-one with people. I had no idea what that would entail, but as I grew older, I found myself fascinated by the healing arts. It's so fulfilling to comfort and care for someone who is injured or ill. It also allows me to share my faith, which is always a privilege."

Mrs. Weaver nodded. "It is, isn't it? Telling someone about God's goodness and what He has done to benefit and protect us should always be considered a privilege, yet it so seldom is." The old woman slipped several biscuits into her pocket as if she were doing nothing more unusual than placing her napkin on the table.

Faith had watched Mrs. Weaver throughout their meal. She was always slipping something into her pocket. At first Faith had thought she was taking the silver, but it soon became evident that the old woman was only interested in food. At one point she had wrapped several sausage links in a well-worn napkin before putting that in her apron pocket. What was she up to? Surely Nancy allowed her the freedom to come for food throughout the day should she need it.

Later, after Mrs. Weaver had retired to her room with a fresh pitcher of water, Faith asked Nancy about the situation.

"I used to think she had a hidden pet—that perhaps she had slipped a cat or dog in among her crates. I thought that was also the reason she refused to use the community facilities and instead insisted on a chamber pot. You know, in order to manage the waste. But I've never heard anything that would suggest an animal is on the premises. Surely we would have heard barking or mewing."

"Perhaps because she lived through the War Between the States, she suffered from hunger. The South was very hard hit and deprived in order to force it back into compliance with the North. I've read that many people starved to death—especially in prisoner of war camps."

"Seth suggested the same thing. For me, it really doesn't matter. She has never been difficult to manage, so I refuse to interfere. The few times I have gone into her room, I never find it in disarray. In fact, she keeps better house than I do."

Faith laughed. "I find that doubtful."

"Well, overall," Nancy said, getting to her feet as she began to collect dishes, "I'm rather glad to have less work. Especially now."

"Why especially now?"

Nancy smiled. "I've been dying to tell someone, but I wanted to be certain. I believe I'm going to have a baby."

Faith beamed. "Truly? That's wonderful news. Have you told Seth?"

"No. I wanted to be sure. I suppose I'm still not completely sure. I've wanted a baby for so long. The entire eight years I was married to Albert, I longed for a baby and never once did I conceive. Now I've only been married to Seth for four months, and during that time I've ceased having my monthly times. That's never happened before."

"A wedding night baby." Faith couldn't conceal her joy. "Why don't you let me check for sure? By now I can probably tell from the feel of things."

Nancy abandoned the dishes. "Right now?"

"Sure, why not? Let's go to your room. Lie down and loosen your waistband. You certainly aren't showing much, but I've seen women carry very low and hardly show at all their entire term."

Nancy wiped her hands on her apron and then pulled the strings. "I would feel better knowing for sure. I thought about making a trip home to see Mother, but I knew if I mentioned it out of the blue, Seth would worry about what was wrong. Besides, we're already planning the trip home for Christmas."

Faith followed Nancy down the hall to her room. "Well, your mother is much better at just knowing than I am. I swear she can look at a woman and tell if she's with child."

"Mother is gifted, but so are you. I hope you know how proud we all are of you."

Nancy undid the buttons on her skirt and climbed onto the bed. Faith pulled the front of Nancy's blouse from the waistband and reached for her abdomen. "My hands are probably cold." Faith paused and rubbed her hands on her wool skirt, hoping to warm them.

"I am sure I won't care." Nancy's grin went from ear to ear. "I'm just so happy. I know I shouldn't get my hopes up, but I can't help it."

Faith felt her cousin's abdomen. It was immediately apparent that Nancy was pregnant. "You are definitely with child. I can feel the top of your uterus just here." She pressed and smiled. "There are measurements that can be done, but from my experience, I would say you are as you thought, about four months along."

"Oh, I can hardly contain my joy. This is more than I ever dreamed possible."

"What's going on?"

The two women turned toward the door to find Seth. Nancy blushed. "What are you doing here? I thought you were long gone. Didn't you have some sort of client meeting?"

Seth was too concerned to answer his wife's question. "Are you ill?" He looked to Faith.

"I'm not sick at all," Nancy declared before Faith could even speak. "Faith was just confirming my suspicions. We're going to have a baby!"

Seth paled. "A . . . baby?"

"Yes." Nancy sat up and swung her legs over the edge of the bed. She hurriedly tucked her blouse into the waistband of her skirt, then fastened the buttons. "And Faith just confirmed my calculations. This is a honeymoon baby, and we should expect this little one in . . ." She looked to Faith.

"About five months. So sometime in May."

The news began to make sense to Seth, and he started to smile. "A baby. In May. Well, I'll be."

Nancy crossed the room and threw herself into his arms. "I've been fairly certain for a while, but I wanted to make sure before I said anything to get your hopes up. I'm so happy. I've wanted a child for so long."

"My dear wife, I couldn't be more pleased." He kissed her with the utmost of tender affection.

Faith looked away and smiled to herself. A baby in the house would be wonderful. No doubt all of the boarders would find the addition a blessing.

Of course, if things went as planned, Faith would graduate in late April and already be thinking of her next move. For now, however, she needed to focus on her studies and classes. She needed to complete her thesis paper as well. At least she was in the final stages of that obligation.

The Friday before Christmas, Faith stepped in front of Mrs. Lakewood's gathering of friends and smiled. She had dressed in her finest wool suit—a dark green trimmed in black piping. She wore a high-necked lacy blouse and knew she looked acceptable. But still, in the back of her mind, she could hear that voice reminding her that she was a half-breed. These women would never have been so accepting and generous had they known the truth, and that bothered Faith a great deal. More and more she wrestled with whether she was doing wrong by claiming her white heritage.

"First, I want to thank you for your kind invitation to come here today, Mrs. Lakewood. It is an honor."

Lakewood's wife nodded and gave a hint of a smile. She and her friends were sedate and serious for the most part. They were some of Portland's finest society and were not easily accepting of unfamiliar people or ideas.

Without further ado, Faith began her speech. "As Mrs. Lakewood mentioned in her introduction, I attend the medical college sponsored by Willamette University. The university started the first medical college in the Pacific Northwest in 1866 and began admitting women in 1877. I am privileged to be among the first."

She could tell by the bored expressions on her audience members' faces that they were unimpressed. Faith steadied herself and smiled.

"I have been involved in midwifery and healing since I was a child. I have helped deliver hundreds of babies and have treated numerous wounds, diseases, and injuries. By the time I was fifteen, I knew that working in medicine was what God had called me to do."

The looks of the women turned skeptical, but at least the boredom was gone. Faith pressed on. "In this world, it is common for women to be attended by women in childbirth. Most deliveries, particularly in rural settings, are performed by women in the family. Midwives are only sent for in cases of distress or emergency. The simple reason doctors are not in attendance is that childbirth is not considered a major event worthy of a doctor's attention, even though it is the most common reason for death in women. Most doctors are male, which is also a strong reason for eliminating them from the birthing room. Women don't want a strange man present in such an intimate situation." At this comment, Faith couldn't help but remember Andrew Gratton referring to himself as a "strange man." The thought made her smile.

"My thoughts on the matter are similar to those of many other women. Childbirth is probably the most important thing we will ever be a part of, and the safety of our babies, as well as ourselves, merits better understanding and consideration. Keeping that in mind, it has been established through various polls that women find the idea of a female doctor to be a comfort in such situations. Further, they also appreciate the idea of female physicians for other circumstances isolated to the female anatomy. All of this is to say that the importance of supporting women in medicine cannot be underestimated. We are quite fortunate that the men of our state took our needs seriously and established a place for female students in the medical college."

She paused, not sure how much time Mrs. Lakewood had allotted for her speech. "Are there questions?"

When no one said anything and Mrs. Lakewood remain seated, Faith continued.

"Our studies are quite vigorous and demanding. We study anatomy in detail, and we also must complete classes in physiology, chemistry, therapeutics, the theory and practice of medicine, surgery, and obstetrics, as well as diseases of women and children. We are required to attend numerous lectures and clinics on all of the practical branches of medicine and to complete a lengthy and detailed paper on a topic to be approved by the college. There is little time for anything else in our lives, as you might guess."

A woman in the second row raised her gloved hand, then looked around the room as if for approval or acceptance.

"Yes?" Faith smiled, hoping to put the woman at ease. "You have a question?"

"I do. Do the men study diseases of men, while the women study the diseases of women and children?"

Faith shook her head. "I've never understood the titling for that course. Obviously, the diseases of children are the same for male or female. Boys and girls alike, if exposed, have the same chance of developing measles, typhoid, smallpox, mumps, and so forth. I assume that those who put the courses together believed male illnesses would be covered in that manner, and that the problems of a woman's anatomy were more numerous and complicated.

"After all, when young men die it is usually from injury or work-related accidents. Older men generally succumb to the same diseases that women face. Women, however, are more likely to die in childbirth or complications from childbirth, as I mentioned earlier, while children are most susceptible to disease. Although accidents are also responsible for a fair share of their deaths."

"Do you truly feel it's proper and acceptable for a woman to treat a man?" an older matron asked in disapproval. "Why, you aren't even married and shouldn't be at all familiar with a man's body."

Faith smiled. "But I have younger brothers I helped raise and care for. I grew up on a farm and know very well the differences in our bodies. It is neither shocking nor of great concern for me to help a man rather than a woman. Just as I believe it's not a matter of impropriety for a male doctor to treat a woman. Our studies and occupations make it so that we look at the human body in a completely different way."

"Impossible." The woman's disapproval was growing, and Faith feared it might spread to the other women before she was able to conclude her talk.

"Might I share an example to better explain?" She looked at the woman, who, after a long pause, gave a curt nod.

Faith thought carefully before beginning. "As women, when you see a baby—an infant in the arms of its mother—what comes to mind?" There was dead silence. Faith nodded. "Many women will think about how that relates to them. For me, a single woman who has no children, I might reflect on how much I would like to have a family of my own. Mrs. Lakewood has numerous children, so she might compare the infant to one of her own, contrasting and comparing the size and weight, the appearance and so forth. Now, think back in time to when you yourselves were small children and you first beheld an infant—perhaps a new sibling. What were your thoughts then? Envy? Love? Excitement for the possibility of a new playmate?" Faith gave them a moment to consider this, then continued. "What about when you see an elderly man? Perhaps your father or grandfather—an uncle or older acquaintance. Are your thoughts the same when you see him as when you consider an infant?"

"Of course not!" the matron declared. "What has this to do with anything?"

"I'm trying to show that we look at people differently depending on their age and gender, their position and social standing. Doctors and healers look at them in yet another manner. When I see a young man limping along, I'm not intrigued by his appearance—whether he's handsome or holds any purpose in my life. I want to know why is he limping and if I can help. When I see a baby with a runny nose, I don't feel annoyed or worried about my clothes should I hold them. Instead, I worry about any number of diseases and whether this is the first stage of something serious."

To her surprise, the woman settled back and seemed to accept her answer.

Faith smiled and looked at each woman in the gathering. "Just as each individual artist looks at the same thing and yet paints something entirely different, doctors look at people as potential patients. We have a drive to heal—to make life better—to ease pain and suffering.

"I appreciate that you would have me here to speak today, Mrs. Lakewood. I am happy to answer any further questions, but I'm sure your friends would enjoy time to mingle and converse."

The ladies clapped in their polite, gloved manner. Faith didn't know whether to retake her seat or just exit as she longed to do. Choosing the latter, she figured someone would stop her if they wanted her to remain. No one did.

She had nearly reached the front door when a male voice called out to her. "Miss Kenner." She turned to find Mr. Lakewood smiling as he approached. "I heard what you had to say and must tell you that I'm quite impressed."

"Thank you." Faith looked around for the butler so she could request her coat.

"I wonder if you might consider speaking to a group of men—potential donors who will gather after the holidays to consider supporting the college. You are able to explain so well what I would like them to understand—especially where it concerns women attending the medical college."

"I would be happy to, Mr. Lakewood, so long as it meets with President Parrish's approval. I wouldn't want him to be offended at my setting up a speaking event on behalf of the department. He must approve."

"Of course." The silver-haired man beamed her a smile. "Parrish and I are longtime friends. I'm certain he will see things my way."

CHAPTER 6

On Christmas Eve, Faith found herself onboard the *Morning Star* with Nancy and Seth, as well as Seth's sister. They were making their way to Oregon City to celebrate Christmas with the family and were excited to reach their destination. Faith cherished holidays. Since she'd been a young girl, she had loved the way her mother's family celebrated the birth of Jesus. It was never about the presents one could give or get. It was about the supreme gift of Jesus, God's most precious gift of love, and how they were to share that love with each other.

Faith found herself growing more anxious by the minute to reach home. She could almost smell the gingerbread and pine boughs. She could imagine them all gathered in front of the rock fireplace—fire blazing and crackling—her mother softly singing. Nancy had done an amazing job of decorating the boardinghouse for the holidays, but it wasn't the same. No doubt Mimi, who'd been left in charge of Mrs. Weaver, would appreciate the plentiful supply of holiday cooking Nancy had left behind, but Faith wished they could have invited both women to come to Oregon City.

Still, they'd had a nice time the night before with Nancy and Seth. The women of the boardinghouse helped decorate the tree. Even Mrs. Weaver had been anxious to do her part, so they'd made an evening of it with refreshments and a roaring fire. The front sitting room was the perfect setting for their festivities even though Seth at first had thought the large dining room more appropriate.

"No one wants to be crowded at dinner by the Christmas tree," Nancy had protested. "I think the front sitting room is perfect."

And so it was.

"Aren't you cold out here?" Captain Gratton asked, breaking into Faith's thoughts. "It's raining, you know."

She laughed. "Captain Gratton. It's good to see you again. But to answer your question, I'm not a bit cold. I'm just enjoying the journey, and the rain isn't even touching me, thanks to the deck covering."

"It probably doesn't dare rain on you. That seems to be the way it is for you."

Faith's eyes narrowed a bit as she cocked her head. "What do you mean by that?"

The captain pulled up his coat collar. "Just as I said. You enjoy the journey. You seem content in life. How could the rain dare to fall on you?"

"There's nothing wrong with enjoying the journey." She shrugged. "I don't have much interest in the alternative. I've known many a man and woman who lived in the misery of their own making. I have no desire to be like that."

"No, I can't imagine you that way." The captain leaned back against the railing. "Are you going home for Christmas?"

Faith nodded. "I am. My classes are done until after the winter break. That's not to say that I don't have plenty of studying to do, however. That's why this will be a short trip. We will head back to Portland on Saturday."

"That's when I'm returning as well."

She laughed. "Then be sure to save us three seats."

"Three? I thought there were four of you."

"There are, but Clementine—she's the redhead—is staying a little longer. She's a teacher and doesn't have to be back to her position right away, so she's staying to spend time with her fiancé."

"The tall man who was with you when I got my arm cut?"

"Yes. You have a good memory, Captain."

"Please just call me Andrew."

Faith nodded. "And you should call me Faith."

They said nothing for several minutes after that. Faith continued to stare out at the waters of the Willamette, ever mindful of how attractive the captain was with his neatly trimmed black beard and mustache. She had always liked facial hair. It often gave men a distinguished look. With Andrew Gratton, it made him alluring and mysterious.

"Well, I should get back to my duties," he said.

Faith looked up to see he had been watching her. She smiled. "And I shall go back inside. I suppose it is rather cold, and I believe the wind has shifted and I'm starting to feel the rain." She noted that he hadn't worn a hat or scarf. "You should bundle up better. You don't want to become sick."

"Thank you, Doctor."

"My pleasure, Captain." She gave him a curt nod and headed off to join her companions.

Andrew's lack of hat and scarf, however, stayed with her, and upon her first step into her parents' house, she asked her mother for yarn.

"What color?" Hope asked, eyeing her daughter with a curious expression.

"I think red would do nicely."

"What are you up to?"

Faith discarded her coat and hat. "I'm going to make the captain of the *Morning Star* a hat and scarf. He apparently has neither and was quite cold on our journey here."

"It seems unlikely that a riverboat captain wouldn't have the proper attire," her mother replied. "But nevertheless, who am I to deny you?" She went to a trunk at the far end of the room and opened it. "I have some nice red wool here that should do the trick. I dyed it myself just a few weeks back." She pulled out several skeins. "This should be enough. Will you knit or crochet?"

Faith pondered that a moment. "Crochet. I'm faster with a crochet hook, and I only have tonight and tomorrow in which to get this done."

"I could help," her mother offered.

"Would you?"

"Of course. All of my Christmas gifts are complete. I wouldn't want you to miss out on giving yours because you didn't have time."

Faith frowned and felt embarrassed. "It's not a Christmas gift. Not really. I just knew he was cold. I would have offered him my scarf, but it's terribly feminine."

Her mother shook her head. "No matter what kind of gift it is, if we don't get to work, we'll never have it done by the time you leave on Saturday."

"You are right, as usual." Faith took one of the skeins and marveled at its softness. "This is so fine and lovely."

"Yes, but it's good thick wool and will make a perfect protection from the damp air. Come now, we'll go to my sewing room and get you a hook. Your father will be busy helping Alex with the Christmas cider, so we'll have some time before our evening celebration."

Faith had a quarter of the scarf complete by the time Father returned and announced it was time to gather at the Armistead house. The Kenner home sat on the same farm property but a decent distance from the big house. Faith had grown up this way, with all her cousins and family close at hand. The exception, of course, had been Aunt Mercy's children, Isaac and Constance, but even they often came to spend the long summer months on the farm. Mama used to say it was to remind them that they were white as well as part Cherokee. Uncle Adam's mother had been half Cherokee, and Faith had heard the stories of her life's difficulties. Uncle Adam had thought that describing to Faith what another woman of Indian heritage had gone through might help her decide how to live her life. It had. It had terrified Faith to hear how that very Native-looking woman had been treated. Few women would have anything to do with her, and the men called her a squaw. No one considered Adam's mother and father legally married, and they considered Adam and his siblings illegitimate. Only in leaving for other parts of the country and saying nothing about their Indian blood had the children been able to live normal lives. Faith supposed it had influenced her own decision to embrace the privilege that came with looking more white than Cayuse.

If anyone were to ask Faith later what she remembered most about this particular Christmas Eve celebration, she would say the laughter. Everyone was in a jolly spirit. There were letters to share from all the absent family members and no lack of stories from the old days.

After the family shared an incredible supper of roasted deer, creamed peas and potatoes, squash, baked ham, and so many other traditional family dishes, they gathered in the living room to sample the mulled cider and sweet desserts.

Uncle Alex opened the Bible, as was the tradition, and began to read from Luke one, verse twenty-six. "And in the sixth month the angel Gabriel was sent from God unto a city of Galilee, named Nazareth, to a virgin espoused to a man whose name was Joseph, of the house of David; and the virgin's name was Mary. And the angel came in unto her, and said, Hail, thou that art highly favoured, the Lord is with thee: blessed art thou among women."

He continued reading, but Faith let her thoughts wander. She had heard this story every year of her life. She had always loved and marveled at the wonder of it, and despite the very different circumstances, she always thought of her mother finding herself with child. No husband. No hope of explaining her situation in a way that would leave her with a shred of dignity or pride. Perhaps that was part of Mary's journey too. No one ever talked in the Bible about her encounters with those who thought her shameful. And who could blame them? An unmarried girl found herself with child. There were no accounts of her making public announcements about the baby being God's, but imagine if there had been. No one would have believed her. Not without God's intercession.

Uncle Alex was reading the part where Elisabeth acknowledged the holiness of the child Mary carried. How that must have blessed Mary. She didn't have to try to prove the truth of what was happening to her. God had allowed her cousin Elisabeth to know.

Alex read on to the end of the first chapter. The second

would be read the following day at the noon meal, when they all gathered again. More of the family would be with them then, and it was always so much fun, especially if smaller children were there as well.

Hope was asked to sing, and with Meg accompanying her on the piano, she did exactly that. Aunt Grace always said that Hope's voice was very much like their mother's. Rich and melodious, with a perfect pitch that never failed.

Faith had never known a grandmother or grandfather, and she always wondered what it might have been like to grow up with an older person in her life. There was Uncle Edward, of course. He had lived in Oregon City with his family, but he was now gone. The family who remained would join them at the farm the next day, but Faith couldn't help but wish for a grandmother, a loving and kind older woman who would offer advice and sage counsel.

The family joined in for a round of Christmas carols and then shared stories from throughout the year—events that had blessed them in particular or that had taught them something important. Throughout this time, Faith continued to crochet her scarf and think of Andrew Gratton.

Nothing can come of this friendship. He's white, and you're not white enough.

Faith frowned but kept her head down so no one would see. She didn't want the others to feel bad for her.

"What about you, Faith? Was there a big blessing in your life this past year?"

Her head snapped up to find everyone watching her. Mother took a seat beside her and picked up her own crochet work. Faith knew her family wouldn't let her get away without replying. She shared the first thing that popped into her head.

71

"The university moved the medical college from Salem to Portland, as you well know. At first that didn't seem like it would be all that important to me, but it turns out it was. I get to live at Nancy's boardinghouse and be close to my family again. I've missed you all very much, and I'm so blessed to be home for Christmas."

"We're blessed to have you here too," Alex Armistead declared. The others immediately chimed in to agree.

"I'm glad she's home for Christmas, even if she is bossy," her younger brother declared. "It gets terribly quiet here, being one of the youngest."

"I've never known it to be quiet when you're in the house," their father teased.

By the time the cider and desserts were gone, most everyone was yawning and anxious for bed.

"Before we head upstairs," Nancy said, smiling in a knowing fashion at her mother, "we want to let you know that there will soon be an addition to the family. I'm going to have a baby in May."

Everyone broke into cheers, and Aunt Grace had tears in her eyes. Everyone knew what this baby meant to Nancy.

"That's the best Christmas present anyone could ever give us," Nancy's father, Alex, declared. He hugged his daughter close. "I'm so happy for you, honey."

Faith felt the air catch in her throat as tears came to her eyes unbidden. She hadn't expected this rush of emotion and regret. Biting her lip, she prayed for God to ease her sadness. She was delighted for her cousin and wanted nothing to suggest otherwise. It wasn't Nancy's fault that Faith was half Cayuse. It was no one's fault.

God, this is so hard. I thought I could bear it well enough—

after all, I'm thirty. I'd come to terms with this long ago, yet here I am, weeping for the loss.

A warm hand touched hers, and Faith turned to see the tears in her mother's eyes. She knew. She understood that Faith wasn't teary in celebration but in sorrow. Their fingers laced together, and Mother gave her hand a squeeze.

"Remember verse thirty-seven of tonight's reading. 'For with God nothing shall be impossible,'" her mother whispered.

Faith nodded. "I'm trying to."

The trip back to Portland had barely gotten underway when Faith went searching for Andrew. She had wrapped the scarf around the hat and carried them just inside her coat. She hoped he'd be pleased with the gift but knew it might be awkward. With that in mind, she'd practiced what she'd say and how she would say it. She knew she could make it clear that this wasn't anything important.

"Miss Kenner, it's good to see you again," Andrew said, coming down from the wheelhouse.

"I thought we had progressed to Faith and Andrew."

He grinned. "Yes, we had. Faith."

"Thank you, Andrew." She reached inside her coat and pulled out the hat and scarf. She pushed them toward him, already apologizing. "Now, don't make more of this than is needed. When I was with you on Christmas Eve, you had no hat and scarf. I decided to make you a scarf, and my mother helped by making the hat. We just wanted to ensure that you are well-protected on your river runs."

"Ever the doctor, eh?" He unwrapped the bundle and considered each piece but said nothing.

Faith could hardly bear it. "It also gave me something to do with my hands while visiting with my family, so please understand that it's not a gift that should make you feel in any way obligated. I simply like to be useful and help people when I can. Speaking of which, I hope Ben is doing well." She knew she was rambling but didn't feel comfortable stopping. "Does he need a hat and scarf as well?"

Andrew looked up. His eyes, such a dark brown, seemed to grow darker still. "They are the best quality. I'm very touched that you would spend your holiday working on them for me."

Faith swallowed the lump in her throat and found her mouth very dry. She nodded and forced a smile. Grief, what was wrong with her? This shouldn't be that hard. It was just a gesture of kindness.

Andrew pulled the scarf around his neck. "I had a good wool hat but lost it on one of my trips. I kept meaning to purchase another." He looped the scarf around and tucked it inside his coat with a smile. "Already warmer." He took off the billed hat that he usually wore and pulled on the red cap. "It's a perfect fit." He smiled. "Thank you, Faith. I wish I had something to give you in return."

"That's not necessary. I didn't do it for that reason." Her voice was barely a whisper. There was something about this man that made her feel small, yet they were almost evenly matched in height. He might have two or three inches on her, but no more.

"I know, I'll give you free passage on the *Morning Star* next time you sail. Although I'm sure to be getting the better part of this exchange."

Faith felt herself begin to relax. "I'm glad you like it."

"The fact is, I like you. You have a spirit that few women exhibit. You are fearless and face the world with a sense of authority. Few women could have done what you did, taking charge of my wound. You're studying to be a doctor, so I know the things you see and deal with must be more than most women could bear."

"Women bear a lot and get little credit for it." Faith thought of all the injuries she and her brothers had endured over the years of their youth. Her mother was always there to patch them up. From time to time, she had to tend Father's wounds as well.

"Still, I've never known anyone quite like you, and I admire you."

Her cheeks grew hot. "Thank you, Andrew. I admire you as well. Your kindness to people of color, Indians in particular, impresses me. Few white men consider Indians to be human, much less their equal."

He shrugged. "Maybe they've just never bothered to get to know one."

"Probably not."

"Maybe they'd be better men if they did."

CHAPTER 7

College classes hadn't yet resumed, but Faith saw Gerome Berkshire was giving a lecture and pondered the possibility of attending. She knew enough to be wary of him—even suspicious of the topic of his lecture—yet she felt drawn to the event. At the last minute, she slipped into the back of the room, hoping she'd blend in nicely with the others. If she was fortunate, Berkshire would never even notice her there.

"I am honored to speak to you tonight," Berkshire declared after another man announced him. The man had sung Gerome Berkshire's praises and no doubt left the pompous fool feeling infallible.

"Most of you have heard me speak before, and during those orations, you probably remember the strong stance I took against black residency in Oregon."

There were some murmurs and nods. Faith tried not to show her feelings one way or the other.

"Tonight I want to speak to you about why my stand in this matter is so critical to our state and why it should be important to you." He took a sip of water and continued. "As you know, when the great migration west began, people in this territory chose to implement laws that made it illegal for a black man or woman to reside here. The wagon masters of the Oregon Trail were charged with refusing passage in their trains to any people of color who intended to settle in Oregon.

"After all, we already had the Indian to deal with. Those were dark days in many ways, and we were misjudged and condemned by some Easterners for our desires and beliefs as it pertained to race. Now, lest you misunderstand me, hear me out. I am not, as some people think, one of those who believes the only solution to deal with the Indian or black is to kill them. I am quite amenable to rounding them up and assigning them land elsewhere or even removing them to nations of people of their own kind."

Faith was amazed at the number of people who nodded in approval. How could they believe that such things were acceptable—that God approved the driving away of one race for the so-called betterment of another?

"Many of us who believe in segregated living are often condemned, but even the Bible shows how God called the Jewish people to live apart from other tribes. They weren't to intermarry with non-Jewish people."

Faith rolled her eyes and might have commented on how Jesus made it clear that there was no longer to be Jew or Gentile, but Berkshire was already well into his next thoughts on the matter. She couldn't believe these people openly accepted his philosophies.

"Now, I've also heard the arguments against the progressive idea that the blacks, Orientals, and Indians aren't human. But it's clear that the various skin colors signal different bodies and functions. I've heard that blacks have an entirely different muscular system than that of the white man. How, then, can we be the same? It is more than skin color that separates us and more than having two legs and walking upright that might join us together as human beings."

Several men responded with a rousing, "Hear! Hear!" Faith felt ill. How could people think this way? She had heard plenty of people who held the same opinion, but as always, when confronted by it, she was almost stupefied. She remembered some of the classes she'd attended where she'd been introduced to such thinking. At first it had been impossible to believe that anyone would accept such philosophies as truth. Then another book or speaker would share their foreign beliefs, urging the youth of the world to open their eyes to new thinking. Craving ideals that separated them from the old, tired standards of their parents, Faith had watch young students soak up the words.

Berkshire's command of the room was growing. Faith could hear how carefully he crafted his comments, increasing his volume or lowering it for effect. She could see how easily persuaded people were to believe that the man on the podium somehow knew all the answers that they so desperately sought.

She'd had enough. When the man beside her began coughing and excused himself from the lecture, Faith followed as though she were his companion.

"Are you all right, sir?" she asked when he looked back at her.

"Just a bit of winter cold lingering." He smiled and gave her a bow. "Thank you for your concern."

He turned away and left her standing just outside the lecture hall. Faith shook her head. She felt contaminated, but not from the man's cough.

"Miss Kenner."

She looked up to find Mr. Lakewood. She was certain from things Nancy had said that he believed much the same as

Berkshire, so she had no smile to offer him. Still, he was an important donor to the college. She needed to be civil.

"Mr. Lakewood."

"Are you ill?"

She pulled her wool wrap more tightly around her shoulders. "I was feeling a bit under the weather and thought I'd return home. Thank you for asking."

"My carriage is just outside. Might I drive you?"

She nodded without thinking. "That would be kind." Only then did she think of what some people might say about her riding alone with a man who wasn't a family member.

Grief, I am always breaking societal rules, whether it's because of my bloodline or being a woman practicing a man's profession. One carriage ride isn't going to ruin me.

He offered her his arm, and they headed outside. "I am sorry that you're feeling unwell. I am counting on you to speak to my gathering on the twelfth."

"I'm sure I'll be much recovered."

He smiled and waved to his carriage driver, who immediately brought the closed carriage to where they waited. Lakewood gave the driver the address of Nancy's boardinghouse. Faith was surprised that he knew it by heart but said nothing. Her head was starting to pound.

Mr. Lakewood handed Faith up and then took the seat opposite her in a very proper manner. He rapped the roof with his hand.

"There. We'll have you home very soon."

Faith pressed her fingers to her temples. "I am sorry to make such poor company."

"It was quite warm in the lecture hall. Of course, you add Berkshire's hot air, and it doubles the heat."

Faith smiled. "I thought you agreed with Mr. Berkshire." She hadn't meant to speak the words aloud, but now that she had, there was no choice but to endure whatever comments he might offer.

"I agree with much that Berkshire has to share. I do believe that had we been a nation of only white-skinned men and women, we never would have suffered through the War Between the States. Had there been no black—no slave—we would have worked through the issues of state's rights without the need for war." He lowered his head slightly. "I lost good friends and family to that war, and for what? To proclaim that a man with brown or black skin is as human as those with white? I never said they weren't human. That's Berkshire's nonsense."

"But you would have them removed from America in order to cleanse the country of colored skin?"

He looked at her and nodded. "I suppose I would. I further suppose you think me extraordinarily cruel to host such beliefs, but keep this in mind—I heard a lecture by a man who had been torn from his family in Africa and forced to come to America to be bought and sold many times over. He longed for home—for the family he'd been separated from, for the land of his birth. I saw grown men—white men—weep for the pain of that man's spirit. Surely that man was not alone."

"But many of the slaves set free were born right here. They have no memory of Africa or Jamaica or any other place from where black men and women were taken. America is their home. To where would you send them?"

"To a land where they could live in the manner that their nature demanded." The carriage rolled to a stop, and the driver was soon at the door.

"Their nature?" Faith couldn't help but ask.

Lakewood nodded. "Their nature. We are not all alike. We do not all long for the same things."

"Like food, shelter, and provision for our families?"

He smiled. "Those are universal needs. All I'm saying is that it's not their natural state to be educated or civilized."

It was difficult to keep her temper from getting the best of her when such ignorance was spouted as knowledge. "And such things are the natural state of white men? I have yet to deliver a baby who can speak or walk, much less read and write. We all must learn, Mr. Lakewood. Unfortunately, I believe some of what is being taught is more dangerous and despicable than useful. If we are not careful, we may well find ourselves fighting a bigger war than we've ever imagined possible."

Faith could see that the rain had started to pour in earnest and knew that her opinion wasn't going to change his mind.

"Thank you for the ride home, Mr. Lakewood. I am sure I will feel fit in time for your gathering of donors. I wonder if you would mind if I bring someone along with me."

He shook his head. "Of course not. Whom did you have in mind?"

"One of the ladies at the boardinghouse. In fact, there are two. They are teachers and mentioned that they would be interested to hear what I might say."

He smiled. "Of course. I will send my carriage for you. My man will be here at six forty-five precisely."

Faith allowed the driver to help her down. "We'll be ready."

"And then he drove away."

"Oh, Faith, what were you thinking, riding home alone with

that man?" Clementine shook her head. "The things I've heard him say suggest he's just as dangerous as Berkshire."

"I agree." Nancy stood and put a hand to the small of her back.

Faith noticed that Nancy was showing quite a bit more than she had prior to Christmas. "Look at you. You're rounding out nicely."

"Sometimes my lower back aches, and I'm certainly more exhausted at times." Nancy smiled. "However, I'm so delighted to be in this condition that you will not hear me complain about a single thing."

Smiling, Faith got to her feet. "I'm spent. After listening to Gerome Berkshire's nonsense in that overheated hall, and then hearing Samuel Lakewood drone on, I could use a bath."

"I believe there is plenty of hot water and fresh towels."

Clementine walked to the window and pulled back the drapes just enough to peer outside. "I wish the rain would stop. I can't bear the idea of dealing with flooding, even if we aren't in any real threat here."

"I agree. The rain has been quite tedious." Nancy suppressed a yawn. "I hope Seth gets back soon. I know he'll be soaked to the bone."

"Where did he go on such a foul evening?" Clementine asked, coming away from the window.

"It was a deacons' meeting at church. I'm sure it won't last much longer, and he has the carriage, so hopefully he'll make the trip quickly when they conclude."

Faith turned to Clementine. "Oh, I nearly forgot. I asked Mr. Lakewood if it would be all right to bring you and Mimi to his donor meeting. You mentioned wanting to hear me speak, and I thought it might give me some additional protection. Berkshire will no doubt be there."

"I'd love to come. I'm sure Mimi would—"

A thunderous crash sounded from the second floor. Nancy gasped and headed for the stairs. "You don't suppose Mrs. Weaver has fallen, do you?"

She raced up the stairs despite her expanding abdomen. Faith and Clementine followed without delay.

Mrs. Weaver's room was near the back stairs at the end of the hall, and it was clear that some sort of ruckus was going on inside.

"Mrs. Weaver, are you all right?" Nancy didn't wait for an answer but produced her key and unlocked the door. "Mrs. Weaver?"

"I'm—I'm quite . . . all right," the old woman replied, her voice barely heard.

Faith made certain they had light before assessing the situation. If Mrs. Weaver had fallen, she would need to examine her. But there was no thought of that once Faith turned back to where Mrs. Weaver lay tangled in her covers—on the floor. The slats in the bed had broken or shifted enough that the collapse had caused a terrible crash.

But this was not the reason for everyone's immediate silence and dropped jaws. There beside Mrs. Weaver in the rumpled mess was a small black woman who stared back at them as if she feared for her life.

CHAPTER 8

The wide-eyed black woman clutched the covers to her neck as her gaze darted from face to face. Faith could see she was terrified and knelt beside her to offer reassurance.

"I'm a doctor. Are you injured?"

The gray-haired woman shook her head. Mrs. Weaver, on the other side of the bed, finally spoke. "Help me up from this mess, please."

Clementine pulled back the tangle of covers and assisted Virginia Weaver to a sitting position. The mattress was lopsided, with part of the top and right side still positioned on the rail, while the left side and lower part had landed on the floor.

Mimi burst into the room. "What on earth happened?" She stopped and gaped when she saw the small black woman.

"Are you all right, Mrs. Weaver?" Nancy asked as the old woman adjusted her mobcap.

"I am well." She got to her feet with Clementine's help and reached for her flannel robe. "What a disaster, and now my secret is known."

Nancy smiled. "Can you explain what's going on?"

Mrs. Weaver allowed Clementine to help her with the dressing gown. "This is Alma. We've been together since childhood, and I will not be parted from her. She was my slave, but I freed her, and she has long been my friend."

Faith again smiled and offered her hand to the elderly black woman. "Might I help you to your feet?"

Alma gave a hesitant nod.

Taking great care to cause the woman no pain, Faith all but lifted the tiny soul from the floor. She couldn't have weighed more than eighty pounds, nightclothes and all.

"Well, I must say, this is a surprise," Nancy said, shaking her head.

"I did not intend to cheat you of revenue," Mrs. Weaver declared. "That was certainly never my intention, but we know about the laws against blacks here. Once, when my husband and I were newly arrived, we saw another family with a black maid, and what happened was appalling. They whipped that poor servant and then forced the family to send her away. Over the years, we've heard much threatening talk, and I've even read about some physical displays in the paper. I couldn't risk that for poor Alma."

"So you kept her hidden? That must have been quite difficult." Nancy's tone was compassionate and not in the least accusing.

Mrs. Weaver nodded. "It seemed the only thing we could do. If folks knew we had a black woman living in our house, they would have come to make her leave."

"I'm sorry you've had to endure so much." Nancy shook her head. "Why don't we go downstairs and have some cocoa? When Seth returns, I'll have him repair the bed. He should be home any moment."

"But what about Alma?" Mrs. Weaver asked. "I cannot bear for her to be put onto the streets." She went to the black woman and put her arm around her. "She is dearer than a sister to me, and without her I would surely die. She has cared for me since infancy."

"I would never consider separating you," Nancy replied. "Honestly, Mrs. Weaver, if you had just come to me, I would have seen to it that she was safely kept with you. I am not like those who would cruelly take her from you. Although I understand why you didn't tell me. Trust is required for such a thing, and you didn't know me well enough to know that you could trust me with your secret."

They adjourned to the first floor, and while Clementine went to the kitchen to see to the cocoa, the other women gathered around the dining room table.

Faith could see that the black woman was still quite fearful. "I'm Faith Kenner, Alma. I'm pleased to make your acquaintance. I think you'll find that everyone here is quite accepting of people, no matter their skin color."

Alma glanced to Mrs. Weaver, who nodded. "It would seem," Virginia Weaver declared, "that we are among friends."

"Of course you are," Nancy countered. "Oh, I wish you had just come to me. I have no desire to see you and Alma separated."

"But most whites do not feel as you do." The old woman looked at her friend. "We have been together since my birth. Alma is three years older than me, and her mother was my mammy. Alma was my childhood companion and later my maid. When I married, my father gave Alma to me as a gift. When my husband decided we would move west, there was never a question of whether we'd invite Alma to accompany us."

Mrs. Weaver paused to smile at Alma. "So she decided to come with us, only to learn that blacks were not welcome in the Oregon Country. We witnessed many horrible things involving the Negro people. Many were whipped and forced to leave, never to be heard from again. I couldn't let that happen to Alma.

"My husband had purchased a house in the country, and there we felt fairly safe. Alma was able to live without fear to a degree, but whenever people came calling, we were careful to hide her away. We had a nice room set up for her off the chicken house. This was only for those times when people came calling and were in the main house. Otherwise Alma had her own bedroom upstairs in our house."

"Why did you need a separate hiding place off the chicken house?" Nancy asked.

Virginia nodded, as if anticipating the question. "We couldn't risk someone being with us downstairs and hearing her footsteps or the creaking of the floorboards upstairs. We had to constantly keep such things in mind."

"That would be terrible."

"We made sure there were lots of places she could hide on the property. We wanted to make sure she'd be safe no matter what. No one ever knew she was with us."

"How awful to have to hide away all the time," Nancy said, shaking her head.

Virginia cast a sorrowful gaze at Alma. "When my husband died and I was forced to sell everything and move to the city, I actually considered returning to Georgia, but I knew it would cost every cent I had. We'd be dependent upon family to care for us, and I couldn't be sure they'd accept Alma. I told her we would simply have to sneak her into the boardinghouse, so she hid herself in the blanket box that I packed with my clothes and sentimental articles. She would hide there when you came to see me in my room. Sometimes, though, there wasn't time, and she would crawl under the bed."

Faith couldn't imagine the old woman having to do that. She and Mrs. Weaver were at least in their sixties, and just watching Alma as she came downstairs, Faith felt certain the black woman was arthritic.

"Well, there will be no more of that." Nancy frowned. "I am so sorry for what you've endured, Alma. I have little tolerance for the harsh judgment that is passed on a person because of the color of their skin." She looked back at Mrs. Weaver. "How can we best remedy this, Virginia? Would a bigger room help? We have the room the Clifton sisters used to occupy. It's a little bigger. I have empty rooms downstairs that I plan to convert to bedrooms, as well. Seth and I could move ahead on that project, if that would benefit you and Alma. In the meantime, I can certainly provide two beds instead of one."

"We don't wish to be trouble. It's a blessing that you would allow Alma to stay." Tears came to Mrs. Weaver's eyes, and she looked down as if embarrassed. "I can't afford to pay much more, however."

"We won't worry about that just now. Instead, we want to make sure Alma has what she needs."

Clementine brought a tray of cocoa and cups. "Here we are. This should fortify us."

The rain began to fall quite hard outside. Faith could hear the pounding on the roof. It sounded as if someone were pelting the house over and over with rocks. The others noticed it as well.

"I'm sorry Seth has to be out on a night like this," Clementine declared, pouring cocoa into each cup. "I saved a mug for him on the stove. Hopefully it'll keep warm."

Nancy nodded. "I'm sure he'll appreciate that."

"I don't think you should worry, Mrs. Weaver," Mimi said, reaching over to give the older woman's arm a squeeze. "There may be laws against the blacks living in Oregon, but few people are enforcing them. The black community has its own church and school, and many blacks even own businesses and homes. I believe better heads have prevailed against those ugly laws."

"Yes, but they haven't changed them." Virginia Weaver looked at each of the ladies as if she were hoping someone might contradict her comment. No one did.

The truth was that the laws were clearly on the books, and if someone chose to make a case out of it, the law would support ridding the town and state of anyone who was black. Faith could understand Virginia Weaver's fear. It seemed better to her to hide her friend away in a blanket box than to risk losing her altogether.

"It's true the laws haven't been changed," Nancy said between sips of cocoa. "But they should be."

"Still, with men like Gerome Berkshire fighting to rid the state of blacks and Indians, we can't be too careful." Faith looked at her cousin. "We can, however, continue to keep this secret."

Nancy nodded. "Absolutely."

"We won't say a word," Mimi agreed.

"You can count on me," Clementine promised.

Mrs. Weaver exchanged a look with Alma. Tears streamed down her cheeks. "I don't know what to say but thank you. I know that's not enough, especially after deceiving you as I did."

"You did what you thought best for your friend." Nancy gave her a warm smile. "I would have done the same and cannot fault you for your love."

The front door opened, and the ladies all glanced toward the arched entry to the dining room. Seth came down the hall drenched, clearly intent on making his way to the bedroom. He stopped when he saw the women, however.

"Is something wrong?" he asked.

Nancy got up and handed him a tea towel from the sideboard. "Besides the fact that you're soaked to the bone, we had an incident with one of the beds upstairs. The slats fell out."

He took the towel and wiped his face. "I'll get some dry clothes on and see to fixing that." Then he noticed Alma. He looked at Nancy, his brow furrowed.

Nancy made the introductions. "This is Alma. She's Mrs. Weaver's lifelong friend and our new boarder."

"Welcome to the house," Seth said, his expression relaxing. "You picked a doozy of a time to come, but you're always welcome. Now, if you ladies will excuse me." He headed down the hall before anyone could reply.

Nancy smiled back at Mrs. Weaver and Alma. "See there, he doesn't mind a bit. If you'll excuse me, I'll see if I can help him get changed."

"So she was hidden in the blanket box?" Seth asked after the bed was repaired and everyone but Faith and Nancy had retired for the night.

"Virginia was so afraid Alma would be beaten and sent away that she felt she had to hide her. Isn't that terrible?"

"It is. Sadly, I know it's widely accepted behavior. We have a lot of prejudice in this country, and the Indian wars over the years have only served to make whites question the need for any person of color. Just last week, a Chinese man was found severely beaten behind one of the saloons." Seth sipped his cup of hot chocolate.

"People are cruel." Faith knew this from patients she'd cared for on her hospital training rounds.

For several minutes, no one said anything more. Resolution was a long way off, and they all seemed to feel the burden of this in their silence.

"Thank you for the hot chocolate," Seth said. "I finally feel thawed."

"I wish it would stop raining," Nancy said again as she began to gather the cups. "Everything is so damp and cold. I can't seem to get warm enough, no matter what I wear."

Seth grinned. "I'll keep you warm."

Faith laughed. "I believe that's my cue to leave you two." She got to her feet. "I hope you know how much I appreciate your acceptance of Alma. And for that matter, me. I sometimes ponder the choices I've made and wonder if I'm doing wrong by living the life of a white woman." She had given Nancy permission to share the truth of her birth with Seth, especially now that he was family.

"You are equally white and Cayuse," Nancy replied. "I see nothing wrong with choosing one or the other. I would see nothing wrong if you wanted to live as both, although I know the world would never accept that and brand you Indian alone."

"It's true," Seth replied. "I think you can help the most people with your medical training, and that means continuing to pass as white. Otherwise I'm afraid all opportunities would be closed to you."

"I know you're right. I look at the laws and the problems the Indian people are facing. They have so few who will advocate for them. Although I did meet a woman in Colorado a few years back. Her name is Helen Hunt Jackson. We became fast friends when she learned I was studying to become a physician. She had lost two sons, one to diphtheria and one to a brain disease."

"How awful." Nancy rubbed her growing belly. "I don't think I could bear such a thing."

"She is a remarkable woman, but her pain was evident. Still, she was troubled by the treatment of the Indians, and last year she attended a lecture in Boston where she heard the Ponca Indian Chief Standing Bear describe the government's removal of the Ponca in Nebraska. She wrote to me, knowing that I held great interest in the matter of Indian affairs. She was heartsick at all that had happened to the Indians. The government had been cruel. Many starved to death, and others were beaten and abused. It was then that she decided to take up the Indian cause full-time. She wrote to tell me she plans to pen a book that will detail the terrible things that have been done."

Nancy's face lit up. "Then perhaps, dear cousin, that is exactly what you are here to do. Didn't you tell me you were speaking to a group of donors next week? Men who will donate large sums of money to the medical college?"

"Yes. But I won't be speaking about the problems between Indians and whites."

Nancy smiled. "Maybe you should. Maybe as a physician, you can speak to the fact that we are no different. I remember my mother working on a poor Indian woman. She had been injured in a fall, and I remember my mother pointing out that her blood was no different than ours—that her internal organs and bones were made just as ours are."

"It's true. I've done many dissections on Indian bodies as well as whites. There is no difference inside. We are the same.

Blacks and Chinese as well. As far as science has proven to me, once you peel away the outer skin, we are basically the same."

"So maybe you need to work that into your speech. While you defend the need for female doctors, maybe that tidbit of knowledge could be shared as well."

"I think Nancy makes a good point," Seth chimed in. "Maybe with your education and knowledge of the body, you will be able to persuade others to reconsider their opinions. After all, other doctors know the truth as well."

Faith smiled. "You might have a point there. I'll give it some thought."

"Perhaps Mrs. Jackson can even offer you advice on how to approach your audience," Nancy said.

"I'm sure she could. She truly is a remarkable woman. I hope you get to meet her one day."

Such thoughts filled Faith's dreams that night, and the next morning as she made her bed, she continued to ponder what Seth and Nancy had suggested. The idea behind speaking about being a female doctor was to raise financial support for the college. If she expressed her own feelings against racial prejudices by using her educational experiences, she had a feeling it would only defeat the first purpose. Yet how could she stand by and do nothing?

A light rapping sounded on her door. "Come in." She plumped the pillow and waited to see who it was.

"Good morning, Faith." Clementine beamed at her. "Nancy asked me to give you this letter. It came yesterday, and she forgot all about it until this morning."

Faith took the missive and glanced at the writing. "It's from my mother."

"Always good to have news from home. I'll leave you to read it."

Once Clementine was gone, Faith opened the envelope and scanned the page. She had to smile at her mother's concern about her staying warm enough and keeping dry. She supposed no matter what her age might be, Faith would always be a little girl to her mother. She continued to read.

Your father and I heartily approve of your work with the other college students to hold lectures to promote unifying people of all colors. We want to help with that in any way we can.

Faith had written to express her concerns some weeks before her trip home for Christmas. There had been little time to discuss it over the holidays, but now that she was refocusing on her final semester of school, Faith felt an urgency to do whatever she could to help further the cause. Last night had driven home a point to which she had given little thought. People were suffering because of prejudices and bad laws, and it was her duty to help get those laws changed and see that all people were treated equally. She might not be able to vote, but that didn't mean she couldn't work to influence others.

Your father plans to come to Portland and set up a bank account for you. The money can be used for your personal needs but also for helping fund your lecture plans.

Faith couldn't contain her smile. Her parents were always generous, and her father would know exactly the kind of funding they would need to rent out speaking halls and have flyers printed.

We are proud of you, Faith. You have always been so tenderhearted toward people of all colors. Your kindness and determination to see people treated as God would treat them serves to make you all the more admirable.

To know that her parents were proud of her brought tears to Faith's eyes. She had always worked for their favorable opinion and approval, and now it was clear she had both. She could hardly ask for more than that.

Faith went to her writing desk and took a seat. She would send a thank-you note back to her folks, but first she would write to Helen Hunt Jackson. With the funding provided by her folks, it seemed clear that God was calling her to take up the cause, and Helen would be able to advise her as to how to start.

Perhaps she could even favor us with a visit! Faith picked up her pen.

CHAPTER 9

With her classes resuming next Monday, as well as her speaking event for Mr. Lakewood the same evening, Faith began to feel overwhelmed. It was already Friday, which gave her only two days to see to schoolwork and her speech, because she wanted to keep her Sabbath as a day of rest. When Seth mentioned that the *Morning Star* had docked sometime in the night, Faith knew she could find solace in visiting Captain Gratton. It seemed unreasonable to waste precious time, given that nothing could ever come of their friendship, but she told herself that perhaps nothing needed to come of it. Having a good friend in the captain was reason enough to continue the relationship. She didn't need to think of him as a potential mate. Wasn't there a certain liberty in that?

Of course, there was still the issue of her studies looming over her. Perhaps since church didn't start until ten o'clock, she could sleep late that morning. That way she could stay up late on Saturday to finish her assignments and finalize her speech. She wanted to make a good impression on Mr. Lakewood and his friends.

When Faith drew near to where the ship was moored, she

spied Andrew on the lower deck, speaking to a couple of crew members. He saw her and waved her aboard without hesitation.

"What brings you down here today?" he asked, helping her with her final steps up the gangplank. "We aren't taking passengers until this afternoon."

"I heard you were in town and wanted to see if you had fully recovered from your injury." She knew it was a lame excuse, but at the moment she couldn't think of anything else to say.

He smiled. "I'm fit as a fiddle. Had a great doctor and knitter." He tugged on the red cap she had made him.

"Crochet," she corrected. "The hat and scarf were crocheted, not knitted." She smiled. "But I'm glad to see that you're using them."

He chuckled. "I'd be a fool not to. They're very warm and suit me well. Now, come meet the boys." He moved toward the two crew members who were awaiting him. "Gentlemen, this is Miss Faith Kenner, a good friend of mine and a fine physician." He looked back at Faith. "This is Joe and Festus."

Faith smiled. "I'm pleased to meet you both."

The men smiled, but Joe was the one to speak. "I've heard of women learnin' to be doctors and figured that was an oddity. Guess I wouldn't mind if she was as pretty as you."

Andrew was having none of his flirting. "Joe, go find Remli and tell him I need coffee for two in the saloon. Maybe some of those cheese biscuits he made earlier. Then I want you two to get back to loading. Finish that and then see to these repairs."

"Sure thing, Captain."

Andrew looked at Faith. "Come on, let's get inside. The wind is making the morning impossibly cold."

"I agree." She followed him to the passenger saloon and

was grateful to get inside out of the breeze. "Thankfully it has stopped raining."

"It's bound to start up again. At least that's what my—what Ben said at breakfast." He looked momentarily uneasy. "He, uh, always seems to know about the weather."

Faith took a seat at one of the tables, and Andrew joined her. "How are your classes coming along?" he asked.

"We've been on a break for the holidays, but they start back up on Monday, and then we must all press our noses to the grindstone. Graduation is in April, and I have to complete my thesis paper on childbed fever and modern innovations to prevent its occurrence, as well as attend a great many lectures. And, of course, there will be the inevitable tests." Faith unbuttoned her coat. "I've also been asked to speak at a gathering of gentlemen who are being encouraged to donate to the medical college."

Andrew frowned. "A gathering of men only?"

Faith shrugged. "I honestly don't know. Mr. Lakewood spoke only of men, but I suppose it's possible he said that because they will be the ones deciding whether to give money to the cause. Hopefully some of their wives will be present as well."

His frown deepened. "You won't be going alone, will you? Maybe your cousin and her husband could accompany you."

She was touched by his concern. "I have two of the boardinghouse ladies accompanying me. They wanted to hear me speak."

"I'm glad to hear it. So what will you be saying to them?"

"That's partly what I wanted to talk to you about. My family believes that besides speaking on the virtues of women as physicians, I should use the opportunity to speak about the unjust treatment of the Indians and other people of color. Especially since it is a topic that touches me deeply."

"Why would you need to speak to me about that?"

Faith shrugged. "I guess I just need an impartial opinion on the matter. My friends and family always have in mind what I should do or say, but I thought that since you are a newer friend, someone who doesn't know everything about me . . . well, I thought you might be able to advise me."

"I see. I'm not sure that's the case, but I'll try. You say you were asked to come and help influence donors to give money to the medical college. Do you have people of color attending the college?"

"Mercy, no. It's hardly acceptable that women are there."

He nodded. "So it's not going to promote donations to digress and talk about something unrelated to the college."

"That's true." Andrew was echoing her own concerns about possibly hampering the fundraising effort. "There are a group of students at the college who feel as I do about the injustices done to people of color. We want to start a series of lectures. My folks have even decided to help by donating money for us to secure lecture halls and create advertising."

"It sounds as if you will have ample opportunities to speak out against the problem of racial injustice."

"Yes. Yes, I will." She smiled. "So it's probably wise just to speak about the topic I've been asked to speak on and leave the other for another time."

A stout man entered the saloon, carrying a tray. He was of mixed race, black and perhaps Indian or Mexican. He beamed Faith a smile.

"I see the captain is entertaining. Ain't never seen him do that before."

"Don't be making something out of nothing," Andrew warned. "This is the woman doctor I was telling you about. The one who sewed me up. Faith, this is Remli. He's been cooking and cleaning for the *Morning Star* for over ten years."

She nodded. "Mr. Remli."

"No *mister*," he said, depositing the tray. "Just Remli." He smiled. "Glad to meet you, ma'am."

"Faith. Just call me Faith, Remli."

The black man's smile widened.

"Thanks for the refreshments." Andrew was already slathering butter on one of the biscuits. "You have to try this, Faith. Nobody makes biscuits like Remli."

She pulled off her gloves. "I'm excited to sample them."

Andrew handed the buttered piece to her. Faith took a bite and had to marvel at the cheesy flavor. "This is wonderful. How did you make them?"

"I just mix up a batch of biscuits and then throw in some seasonings and grated cheese. You can put jam on 'em too." Remli uncovered a pot of what appeared to be blackberry preserves. "The cheese goes along real nice."

Faith picked up a spoon and added some of the jam to her biscuit. She took another bite. The flavors were delightful. "Mmm. Heavenly."

Remli grinned. "Glad you like 'em. Captain, if you ain't needin' nothing else, I got four meat pies in the oven."

"By all means, see to it. That's our supper."

"Nice meetin' you, ma'am. Faith."

"And likewise you, Remli."

She waited until he'd gone to finish her biscuit, while Andrew poured the coffee. She liked the way Andrew's crew felt like family rather than employees.

"Would you like some cream or sugar for your coffee?" he asked.

"Just cream." She leaned back in her chair and smiled as Andrew added an ample portion of cream. Here was this rugged ship's captain playing hostess at an impromptu tea party. Or coffee party, in this case. Faith had to admit she was smitten.

"Now that we've resolved your questions about the lecture you'll be giving, what else should we discuss?" he asked, handing her the cup.

Faith took the coffee and cherished the warmth in her hands. "Why don't you tell me about the journeys you've made since I saw you last?"

"Mostly back and forth from Astoria and Fort Vancouver and then down to Oregon City. Routine shipping—a lot of flour and grain."

"Any problems?"

"None to speak of."

"No pirates to attack you and steal away your booty?"

He blinked at her, then burst out laughing. "No pirates. Although there was one cranky customer who thought we had shortchanged him. We sorted out the details, however, and he clearly saw his mistake and went away content."

She nodded and sipped the coffee. It was strong, but the cream mellowed the bitterness. She felt so at ease with Andrew that it was almost startling. Here was a man she knew very little about, and yet she felt as if they'd been friends for years.

"Are your folks or siblings in the area?" she asked.

He shook his head. "I was the only one of my folks' five children who lived to see adulthood. My mother died after my siblings, and then my father. He was pretty well up in years."

"I'm sorry to hear that they're all gone. That must be lonely at times. I love my family, and I don't know what I'd do without them."

"The crew of the *Morning Star* is my family now." He seemed rather uncomfortable and stared down at his cup.

Faith decided to change the subject. "How did you become a riverboat captain?"

He shrugged. "A lot of hard work. I started out as a loader and point man. I kept an eye on the river and looked for things that could cause snags and problems. I worked from boat to boat, seeking whatever promotion I could get—learning each and every job until I found someone willing to take me on and teach me how to pilot the boat. I've worked stern-wheelers like the *Morning Star*, side-wheelers, tugs, and just about anything else that floats. I've even done my share of ocean voyages. I prefer the river. The ocean is always changing—the river too, but she's less unpredictable."

"I've always loved the Willamette, and you're right. There is a predictable nature to her. I remember when I first came to live in Oregon City after growing up on the Rogue River. I could see the outward differences in the nature of the rivers, but there were also differences that couldn't be seen—beneath the surface, sometimes deep down. It made me think of God and how He doesn't look at the outward appearance but at the heart of man."

"I've never heard anyone compare things quite that way. I'll take my chances with the river before doing the same with God."

Faith frowned. "What do you mean? God is hardly unpredictable. The Bible shows us His character and nature from start to finish. He is constant. The only constant in the entire universe. He is the same yesterday, today, and forever. What's to take a chance on?"

He shrugged. "I'm sorry. I didn't mean to rile you. I can see you're even more passionate about preaching than doctoring."

Faith flushed. "I wasn't trying to preach. It's just that when people make suggestions about God's character that contradict what I know it to be, I feel the need to defend."

"Defend God?" Andrew smiled. "Do you really suppose He needs our defense?"

"Perhaps not defense so much as support."

"So you are making yourself a character witness for God Almighty?" Andrew grinned.

"I remember you saying that you were acting like a Christian by saving Benjamin, but now you sound almost sarcastic about faith and a relationship with God. I thought you believed in Him."

"Of course I believe in Him." Andrew reached for a biscuit and tore off a piece. "I just don't think the Maker of the universe has time to worry Himself over me. I believe His underlying current—since you compared Him to the river—is too powerful for the likes of me."

"I didn't compare God to a river. I merely suggested that like the river, man has things that he hides out of sight. At least, I was getting around to that. I only brought God into it because the Bible says He looks not on the outward appearance of man but at the heart."

"Big storm coming up. Miss Faith better go."

Faith couldn't be sure when Ben had entered the room, but there he stood, smiling and offering his advice.

"Good morning to you too." Faith smiled at Ben. "Thank you for letting me know about the weather. I have no desire to be drenched."

"It's gonna be a bad one." The old Indian shook his head. "Bad like when I was a boy."

Faith frowned. "Then I'd best hurry." She had no doubt Ben

knew what he was talking about. "Thank you for your hospitality, Captain." She gave him a smile and grabbed another biscuit. "I'll take this to sustain me in case the rain starts before I get home. I'd love to continue our conversation another time."

Andrew followed her outside, where they found the wind had picked up and the temperature had dropped. The sky was heavy with rain-laden clouds.

"It looks like we're in for it, just as Ben said." Faith secured her coat's top buttons and then pulled on her gloves. "Hopefully I'll see you again soon."

"Be careful," Andrew said, his dark eyes narrowing. "I'm sorry if I upset you in our discussion."

She shook her head. "Not at all."

"I'd walk with you, but I need to make certain the ship is secure."

"Don't worry about me. I'll be just fine. I meant it when I said I would like to pick up our conversation another time. You'll find I'm not easily frightened away when it comes to defending my beliefs."

He smiled. "Or supporting them, as you suggested."

They were standing so close, and to Faith it felt natural to offer him a hug. Had they been close friends or promised to each other, she might have.

But she didn't, because they were neither. Andrew was a fine man, and the fact that he seemed to enjoy her company as much as she did his blessed her. She knew it was dangerous to allow such feelings, but for the life of her, she couldn't force them aside as she'd always done in the past.

"Good-bye, Captain Gratton." She took a bite of her biscuit and walked away.

"Good day to you, Miss Kenner."

She glanced back when she'd gone nearly a block, but Andrew was already gone. No doubt, with the storm he had a great many tasks to see to. Faith turned to make her way home. She had wanted to stay and hear Andrew's perspective on God.

A blast of cold air almost knocked her to the ground and put her thoughts on the impending storm. The wind lessened almost as soon as it delivered the punch, but she picked up her pace. This close to the docks, there were few places a lady could seek safe refuge should the storm cut loose in the next few minutes.

She wasn't all that far from the *Morning Star*, however, when another gust came, and then another. Before Faith could steady herself, the wind was blowing steady with gale-like force and whipped the biscuit from her hands. It was just as well. She needed to hold on to her hat and skirt. She placed her hand atop the hat and put her head down in order to press on, but it was like fighting against a giant's hold. All around her, merchants were battling to get their wares inside. Customers and dock workers were running for shelter.

The wind's roar seemed to grow ever louder, and a terrible screeching of metal on metal sounded from her right. Faith glanced up just as a huge piece of roofing pulled away from a store. Debris appeared all around her and swirled in a strange sort of dance. It was almost mesmerizing. Merchants continued battling to retrieve various items, but it was a hopeless task. The wind was too powerful.

Faith hesitated. She wasn't at all sure which way to go. The ship was closer. Perhaps she should return to the *Morning Star*. There was no possibility of reaching home in this gale. The streetcars wouldn't be running, and no cab driver was going to risk his horse and carriage. She saw a large basket careening down the road, seeming to take direct aim at her. Faith side-stepped it at the last minute, but mud stung her eyes, making it impossible to see the other things coming at her. How was it possible for mud to be picked up by the wind? Yet there it was, smeared against her clothes and no doubt her face. Faith struggled to wipe her eyes. She was pelted by a variety of debris, none of which she saw. Putting her arm up to shield her head, she wasn't surprised to find the wind had ripped her hat away.

She tried to cry for help, but the wind choked the words back and not even the tiniest sound came from her throat. Things were getting desperate, and she decided to head back toward the *Morning Star*. It was just a few blocks away. Surely she could make it.

But before she could move, another cacophony of tearing metal and wood rose above the wind's roar. It sounded like an entire building was being ripped apart, and when she managed to look to her left, it seemed the entire block was dissolving.

Faith saw the sign from O'Brien's Warehouse rip off its hinges and fly directly at her. She turned to run but found it almost impossible to move, as the wind seemed to blow from every direction. The sign hit hard against her back, sending her forward into the muddy street as it flew over her and moved on down the road. Before Faith could assess herself for damage and get back to her feet, however, something hit the back of her head.

She fell forward onto the street. Rolling to her side, she reached her gloved hand up to where she'd been hit. The ground seemed to whirl beneath her. Were they having an earthquake as well as a storm?

She touched her head. It didn't hurt, so she hoped the damage was minimal. When she withdrew her hand, however, there was blood on her glove. A lot of blood.

She tried to get up but found she hadn't the strength. All around her, the world was coming apart piece by piece, and all she could do was lie in the street and ponder what she was going to do. How she wished Andrew would come searching for her. She imagined him finding her and saying something sarcastic about her having to tend herself. She could almost see him smiling down at her—promising her she'd be just fine, that he'd see to it.

And then the roar of the wind grew even louder, and the light faded from the sky. Faith closed her eyes, giving in to the darkness, wondering if Andrew and the *Morning Star* would survive the storm.

CHAPTER 10

Nancy heard the rise of the wind but thought little of it until one of the shutters began banging wildly against the house. She went in search of the culprit and found that one of Mimi's windows was to blame. Opening the window, Nancy leaned out as far as her belly would allow and grabbed the wooden shutter as it came flying toward the house. The snap of the wood against her cold fingers hurt, but Nancy was determined to secure it. When the wind tried to rip it from her grasp, she heard a cracking sound, and for a moment she thought the shutter was ripping away from the house. Instead, she glanced up in time to see the neighbor's large fir tree fall across the street and yard.

She froze. She looked heavenward and saw the heavy gray clouds that swirled and roiled. She couldn't remember ever seeing such a storm. The wind picked up again and blew a steady gust of icy air. Nancy wrestled the shutter into place and locked it, then brought its counterpart forward to hook them together. It would provide the window with a minimum of protection. She hurried to secure the rest of the shutters. It was the first time since she'd moved into the house that she'd ever needed to worry about such things.

She went to Clementine's room and then to the empty bedroom at the end of the house and fastened the shutters. Again, a cracking sound split the air. This one sounded much closer.

Nancy knocked on Mrs. Weaver's door. "Ladies, we should make our way downstairs." She didn't wait for Mrs. Weaver's invitation to enter the room. She found the two women sitting close to each other, far from the window. "I need to secure the shutters, and then I suggest we seek shelter in the pantry. I have a feeling, with the trees being uprooted, we may very well see damage done to the house. The pantry runs under the stairs and offers the most protection."

"Goodness, it sounds like the end of the world out there," Mrs. Weaver said, gathering a few things. Alma looked to her for instruction while Nancy secured the windows.

"There, that's the best I can do here. Let's go. Bring your coats in case we cannot make it back upstairs."

"Why would we not be able to return?" Mrs. Weaver asked, her winkled brow furrowing even more.

"The trees are being uprooted, and we have several that could fall against the house. Come on, now. We must hurry."

Virginia Weaver nodded and went to the coat tree, while Alma retrieved her things from the blanket box near the door. Nancy escorted the two ladies downstairs and made her way to the dining room. The wind's roar made it difficult to hear anything, so she guided the women by hand signs. She grabbed the outdoor lantern as she passed the counter, then opened the door to the pantry.

Once they were inside, Nancy quickly realized there was no place to sit. "You ladies stay here, and I'll grab a couple of dining room chairs."

She stepped from the pantry as a tree in the backyard gave way and crashed against the house. A scream escaped her throat as her hand went to her abdomen. What in the world was going to happen to them?

"Are you all right, Nancy?" Mrs. Weaver asked from the pantry doorway.

She glanced back and nodded. "Get inside. A tree just hit the house." She grabbed two chairs and dragged them back toward the pantry. Alma was there to take them in hand.

"You come on, now," she said in an uncharacteristically bold manner. "There's a little stool here. I can sit on it right fine."

Nancy nodded and went into the pantry, pulling the door closed behind her. Mrs. Weaver had already lit the lantern. The shadows cast by the dim light were ghostly and ominous.

"We need to pray," Mrs. Weaver said.

Nancy was still in shock. She sank onto the chair and nodded. Any words she might have offered were stuck in her throat.

"Father, we ask for your provision and protection," Mrs. Weaver began. "There's a mighty storm blowing around us. We have no idea what to do other than to hide away here. But we know that You know where we are and what we need. Father, help us now. Be our strong refuge in this time of trouble."

"Amen," Nancy managed to whisper.

It sounded like a war was going on outside, but Nancy comforted herself in the fact that the house was well built. Her first husband had insisted the place be constructed sparing no expense. He wanted the very best, and he oversaw the details to ensure everything was done to his standards. Hopefully that meant the house would be able to withstand the heavy winds, since there seemed to be no sign of them stopping anytime soon.

"Might we sing some hymns?" Mrs. Weaver asked. "I always find that settles my nerves."

Nancy drew a deep breath and nodded. "Yes, I think that would be calming."

"'Behold what wondrous grace the Father has bestowed on sinners of a mortal race, to call them sons of God!'" Mrs. Weaver sang with surprising clarity, and Alma joined in with strong alto harmony. "''Tis no surprising thing that we should be unknown; the Jewish world knew not their King, God's everlasting Son.'"

Nancy was unfamiliar with the song and contented herself with listening to the two women sing. She felt a surprising peace despite their situation and closed her eyes to pray for Seth and the others who were out there in the storm. She hugged her abdomen and imagined God hugging her close as well.

"'If in my Father's love I share a filial part, send down Thy Spirit like a dove, to rest upon my heart. We would no longer lie like slaves beneath the throne; my faith shall Abba, Father, cry, and thou the kindred own.'"

As the last notes faded, Alma took up the call. "'Amazing grace, how sweet the sound.'"

Nancy smiled at the familiar words and joined in to sing. "'That saved a wretch like me. I once was lost, but now am found. 'Twas blind but now I see.'"

They continued to sing as the storm raged. As the minutes and then hours passed and still the storm held fast, Nancy's spirit continued to calm. God truly was the only refuge and strength that would last. Her fine house and beautiful yard would be destroyed. If not in this storm, then in another or simply by time itself. Why did people worry so much and put such stock in their possessions? As the Bible said in Matthew sixteen, "For what is a man profited, if he shall gain the whole world, and lose his own soul? or what shall a man give in exchange for his soul?"

Even her concerns for Seth and the others diminished. No matter what happened, Nancy rested in the knowledge that God held the reins. It hadn't been her first inclination, but as she sat and waited, she realized it was the only solution. Nothing else came even close to equaling God's sovereignty and power. Just as He could bring such a storm in the first place, God could quell it. And through it all, He alone could bring peace to Nancy's battered heart.

When his large office window shattered, Seth grabbed his coat and went in search of his employer, John Lincoln.

"John, I think we should seek shelter away from the windows. Something came smashing through mine. I didn't even see what, but I have glass all over my office."

"I heard the crash and was just coming to see what happened. I've lived here for over twenty years and never witnessed a storm like this. I thought it would pass, but this one seems determined to linger. I pray our wives are safe."

Cyrus, their secretary, entered John's office. He had several bloody scratches on his face. "The front window is gone."

"Are you all right?" John asked, moving to his side. "You're bleeding."

"It was a large board—perhaps a sign or a post." It was clear Cyrus was in shock.

"Let's move down the interior hallway, well away from the front entry. There are no windows down there," Seth suggested as the sound of debris hitting the building threatened more trouble.

John guided Cyrus, and Seth followed. There was little else they could do but seek protection and wait out the storm. Others who rented office space in the building soon joined them. Everyone wore the same look of confusion and surprise.

No one anticipated the storm lasting for four hours. It wasn't until around two o'clock in the afternoon that the wind died down and the rain stopped. Seth had thought of nothing but Nancy the entire time, and now that there was at least a break in the storm, he intended to get home to his wife.

"I'm leaving," he told John.

"Be careful. Things are certain to be a mess out there. Flooding and debris can create traps."

Cyrus was more himself after John and Seth had seen to his cuts, but the younger man was still quite shaken. He said nothing as he huddled in the corner.

"Can you make it home on your own, Cyrus, or should I assist you?" Seth asked.

"I'll be fine." Cyrus shook his head. "I've never seen such a storm in all my life."

"No one has, son." John Lincoln touched his shoulder. "Come, we'll head out together."

Some of the other office workers led the way, and the trio followed, not exactly hesitant, but guarded at the thought of what they might find.

They stepped from the building and gazed at the destruction around them. Seth thought it looked as if a giant had stepped on many of the buildings. Windows were broken and roofs ripped off. Telephone and telegraph poles had been torn from the ground and plunged into the sides of some buildings, while others lay wrapped in their wires and twisted together with other debris.

"Gracious," one of the other men said. "We had tornadoes in Kansas, but nothing like this. Nothing that lasted for hours on end."

"I have no idea what the authorities will ask of us," John said in disbelief. "Perhaps I should box up all the records and take them home. However, with the streets full of debris, I wouldn't be able to get the carriage here for transport."

"Why don't you put the more important papers in the safe, and we can figure out the rest later? Look, the police are already out in force. They'll no doubt keep looting to a minimum." At least Seth hoped they would. Right now, however, there was probably more concern about injuries. That again reminded him of Nancy and the ladies at the boardinghouse. "I need to get home."

He took off at a jog, doing his best to avoid the worst of the wreckage, but as he reached the more residential neighborhoods, he had to slow his pace considerably due to fallen trees strewn across the roads and yards. It was clear that the weeks of rain prior to the storm had weakened the ground. The trees had been pulled out as if they were rooted in sand.

People were starting to emerge from the houses. Many of the women were crying, and the men were doing their best to offer comfort. No one could figure out what had happened or what they were supposed to do now.

The sky overhead was still ominous, and from time to time the wind whipped with an ugly reminder of its power. Seth feared this was nothing more than a lull in the storm. He quickened his pace but found it impossible to hurry. There was just too much to overcome. Fallen trees were a considerable obstacle, especially the evergreens. Their branches were full, and it required great skill to pick a path through them. Seth found himself exhausted by the time he reached his own neighborhood.

When he turned onto his own street, a gasp escaped him. Trees were everywhere, and most of the houses were damaged either by those same trees or the wind's relentless power. One beautiful Queen Anne house he'd often admired had been cut in half by a huge fir.

Seth picked his way through the branches of fallen trees, some of which didn't even belong in his yard, to make his way to the front porch of the boardinghouse. A large white oak from the neighbor's yard now stretched across the end of the porch. His breathing quickened and his heart picked up its pace.

He opened the front door and entered, calling Nancy's name. He tried to ignore the dread that soured his stomach as he glanced around the sitting room. The front windows were undamaged, probably due to the porch's protection. It gave him hope.

"Nancy!"

"We're here!" she called back. "In the pantry."

As he reached the dining room and then the kitchen, he found his wife and Mrs. Weaver emerging from the pantry. Alma followed them. Seth reached for his wife and pulled her close.

"Are you all right? Is the baby all right?"

"We're both fine, as far as I can tell. What about you?" She looked up to search his face.

"I'm unharmed. The storm has destroyed a good deal of downtown. I wasn't sure I could even get through. Trees are everywhere, along with telegraph poles." Seth continued hugging Nancy. "Are you certain you're all right?"

"I am. We were quite shaken by the storm, but then we prayed and sang hymns, and the time passed quite easily." She smiled up at him. "We prayed especially for you. I was so worried."

"Where are Faith and Clementine? And Mrs. Bryant?"

116

"I've been wondering about all of them. Faith left early— shortly after you—but I have no idea where she is. Clementine and Mimi should have been at the school, since classes have started again, although I don't know what their situation is like. That school building is an older house. It might not have been strong enough to withstand the storm."

Seth nodded. "Don't fret. Worry won't change a thing. I'll go to the school after I check the damage to the house. I won't leave you here if there's a chance the place will collapse." He sighed. "I'll get to it now and then go check on the others."

As much as he hated to leave her there, Seth made his way upstairs and went room by room to check for damage. He kept thinking of what he'd seen as he made his way home. What if Clementine had been injured or killed? No doubt there would be deaths. How would he ever tell their parents . . . or Gabe?

"God, please spare my family and friends from any harm." He went to Clementine's room first. The scent of her perfume brought a smile to his face. "Protect my sister, Lord. Please let her be all right." Seth continued his search.

The shutters had kept the windows from shattering, and although one large tree had crashed against the house, there was only minimal damage, as far as he could see. Once he was outside, Seth could see there was a lot of pitting and exterior damage to the house, but it wasn't anything that would keep them from being able to live there. Part of the porch had col- lapsed under the neighbor's tree, but it didn't look to threaten the house's stability. The worst of damage was at the back of the house, as well as the carriage house. One of the larger trees had collapsed the south side of the carriage house. He managed to force his way through the mess to find that the horse was dead.

"Poor boy. You had no idea what hit you." Seth knelt and

stroked the animal's head. Beams from the roof had crashed down on him, leaving him badly broken. Nancy would be saddened at the loss, but all the more so at the thought of his suffering.

Seth made his way back inside to find the three ladies taking a general inventory of the house.

"One of our bedroom windows is cracked and the windows in the office are broken," Nancy told him. "I think that's the most immediate problem."

"The carriage house roof collapsed." He shook his head. "Racer didn't make it."

"Oh no. Poor beast. Did he suffer?" She bit her lower lip.

"I don't believe so. I think the initial collapse killed him instantly." At least, that was what Seth prayed had happened. He hated to think of the horse struggling beneath the weight of the wreckage. "A tree fell against the back of the house. I need to figure out if it presents any immediate danger or if we can stay here without concern. For once I'm glad we don't have natural gas. First, however, I need to check on Clementine."

"And Mimi," Mrs. Weaver declared.

"Yes, of course." Seth gave the old woman a smile. "I'll trust you to keep Nancy from doing anything foolish."

Mrs. Weaver bobbed her head. "We will take care of her. Don't you fret."

Nancy reached out to touch her husband's arm. "Seth, do you suppose the storm extended farther than Portland? Like . . . to Oregon City and our folks?"

"I doubt it. It was a bad storm, but I can't imagine it was that widespread."

She nodded, and the worry faded from her face. "We'll get the glass cleaned up and see what else we can do."

"Don't cook anything or start any fires. I know it's cold, but I need to make sure the chimneys and flues are working properly."

"We will don extra clothes and wrap up in blankets if need be." She stretched up and kissed his cheek.

Seth took hold of her and bent to kiss her on the mouth. He hadn't realized how frightened he'd been for her and the baby, but now that he was assured of their safety, he realized just how harrowing the entire experience had been. And he didn't yet know whether his sister was alive. He kissed Nancy again and held her for a long moment.

"Don't overdo it. I'll be back as soon as possible."

But before he could take up his hat, there was a knock at the front door. Seth opened it to find one of their neighbors, Mrs. Trent. She was pale, almost ashen.

"Can you come quick? It's my George. I think he's dying. His heart has attacked him, and I can't wake him."

There was no choice but to delay his plans. "Show me the way."

CHAPTER 11

Faith opened her eyes and blinked several times. The surroundings were unfamiliar, but she was warm and felt safe. She felt a rocking motion and wondered at it. How could she be in a rocking bed? She closed her eyes, and when she opened them again, a man was sitting beside her.

"Andrew?"

"Glad to have you back among the living. Or maybe I should say the conscious."

She heard a pounding in her ears. Was that her own heartbeat? "What happened? Where am I?"

"You're on the *Morning Star* in my quarters. You were hit in the head by debris. Do you remember anything?"

She closed her eyes again. "I remember the storm. There was a fierce wind and . . . yes, there was a lot of debris flying around." She thought about it for a moment.

When she opened her eyes again, Andrew had moved. Now, instead of sitting on the bed beside her, he sat in a chair.

"I see you're back again," he said.

She shook her head. "What are you talking about?"

"You've been in and out of consciousness for nearly five hours now."

"Five hours?" Faith tried to sit up, but a wave of dizziness sent her back to the pillow. "What happened?"

"You were hit in the head with debris from the storm. Ben sewed you up. He said to tell you he put in four strong stitches."

She touched the back of her head and felt a bandage. "Tell him I said thank you."

"You can thank him yourself. He's been here checking up on you every twenty minutes or so."

"My family will be worried sick."

"As soon as you're up to it, I'll get you home."

"I can take myself. The cable car goes right to the corner."

"The cable cars aren't running. You don't realize it, but our little storm destroyed most of Portland."

"What?" Faith tried to comprehend what he was saying. "It was just some wind and rain."

"A wind and rain that lasted four hours. The Army Signal Corps said the barometric pressure dropped to just about the lowest point they'd ever seen. It was like a hurricane. It tore out the telegraph and telephone lines, ripped off roofs, and tore buildings apart like so many matchstick figures."

"There must be a great many injured people. I should collect my things and make myself useful."

"You aren't going to be of use, because you're one of those injured people." Andrew shook his head. "I thought we might lose you. You bled a lot and were unconscious nearly all this time."

What he said made sense. She could remember waking up to snippets of conversation and momentary thought. "I remember the storm getting worse. I think I was trying to get back here. How did you find me?"

"When I realized how bad things were, I went looking for you. I even found myself praying, which I haven't done with any real thought of being heard in a long, long time."

Faith smiled. "And God heard you."

"He was probably only listening because it involved you."

That made her laugh. She shook her head and regretted the movement. She held her head between her hands, hoping the pain would fade. It didn't. "Grief, I make a poor patient. I can't bear being put to bed. There's so much I need to do."

"Right now you must see to yourself."

"You're awake. That's good," Ben said, looking in through the open doorway.

"I understand you put in four strong stitches," Faith said, dropping her hands and giving Ben a smile. "Thank you."

"You bled plenty, but head always bleeds more."

"It does indeed."

"You want tea to help with pain?" Ben asked.

Faith gave a slight nod. "That would be wonderful. Thank you."

When Ben was gone, she turned back to Andrew. "Is the town really in that bad of shape?"

"It is. I wouldn't even bother trying to get you home, but I'm sure your family is worried."

"If they're all right themselves. I hope the storm didn't cause them as much trouble as it did me. How widespread was it?"

"I can't tell you that. I suppose no one will know for a while. Word has it there's neither a telegraph line in place for miles nor an open rail line. The river is full of debris, making it too dangerous to head out. We're stuck right here, with no word in or out to let us know how the rest of Oregon fared."

"I've definitely endured worse quarters and company," she

said, smiling. She wouldn't tell him what an effort that smile took.

Andrew returned the smile. "I've never met anyone quite like you. You even have me reconsidering God."

"It's not me. God is calling you back. He must have some need of you—some desire for communion with you. You know He truly does want that with each of us. At the very core of our existence, we were made from love—His love—and He longs for us with a protective nature that speaks to the deepest longing in us."

"You are a strange woman, Faith Kenner. I've never met anyone who talks about God like you do."

The throbbing in her head was nearly impossible to bear, but Faith was encouraged by Andrew's willingness to speak about God. She wouldn't stop now.

"I've done a lot of studying, Andrew. I started reading when I was two years old."

"Two? That's impossible."

"Not at all. I wanted to know what those letters were and the words they made. Mama said I learned so fast, she could scarcely keep up. Anyway, when I was a young girl, I was encouraged to read books. All sorts of books. I think sometimes people just wanted to keep me occupied, but other times, I think they pushed me that direction because they knew that I had so much longing to know everything—at least as much as I could.

"One of the places I was able to borrow books from was a minister friend of the family. He had a library of history books that related to the church. I used to pore over them. He would see me reading them and then reading the Bible and puzzling over something far too grand for my ten-year-old mind. Eventually he asked me what I thought of all that I had read. Had I learned anything valuable? Had I figured out the meaning of life and the universe around us?" Faith could almost hear the old man's questions.

"And what did you say?" Andrew asked, looking as if she might impart the answer to that very question.

"I told him that while the books were interesting, I was constantly going back to the Bible. No matter what one man or another had to say, if it didn't agree with God's Word, I wasn't interested, and when it did agree, it only served to draw me deeper into God's Word. Does that make sense?"

Andrew sat for a long time and said nothing. Faith thought, from the frown on his face, that he must think her mad. Finally, however, he looked at her with an expression of wonder. "What did your friend say?"

She smiled and shrugged. Again, the pain of moving reminded her of her predicament. "He said he'd studied his entire sixty-seven years to discover what God had revealed to me in ten. He told me that God must have a powerful work laid out for me. It terrified me."

"Here's some tea," Ben said, coming into the room with a mug of steaming liquid. "It will help, and you can sleep until you go home."

"I really should go as soon as possible." She took the mug and sampled it. Willow bark, honey, and something else she couldn't identify. She wasn't worried, however. Something about Ben made her feel as if she were with family. "This is very good, Ben. Thank you."

"You plenty welcome, Miss Faith." He gave her a smile, then looked at Andrew. "You can stop worrying now. She gonna be well soon. She very strong."

"She is that," Andrew said, glancing back at her as he stood. "I need to check on a few things. I hope you don't mind. Just rest and drink your tea. I'll be back in a while."

"What time is it?" Faith glanced around the room for a clock.

"It's nearly four-thirty. I promise I'll get you home before much longer. After I see to the ship, I'll figure out a way to get you back to your family."

She nodded and took another sip of tea. Already she could feel the pain diminishing. It was probably more the company than the willow bark, but it was welcome no matter the source.

"She looks good," Ben said as he and Andrew made their way down below.

"She might not even be alive if not for you. You did a good job, Grandfather." Andrew put his hand on Ben's shoulder. He spoke in Nez Perce, knowing it pleased the old man. "I am grateful for your skills. You have helped my friend, and it has made my heart glad."

"She is more than a friend, I think. I think your heart is glad for reasons that you will not speak." The old man smiled and turned to leave. "I think your heart has found love."

Andrew watched his grandfather walk away and knew he had spoken the truth. He had fallen in love with Faith Kenner. He had carefully protected his heart all of his life, for all the good it did him. He knew the limitations and problems he could face as the laws of the land became more and more stringent in regard to bloodlines. The Civil War had only deepened the hatred of races mixing, and now most states had laws about people of various races intermarrying. Oregon's laws were quite strict.

Andrew's father had been half Assiniboine or Hohe and half English, a fur trapper who'd fallen in love with a woman who was part white, part Nez Perce and Cayuse. Her father was Benjamin Littlefoot. That left Andrew few choices when it came to marriage, and none of them included a white woman like Faith Kenner.

He drew a deep breath and thought of how much she fascinated him—how quickly she'd managed to win him without even trying. He wanted to spend his life with her—to never leave her side. He wanted to watch her use her skills as a fine surgeon. He wanted to talk to her about all those great books she'd read and how she'd come to understand in ten years what it had taken a schooled man of God decades to learn.

A band seemed to form around his chest. *You can never have her for your wife. She's not for the likes of a mixed breed riverboat captain,* a familiar accusing voice said from deep inside him. *You have nothing to offer her. Nothing at all.*

Gerome Berkshire sat across from Samuel Lakewood, frustrated that the older man wouldn't hear him out.

"If we do things my way, we can lay low for a time and let others take the blame for the guns and whiskey. Once they're arrested and put in jail, we can go back to our plans."

"How easily you sell out your friends," Lakewood said, shaking his head. "The fact of the matter is that right now Portland needs our attention."

"But listen to me, please. The destruction from the storm is the perfect chaos to push our plans forward. With all of this mess tying up the legal authorities as well as the army, we can move a great many firearms to the reservation at Warm Springs and let those being sent to Grand Ronde be discovered. It wouldn't be the new guns, just the old ones that are missing all their firing pins. Think of it. It would allow me to give the army something that would make them trust that I'm truly working for them. Otherwise I'm afraid they're going to throw me in jail for not giving them more useful information."

"We don't even know if those places were affected by the storm," Lakewood countered. "They may both have suffered as we have."

"It seems unlikely that a storm would cover such a distance. Why don't we get someone to ride out to each of the reservations and bring us back a report? Someone fast enough to get out there and back without delay." Gerome shifted in his chair. "You don't know how these people work. They are determined to shut us down once and for all. The storm damage will buy us some time and create enough confusion and disorder that we can accomplish a great deal. The men at the reservation are primed and ready to go to war. Just think about it. The city is in shambles and the Indians rise up. Imagine the trouble that will cause and the fear it will put into the hearts of neighboring people. More important, the government will see me as a true informant. That's to our benefit."

Lakewood tapped his fingers together. "You may be right. The storm's destruction will serve us well in this matter. Let's first find out just how far the damage extends. Then we can decide how to proceed."

"I'll get on that," Gerome said, smiling. "What the army doesn't realize is that I have made friends with the soldiers. For a little bit of money, those friends share information with me. Information that nicely aids our cause."

The older man nodded. "Find out what they know about the extent of the area hit by the storm and report back to me. Let's figure out how to make this work to our advantage."

CHAPTER 12

It took over an hour for Andrew and Faith to pick their way through the city. Not only was the wreckage an obstacle, but Faith often needed to rest. By the time they reached Nancy and Seth's house, it was dark and quite cold.

"Please come inside and warm up," Faith encouraged as Andrew helped her up the porch steps. "I know everyone will want to thank you for what you've done."

Andrew said nothing, but when Faith reached for the door-knob, he stopped her. "I'll say hello to your family, but first I want to thank you for the way you share your beliefs without hesitation. I've believed myself to be a Christian for a great many years. My mother taught me that Jesus is God's Son and that He died in my place. As a child, it was hard to really understand, but as an adult who read and tried to understand the Old Testament, I could see the complications of the life the Jewish people lived and their need for someone to come and reconcile them to God. All the sacrifices they made—the blood they spilled for their offerings and sins—it was never enough."

Faith nodded. "I saw that too. I remember being so grateful

we didn't have to slaughter animals for sacrifice anymore. I don't think I could have done it, and yet that was the law."

"None of us could ever have kept up with that law," Andrew replied.

"No." Faith glanced toward the window where the soft glow of lamplight made the house look inviting.

For several long seconds, neither said anything, and Faith found herself wondering about Andrew's reasons for commenting as he had. She'd never been shy about asking difficult questions, so she decided to simply ask him about his heart. But before she could, Andrew spoke again.

"I've never met someone who puts their beliefs into action as you do. You truly don't seem to notice skin colors or people's cultures. You spoke of God not seeing man on the outside but looking at his heart. I fear when He looks at my heart, He'll be disappointed. I've closed it off and tried to avoid people and conflict. Then you came along and wormed your way in." He gave a nervous chuckle. "I didn't mean that to sound insulting at all."

Faith laughed. "I wasn't insulted. But if my worming has helped put you on a course of reconciliation with the Father, then I'll gladly take the analogy."

"I guess I'm just trying to say thank you. I was angry, and my heart was steel. The way of love—of God's love—was something I truly did not comprehend. But I'm beginning to see it now. You've opened my eyes with your honesty and kindness."

Faith lowered her face. She hadn't been totally honest, and in recognizing that aspect of their relationship, she felt awash in guilt. How could she pretend to be so open and honest—so immersed in God's Word and ways—when she hid part of herself? The part of herself that would limit her acceptance in most social circles?

"Come on. It's cold out here, and my head is really starting to hurt." She opened the door. "Nancy? Seth?"

Her cousin came rushing to the foyer, where Andrew was shutting the door as Faith removed her coat. Faith looked at her coat, amazed at the cleaning job Ben had done. There wasn't a sign of blood anywhere.

"We've been so worried. Are you all right?" Nancy asked, embracing Faith. "Oh, you're frozen."

"I'm fine. Some debris hit me in the head and cut me. I have four stitches and a tremendous headache." She pulled back and smiled. "You remember Captain Gratton, don't you?"

"Please call me Andrew." He extended his hand as Seth joined them, followed by two ladies.

"Andrew, this is my cousin Nancy and her husband, Seth. They were on the *Morning Star* when we sailed to Oregon City at Christmas. Behind Seth is Mrs. Weaver."

"It's nice to meet you, Mrs. Weaver."

The old woman gave him a nod.

Faith continued. "I went to see Andrew just before the storm struck. I left the boat thinking I could make it home but instead got waylaid. Andrew found me and took me back to the *Morning Star*, where I recuperated until it was safe to come home." She turned as she pulled the scarf from her head. "See, I have a bandage on the back of my head. Ben no doubt had to cut away some of my hair to stitch me up. Won't that make for an interesting obstacle to overcome when arranging my hair?"

"He was very careful. I think you'll be impressed," Andrew countered.

"We've been so worried," Nancy admitted. "The police are insisting people remain home, and Seth has tried twice to get to the school to see if his sister and Mimi are all right. We've seen nothing of them."

"We encountered the police and soldiers," Faith acknowledged. "Once they realized we were headed home, they weren't quite so harsh. Maybe if Seth pretends he's on his way home instead of going to the school, they'll let him pass."

"I was just waiting for dark to try again," Seth admitted.

"I could go with you," Andrew volunteered.

"Thank you. That would be helpful. Especially if they're trapped."

"Perhaps we should bring some tools."

"That's a good idea." Faith turned to Seth. "If you have, say, an ax and shovel, you can even tell them you're going there to help clear the debris." She glanced around. "Is everyone else all right?"

"Mr. Trent from next door died. The storm upset him so much that he had a heart attack. We tried to help but couldn't get him to the hospital because of the debris."

"I wished I'd been here." Faith shook her head. "Perhaps I could have helped."

"I wish you'd been here so you might not have been injured," Andrew threw in.

"I'm sure folks have plenty they wish was different tonight," Nancy added.

Seth turned to Nancy. "I'm going to try again. I'll be back as soon as I can." He donned his coat and hat, then gave Nancy a peck on the cheek.

Faith looked to Andrew and smiled. "Thank you for getting me home safe and for helping my family."

He nodded but said nothing more.

Once the men were gone, Mrs. Weaver and Alma, who had

been sitting on the back stairs, went back upstairs. Faith closed the front door and turned to Nancy. "What a day. I've never seen anything like it. I feel I should be out there helping, but with my head wound, I know I should rest."

"I'm so glad you're safe. Mrs. Weaver and Alma and I hid in the pantry. I thought the entire house would fall down around us."

Faith noted that Nancy looked pale. "You're exhausted. Why don't I help you get to bed? Have you eaten?"

"No. Seth only just got around to checking the flues and chimneys. He believes we'll be all right to cook."

"Good. Then while you rest, I shall do what I can to make something." Faith put her arm around her cousin. "We have leftovers, and I'm sure we won't starve."

Nancy started to say something, but all that came out was a moan. Her knees gave way, and Faith barely caught her before she fell.

"Mrs. Weaver! I need some help." Faith struggled to lower Nancy to the floor. "Nancy? Can you hear me, Nancy?"

She was out cold.

Faith frowned. "Mrs. Weaver! Come quickly and bring Alma."

It was less than a minute before both women arrived. Mrs. Weaver's eyes grew wide at the sight of Nancy on the floor. "Goodness. What happened?"

"She fainted. I need help to get her to her bed."

"We can help. If you can get her upper body, we can get the lower," Mrs. Weaver declared, nodding toward Alma.

Faith had her doubts that the two women were strong enough, but they quickly proved themselves more than able. It was Faith who struggled with the weight of her cousin. It wasn't that far down the hall to Nancy's bedroom, but Faith felt her head pound with each step. She should be resting right alongside Nancy, but she knew that wasn't going to be the case. Someone had to take charge.

They managed to get Nancy up on the bed. Faith sat beside her for a moment, pretending to feel her pulse when in truth she was waiting for a dizzy spell to pass. "I'll get her changed and tucked in. Could you put on some tea? Nancy said Seth had checked the stove and flue. We should be fine to light some fires as well."

"We'll take care of it," Mrs. Weaver said, nodding toward Alma. "We can manage together just fine. You take care of our sweet Nancy."

"Thank you. Maybe heat some leftovers. She hasn't eaten."

When they'd gone, Faith went to Nancy's dresser and searched for her nightgowns. Once she located them, Faith went back to the bed and began to undress her cousin. She talked to her the entire time, hoping Nancy would regain consciousness.

"You've overdone it today, that much is clear." Faith un-hooked the buttons on Nancy's boots. "Then the stress of this storm was enough to cause your fainting spell, even if you weren't expecting a baby." She undid the buttons on Nancy's skirt just as her cousin began to wake up. "You're doing just fine, Nancy. I have you in bed. Don't fret."

Nancy's eyes fluttered open. "What happened?"

"You fainted. Nothing to worry about. I have Virginia and Alma making tea and warming food. Then they'll be laying some fires. I'll get one going here in your room in just a minute. First I wanted to get you undressed and into a nightgown."

"I can do that myself," Nancy murmured.

"I know you can, but with me assisting, it'll get done twice as fast." Faith helped Nancy sit up. "Just let me do the work." She managed to finagle the gown from Nancy's frame, leaving her in her undergarments. Faith folded up Nancy's gown. "When did you last eat?"

"Not since breakfast. The storm came up just before lunch, and then that was all we could think about. When Seth came home, we were both so concerned about his sister and Mimi's well-being that we completely forgot about meals."

"Well then, I'm sure that's the reason you fainted. Do you think you can stand long enough for me to remove your petticoats and chemise?"

"I can. I'm feeling better." Nancy got to her feet, but Faith refused to let go of her as she straightened. "There. See? I'm fit as a fiddle."

Faith laughed. "I don't know about that, but—" She stopped as blood on the petticoat caught her eye. "You're bleeding."

"Is it the baby?" Nancy asked, her eyes going wide. "Did I hurt the baby when I fainted?"

"I don't know. Let's finish getting you changed, and then I can check you. Or, if you prefer, I can send for a doctor."

"You are a doctor, even if you don't have your certificate yet. I trust you to know what to do. After all, you've been helping my mother with babies most of your life." The fear in Nancy's voice was evident.

"Don't worry. It's not a lot of blood, and it's probably just from all this excitement. We'll put you to bed, and things will no doubt be better."

Tears came to Nancy's eyes. "Don't let me lose the baby. Please."

Faith pulled her close and hugged her. "I'll do all I can, but God is the one we should seek. He's the one who created this child and the only one who can protect him or her. Now, try not to cry and further upset yourself."

Once Faith got Nancy changed and back in bed, she did a quick assessment of her cousin's condition. Things didn't look bad. There was very little blood and no dilation.

"I think if you remain in bed for a time, everything will be fine." Faith went to the wash basin. "I want you to stay in bed for a few days and do nothing more taxing than reading or sewing." She cleaned up, then turned back to smile at Nancy. "The baby seemed just fine, so stop fretting."

"It's just that I want this baby so much. I can't bear the idea of losing him."

"So you've decided it's a boy?"

Nancy shook her head. "No. I go back and forth, calling the baby a him and then a her. Seth is always laughing at me." She gave a weak smile. "I know most men want a son first, but I think it would be great fun to have a daughter with red hair like her father."

"Nothing wrong with that," Faith said, drying her hands. "Now, you rest while I see to your supper. I'm sure Seth will be back soon enough, and then you can relax completely."

"Thank you, Faith. I don't know what I'd do without you."

Faith's head hurt worse than before, and she was feeling quite nauseous. Nevertheless, she didn't want to worry Nancy and forced a smile. "I don't know what I'd do without you either."

A loud knock sounded.

Faith looked at Nancy. "Who do you suppose that is?"

"I can't imagine."

"I'll go see to it. Mrs. Weaver is probably terrified someone has come for Alma."

Faith made her way to the front door and opened it just as

the knock sounded again. On the other side stood two women, one rather severe-looking and the other mousy and frail.

"What can I do for you ladies?"

The severe woman spoke. "We used to live here. Our apartment was destroyed today, and we wondered if Mrs. Carpenter might have a room for us again."

"Why don't you step inside, Missus . . . ?"

"It's Miss. Miss Clifton and Miss Clifton."

Faith had heard of the two women and smiled. "I'm Faith Kenner, Nancy's cousin. Please come and warm up." She could see that there were snowflakes on the women's coats. "Is it truly snowing?"

"Indeed it is," the severe woman replied.

Faith shook her head. "What a day." She led the way to the front room, where a fire was already blazing and warming things nicely. Faith was grateful and held out her hands to the flames. "Nancy is in bed, but I'll let her know you're here and what your needs are. I believe your old room is still empty, so I can't imagine that you couldn't reclaim it, but I'll go ask her to make certain."

"Thank you," the sisters replied in unison.

Faith smiled. Both women looked weary. "I'll have some tea in just a bit. Mrs. Weaver is making it now."

"I could help," the severe sister offered.

Faith shook her head, thinking of Alma. "No, just wait here and relax. I'm sure you've had a pressing day if your apartment was destroyed."

She left the women and went back to Nancy's room. Nancy was lying stiffly beneath the covers, her hands at her side. Faith had seen other women in her situation do the same for fear of the slightest movement causing further problems.

"Nancy, you don't have to lie rigid. Relax, or you could cause yourself more trouble than good."

"I'm just so worried."

"And that isn't helping. Try praying or reading the Bible. I'll fetch it for you and turn up the lamp."

"Who was at the door?"

Faith retrieved Nancy's Bible and brought it back to the bed. "The two Misses Clifton who used to live here. Their apartment was destroyed, and they wondered if they might have their old room back."

"Of course. But I thought they didn't want to live under the same roof as a man. You might remind them Seth is still here."

"I will. Meanwhile, what about Alma?"

Nancy frowned. "That is a concern. Let Mrs. Weaver know. Perhaps Alma can hide herself for a few days until we get a feel for what Bedelia and Cornelia might think and how long they intend to stay."

"I'll see if I can speak to Mrs. Weaver."

Faith went to the kitchen and found both women working to put together something for supper.

"The tea is ready," Mrs. Weaver declared. "If you'd like, I can take Nancy a cup."

Faith motioned for both women to draw near. "Look, the women who used to live here—the Misses Clifton—they're back. Their building was destroyed in the storm, and they're seeking their old room. Nancy thought perhaps it would be wise to hide Alma until we can figure what their response to her will be."

Mrs. Weaver nodded. "Alma, it's best if you go upstairs to our room. Take the back stairs so no one sees you."

The black woman nodded. "I'll go now." She left without another word.

Mrs. Weaver retrieved two more teacups and saucers. "I'll make a tray for them. You take Nancy her tea, and then we can deal with the Misses Clifton."

A few minutes later, Faith and Mrs. Weaver sat down with Bedelia and Cornelia. The sisters were a little less pale.

"Nancy is expecting a baby, as you might have heard." Faith held up the cream pitcher. "Would you care for cream?"

"Yes, please," Bedelia replied. "We had heard about Mrs. Carpenter and were very happy for her and Mr. Carpenter."

Faith glanced at Cornelia, who only nodded. Nancy had told Faith about the sisters and how Bedelia generally spoke for both. She poured the cream and then held up the sugar pot.

Bedelia shook her head. "No sugar. We should refrain from sweets in this time of urgency. It tends to stress the heart."

"Very well." Faith's medical training had never suggested such a thing, but she was too tired to argue. She handed each woman her tea. "Now, as I was saying, Nancy is expecting a baby, and she's had a very rough day. I've put her to bed to rest, but she assures me that you are welcome to take your old room. However, she would remind you that Mr. Carpenter is still very much in residence."

Bedelia's expression became even more pinched. "We considered that, but given our circumstances, we felt we had little choice. We have nowhere to turn. So much has been destroyed, and we can hardly go searching for another boardinghouse at this hour."

"Of course not." Faith smiled. "Were you able to get any of your things from the apartment?"

Cornelia began to weep, and Bedelia fixed her with a hard look. "Cornelia, tears will serve no good purpose." She looked back at Faith. "We were unable to claim anything. The building collapsed. We only survived because we were at our church helping with the clothing drive for the poor. Sister and I always participate. Now I fear we may well need to seek help there ourselves."

Cornelia sniffed all the louder, but this time Bedelia didn't reprimand her.

"Well, you are among friends now," Mrs. Weaver declared. "I'm sure we can work together to see that you have what you need. I have an extra nightgown or two that should see you through tonight. On the morrow we can see what needs to be done for the sake of your wardrobe and other personal needs."

Faith could see this idea was acceptable to Bedelia and added, "I have an extra hairbrush—it's new and never been used—as well as a few other things you might find useful. I'll bring them to your room after we finish our tea."

Mrs. Weaver got to her feet. "I am going to take a supper tray to Nancy."

There was noise at the front door, and the foyer soon filled up with Seth, Andrew, and Clementine. Faith could see them from the front room and went to lend a hand.

"Where's Mimi?" she asked.

"She was injured and taken to the hospital," Clementine said, giving Faith a hug. "I heard you were injured as well."

Faith turned so she could see the bandage. "A bit of a head wound, but nothing I can't manage. Why don't you all come in and warm up? We have some company."

Seth peeked around Faith to see who it was. "Ah, Miss Clifton and Miss Clifton. How nice to see you again."

The ladies nodded as everyone collected in the front room. Faith explained the situation. "Their apartment building collapsed in the storm. They've lost everything, but because they were helping at the church, they managed to escape harm. They requested to have their old room again, and Nancy agreed."

Seth seemed surprised. "Well, you are certainly welcome here." He looked around the room. "Where is Nancy?"

"She had a little spell earlier, and I put her to bed. Nothing to work yourself up over, but you might want to see her."

Seth nodded. "Then I will. Ladies, if you'll excuse me."

"Of course," Bedelia said, then took another drink from her cup.

Clementine moved toward the fire. "I'm frozen through."

Faith joined Andrew. "Misses Clifton, this gentleman is Captain Gratton of the *Morning Star*. He's a friend and helped me earlier today when I was hit by debris and injured."

"Captain Gratton, it's good to meet you," Bedelia replied.

Andrew gave a small nod. "Ladies." He looked at Faith. "I should get back to the *Morning Star*. I just wanted to make certain you were all safely settled."

Faith nodded. "We are."

"Then I will go." He turned back for the door, and Faith couldn't help but follow.

Once they reached the foyer, she surprised them both by rising up on tiptoe to kiss his cheek. Embarrassed at what she'd done, Faith backed away and looked at the floor. "Give that to Ben from me." She cleared her throat and tried to settle her nerves. "Thank you for everything. For coming after me, but especially for helping Seth. I'm sure it meant a lot to him, and it touches me that you would so willingly help my family." She forced herself to look up and found him watching her in awe.

"I was glad to help." He gazed at her for a moment longer, then added, "And I'm glad that you're doing so well."

"My head hurts something fierce, but it can't be helped.

Nancy was in no condition to manage things. I'll get some rest soon and be just fine."

He grinned. "I doubt that."

"Doubt that I'll be fine?"

"Doubt that you'll rest soon." He shook his head. "I've got my doubts that you'll rest at all."

Faith couldn't help but chuckle. "You think you know me pretty well, don't you? Well, I'll have you know that there are more than one or two secrets I have that you'll most likely never know."

His dark eyes captured her gaze. Faith sobered and swallowed the lump in her throat. She'd always been glad to keep her secrets, but at this very moment she felt almost compelled to tell Andrew everything.

"We've all got our secrets, Faith," he finally said before turning to go.

CHAPTER 13

As the end of January concluded and the days moved into February, tales of the storm were told far and wide. People greeted each other with the question, "Where were you when the big storm hit?" It made for interesting conversation, even among total strangers, as everyone worked to clean up the town.

At the boardinghouse, Mimi and Faith both healed, and Nancy was soon back on her feet with limited duties. Upon learning of Nancy's delicate condition, the Clifton sisters had stepped up to take on various tasks in return for several months of reduced rent. This, in turn, allowed them to replenish their lost wardrobe and personal items. Seth was the one to approve the idea, making it clear to Nancy that she was to take it easy until after the baby was born. Faith agreed with him, leaving Nancy little choice in the matter.

"It seems a woman ought to have a say in her own home," Nancy declared.

Faith brought her a plumped pillow and smiled. "Why not enjoy the pampering? Read a book, make something special for the baby."

"I suppose I could." Nancy glanced around the front room. "I don't intend to just sit about."

"No one is demanding you do. Just that you take it easy and let some of us take over your heavier tasks." Faith put the pillow behind Nancy as she sat in front of the fireplace. "It's rare enough for women to get any kind of special treatment when they're with child. Most must go on running their households and caring for other children. I'm just suggesting you enjoy the time. You've only a few months, and then you'll be holding that baby in your arms, and your schedule will never be the same."

"I suppose you're right. I should be thankful that God sent Bedelia and Cornelia back to us."

"You should." Faith leaned down to whisper, glancing all the while over Nancy's shoulder. "They are just as you described. I think Bedelia would have made a great physician. She's got a keen eye for detail and lets nothing escape her notice. I hope that won't extend to Alma—at least not until we can figure out how to bring them together."

"I know. We should probably just do it and let them decide if they can live with it or not. I hate to see Alma having to hide in her bedding box."

Faith straightened. "Me too. Now, is there anything else I can get you before I head back to my studies?"

"She'll be just fine," Bedelia declared, coming into the room. She held a glass bell in her hand. "I hope you don't mind, but I've taken the liberty of bringing you this bell. Just ring it should you need anything. Cornelia and I will be cleaning the rooms downstairs this morning, so we shouldn't have any trouble hearing you."

Nancy took the bell and smiled. "Thank you so much. I'm very glad you've returned to us."

Bedelia looked as if she might allow a smile to touch her lips, but then she turned away. If she did smile, Faith and Nancy would never know.

"I'm impressed with the new bathing room you installed downstairs," Bedelia said. "It's spacious and very nice not to have to run upstairs when in need."

"I agree, especially since my room is downstairs." Faith smiled at Nancy and motioned as if she were ringing a bell. "Don't forget, we're here for you."

By the middle of February, Portland had been cleaned up enough that most businesses could operate. There was still plenty to do, but life had to move forward. Word trickled in and then came like a flood that all up and down the coast, the effects of the storm had been severe. As far north as Seattle they had received several feet of snow on top of a record twenty-four inches that had been dumped on them the week before. It was unusual for Seattle to have that amount of snow, and it brought transportation to a halt and shut down the city, leaving many people without proper heat or food. To the south, the storm had brought Salem and Eugene several inches of snow and strong winds, while in Coos Bay the winds had driven a schooner ashore. But it was the damage to trees that seemed most readily noted throughout Oregon. It was rumored that for every ten feet of distance, one tree had fallen. Thousands of trees had been destroyed in the storm along the coast and as far inland as The Dalles. Beaverton alone claimed six hundred trees had fallen across the train tracks, rendering the railroad inoperable.

Nancy's brother Gabe had come to town purportedly to oversee their sawmill interests but perhaps even more to check on the well-being of his sister and fiancée. Meanwhile, the newspaper noted that hundreds of workers had been brought in from California in order to continue the cleanup. Gabe hoped to employ a good number of them for the sawmill. What was clearly an ordeal for the city looked to be a boon for the logging industry.

There had also been a small article in the paper that Faith noticed and brought to Seth's attention.

"It says the army captured several crates of rifles that appeared to be bound for Grand Ronde reservation. What do you know about that?"

Seth shrugged. "Someone tipped off the army as to where they could find the rifles. I talked to Major Wells from Fort Vancouver. He said it was much too orderly to suit him. It almost seemed like the entire thing had been staged, which raises the question—why?"

Faith frowned. Why indeed? From what little she knew about Berkshire and Lakewood, neither man struck her as the kind who would allow something like that to happen by chance, and if it were staged, what were they hoping to gain? Faith gathered her breakfast dishes and headed for the kitchen with that question on her mind.

"Will you be going to classes today?" Bedelia asked.

Classes at the college had been cancelled until all provision could be made to ensure safety. Faith had been glad for the extra time to work on her thesis and rest. It was apparent to her that her head wound was much worse than she'd allowed herself to believe at first. Little by little, the dizziness and pain left, and she found herself able to study again without having to stop due to her injury.

"Yes. We have a couple of lectures regarding the mortality rates of women and infants during and after childbirth. It's quite fascinating. A doctor named Louis Pasteur believes he has narrowed the cause down to tiny microorganisms that you can't see without the aid of a microscope. Years ago, another doctor realized that by washing in chlorinated lime solution between patients, the mortality rate dropped significantly. The two theories are likely connected."

"Any fool knows that cleanliness is vital." Bedelia's expression showed disgust. She turned away and began to fill the sink with hot water.

Faith knew from Nancy that the elder Clifton was critical of modern thinking, and figured she probably didn't approve of Faith's interest in medicine. Yet she was a stickler for sanitation. Faith had hoped her comments might resonate with the old woman's penchant for cleaning and open her mind to think more favorably of women in medicine. That didn't appear to be the case.

Faith gathered her books and papers and put what she could into her large satchel. There were so many times she wished she could just pull a small wagon around from one class to the other.

"Are you heading off to school?" Mrs. Weaver asked.

Faith smiled and nodded. "I have to be there by eight, so I figure I'd better get going." She went to where Mrs. Weaver sat and leaned down. "I'll bring you and Alma some candy tonight. They say Anderson's Chocolate Store is back in business."

"Oh my. Let me fetch you some coins," the woman said in delight.

"No. This is my treat." Faith pressed her hand on Mrs. Weaver's shoulder. "Besides, I don't even know if the rumors are true."

"Don't forget, we shall be working on Clementine's wedding ensemble tonight."

"Oh, that's right." Faith nodded. "Thank you for the reminder. I completely forgot. I'm supposed to pick up several spools of thread. It would have been a disaster if I'd forgotten."

"Well, I know I shall look forward to seeing what you are able to procure." The older woman gave a conspiratorial wink.

Faith laughed and went to get her coat. Once she was properly decked out for the cold January day, she picked up her large satchel. "I'll be home later in the afternoon."

She opened the front door and felt the damp cold permeate to her bones. How she wished the cable cars were running in this neighborhood. It was said they would have things back to normal in another week or so, but that didn't help her now. She would have to walk a good half mile to get to the nearest stop where she could catch a ride.

As she walked, Faith tried not to think about the cold, but rather went over the details of a discussion she and some of the other students had had the day before. They were all excited to work with Faith's aunt and uncle to gather medicine and other provisions for the Indian reservations. Faith had procured a list of items for each of the reservations and spoken at length on the need for medicines and cleaning supplies. She'd also relayed how she'd written to Helen Hunt Jackson and was anxious to receive a reply. Goodness, it was cold.

To her left, an enclosed carriage pulled to the curb and the door opened. A man called out, "Miss Kenner, is that you?"

She turned to find Samuel Lakewood. "It is. Good morning, Mr. Lakewood."

"It's far too cold to be ambling down the sidewalk. Join me in my carriage. I'll take you wherever you're headed."

Faith didn't even attempt to refuse as the driver climbed down to assist her. She hurried to the carriage and climbed inside.

Lakewood might be involved in all sorts of evil deeds, but at that moment, Faith would have taken a ride from the Devil himself. "Thank you. My satchel is quite heavy."

"I'm happy to help. Are you headed to the college?"

"I am. We have lectures today."

"You heard Miss Kenner," he said to the driver. "Take us to Fourth Street between Yamhill and Morrison."

"Yes, sir," the driver said, closing the door behind Faith.

She was grateful when Mr. Lakewood handed her a blanket that had been warming his lap. She pulled it around her, not even bothering to worry about what he would do for extra warmth. It kept her teeth from chattering, and perhaps, if necessary, she could hand it back to him in a few minutes.

Thankfully it didn't come to that. Mr. Lakewood pulled another blanket from beneath his seat and draped it across his legs. "I suppose you've heard about all the damage up and down the coast and elsewhere. Oregon has suffered greatly from that massive cyclone."

"Is that what they're calling it?"

"It was a huge low pressure system, much like a hurricane. I was up at Fort Vancouver and spoke with some authorities on the weather. They've never recorded a storm quite like it. They're calling it the Storm King."

"I can believe it. I've never seen anything like it in all my years."

He smiled. "You aren't old enough to use that turn of phrase, but I am, and I agree."

"How are your wife and children? Nancy told me that you have ten children."

Lakewood chuckled. "I do. My wife, Deborah, is considerably younger than I am. When my previous wife died, I had four children, and they were all under the age of ten. Deborah was a family friend, and she came and helped me with them, and we fell in love. She's given me another six children over the years. I'm delighted with them all. The oldest is now back east, attending Harvard."

"Why send him so far away?"

"It's what he wanted, and my brother is in Boston, so he has a ready home available to him. Although I imagine he spends more time at the college than with his uncle. He aspires to be a Supreme Court justice one day."

"That is a lofty aspiration. A very limited position too. I used to think being a female and wanting to become a certified surgeon was difficult. Your son desires a job that is one of only nine and assigned for life. What are the odds he will ever reach his dream?"

Lakewood laughed. "It will depend on how badly he wants it. And who knows, they only set the number at nine justices a few years ago. Maybe folks will decide we need fifteen or more justices and increase the number by the time he's qualified."

"Still, that's a very limited prospect."

"Well, at twenty years of age, I fully expect his desires will change. He'll probably find some attractive young woman and fall in love. I've seen it happen to more than one driven young man."

"Perhaps he will, but perhaps she will share his dream."

The carriage slowed and then stopped. The driver soon opened the door. "We've reached the college."

Faith pushed the blanket to one side and allowed the driver to help her from the carriage. "Thank you so much for the ride, Mr. Lakewood."

She didn't wait to hear his response but headed up the walkway to the building. The cold was encouragement enough to hasten her steps, but she also wanted to meet with her friends before the lecture. They were going to discuss the talk they were planning to stage on the following Friday, and she wanted to make certain all was in order.

She spied Malcolm first and bid him good morning. "You look as cold as I feel," she said, placing her satchel on the nearest table.

"I walked all the way. The trolley is still unable to make it from my apartment." He smiled. "But I'm glad classes are back in session. I've finished my paper. At least I believe I have. I'm having a meeting with Dr. Albright later today. We'll see what he thinks."

Faith pulled her gloves off and stuffed them in her coat pocket. "I've nearly concluded mine. I keep thinking of things that I want to stress, however." She took the pins from her hat and pulled it from her head. "There, that's better." She set the hat atop her satchel.

"Just remember," Violet said, coming up behind them, "make your statement in such a way that you only have to say it once." She shook her index finger as they had seen one of the lecturers do. "Repetition leads to boredom."

Faith laughed. She would miss these people when their classes were concluded and they graduated from the college. She had enjoyed the friendship of likeminded friends, and once they all went their separate ways, she wondered if she would ever have such camaraderie again.

"Shall we all still meet at the restaurant after the lectures?" Malcolm asked.

"I think we must." Faith looked at Violet, who nodded. "There's still a lot of work to do before we hold our first lecture. We want to come out very strong. I'm going to write to my uncle and see if he can send his right-hand man to come speak. His name is Clint Singleton, and he's an Indian Affairs Regulator. My uncle says, however, that he's very compassionate about the needs of the reservation tribes. I believe he could offer great credibility."

"We can discuss it at the restaurant. I'll see you there at four," Malcolm said, gathering his things. "Right now, I have to speak with Dr. Hall before the lecture begins."

Violet looked to Faith. "Shall we make our way to the classroom?"

Faith nodded. "I hope it's warmer there than here."

"The students are doing what?" Samuel Lakewood asked.

"They are planning a series of lectures designed to raise money for the reservation Indians for additional medical provisions, as well as cleaning supplies and other household needs."

"Who started this?" Samuel eyed the man across the desk with such intensity that he looked away.

"I believe it was a cooperative arrangement with several of the students."

"Is Miss Kenner involved?"

"I believe so."

"Parrish, this must not be allowed to go on. Especially on college grounds."

The president of the medical college, Josiah Parrish, seemed to regain his strength. "We are known for being open to progressive thinking, Samuel. There is nothing wrong with the students working together to better the reservations. God knows they need help."

Lakewood clenched his fists. "If you don't put a stop to it, I will withdraw my support. It was crazy enough to allow this acceptance of women in the college."

Parrish raised a hand to stop him. "You know full well my wife, Jennie, graduated last year and is practicing medicine even now. She is highly regarded, so do not think to disparage women attending medical school."

Lakewood knew Parrish was more than happy with the arrangement and fully vocal about his support for women at the college. He wondered how supportive he'd be of allowing Faith Kenner to continue her studies if he knew the truth of her background. Perhaps it was an argument for another day, however. The clock on Parrish's desk began to peal the hour, and Lakewood knew he was late for another appointment.

"We'll discuss this another time. I am already late." He gathered his hat and coat. "I don't want these lectures happening on school property. I doubt any of our other major donors will either. Give it a lot of thought, Josiah."

Faith knew if she didn't hurry she would be late to the restaurant and the meeting with her classmates. Speaking with her advisor had taken much longer than she'd anticipated, and now she would have to run several blocks or hail a cab if she was to get there in time.

"We meet again, Miss Kenner." Samuel Lakewood tipped his hat as he held the door of the building open for Faith.

"Good afternoon, Mr. Lakewood." She frowned. "You seem to be a very busy man."

He nodded. "Indeed, I am. Are you headed home?"

"No, actually I'm meeting up with some of my fellow students."

He smiled, and Faith thought him a very handsome older man. He always seemed so interested in benefitting others that she sometimes found it difficult to believe Nancy and Seth's warnings that he was dangerous.

"Might I drop you somewhere?" he asked.

"We're meeting at Brickerson's little restaurant. Do you know it? The students like to patronize it because he has a son attending the university in Salem."

"How nice. I'm not familiar with it, but if you give me the address, I would be happy to drop you off."

"Thank you. I'm happy to accept." Faith allowed Lakewood to hail his carriage driver before giving him the address.

"That's at least a mile away. Were you seriously going to walk in this cold?" he asked.

Faith laughed and pulled her collar closer. "I do what I must, Mr. Lakewood. Besides, after a day of lectures, it would have given me time to clear my mind."

"Don't you enjoy the lectures?"

"Of course. They are wonderful. I have always loved learning, and now I'm in a position to compare and contrast things I've learned over the years. It's amazing."

The carriage came to a halt in front of them, and the driver jumped down to open the door for his master.

"After you," Lakewood said, taking hold of Faith's satchel. "Here, let me."

She gave him the satchel as the driver assisted her into the carriage. Lakewood climbed in after her and took his seat. He placed the satchel beside him and shook his head. "That is quite heavy."

"We have a lot of required reading and discussions that can take place at almost any time without warning." She smiled and leaned back against the plush leather. "One must always be ready."

"Yes, that's true, and in the spirit of that, I wanted to ask you about something I overheard."

Faith cocked her head, which made the back of her felt hat snag on the seat. She reached up to straighten it and smiled. "What is it?"

"I heard something rather troubling about you and your friends—that you're planning to hold a fundraiser of sorts to bring in money for the Indians."

"Why would that be troubling to you?"

"I suppose it's not so much troubling as distasteful. This college has always set itself above politics."

"Since when is doing good for our fellow man a political matter? I could have just as easily organized something at church."

"Yes, but you didn't. You've made it a part of the college."

"Only because so many people there feel the same way." She knew little of Lakewood's true political feelings except for what Nancy had mentioned about his prejudices and support of Gerome Berkshire. "It seems to me that a great many people in town raise money to lobby for laws and arrangements to rid the state of people of color and even to cause them harm."

His gaze became icy. "Really, Miss Kenner, it isn't your affair, and you would do well to stay out of it. There are usually consequences for putting your nose into someone else's business."

Faith wasn't about to be frightened. "If you're hoping to intimidate me, Mr. Lakewood, I would think by now you would know me better. I have lived among the Indians and know how grave their situation can be. I know that men like you do not want to see them benefitted in any way and that you would just as soon they die off so you won't be further troubled by them.

You want the money the government gives them, you want their land, and you want their lives."

If Lakewood was surprised by her bold comment, he didn't show it.

Seeing he was going to remain unmoved, Faith continued. "There are other men who oppose your thinking, and thank God for them."

She reached up and hit the carriage top as she'd seen Lakewood do earlier. The carriage came to a stop.

Faith held out her hands. "Now, if you'd please hand me my satchel, I will be going. I wouldn't want to cause you further discomfort by continuing our association. Someone might see us and accuse you of supporting the Indians."

He handed her the satchel, but his gaze never left hers. "Just remember, Miss Kenner, powerful men can make powerful things happen. You need to drop this matter and find something else to amuse you and your friends."

Faith could see blatant hate in his expression. The hair on the back of her neck stood taut, and her hand trembled slightly as she clutched the satchel close. It was obvious Lakewood wanted to scare her, and Faith was certain he knew he'd done exactly that.

CHAPTER 14

"Captain Gratton," the tall, dark-headed man announced, extending his hand.

Andrew recognized Gerome Berkshire from their previous dealings. "Mr. Berkshire." They shook hands, and then Andrew showed him to the table where he generally did ship business. "How can I help you?"

"I have a load of goods to be picked up in Astoria."

"I see. Well, that shouldn't be too difficult." Andrew pulled together the paperwork and handed it to Berkshire. "Fill out the information, give me the details of what you're shipping, who I'm to meet in Astoria, and where I'll find the cargo."

"I'm hoping we can keep the contents of this shipment from being public. In fact, I'd like very much to keep my involvement unknown. There are those who would try to use it against me."

"In what way?" Andrew asked, sitting back. He had never liked Berkshire and knew he couldn't possibly be up to any good.

"I'd rather not say. In our previous dealings, you always treated me well. I also know from my old friend Albert Pritchard that you are a man who can keep quiet when the need arises.

As I understand it, you used to deliver goods to him in a rather unconventional manner in various locations along the Willamette."

"It wasn't so unconventional, Mr. Berkshire. A lot of folks want their goods dropped off along the way, close to their farms. What exactly is it you're shipping that requires such secrecy?"

"Same as Pritchard. Firearms and ammunition. I don't want to arouse alarm or suspicion. I'm simply supplying farmers with the means to protect themselves."

"From what?"

"From any threat that comes their way." Gerome looked at him with a smug self-confidence that made Andrew want to punch him in the nose. "There are many rumors of Indian uprisings. The settlers near reservations are concerned that the government won't protect them—that the Indians will attack and the army won't be able to reach them in time."

Andrew thought the entire matter ridiculous. Reservation Indians were in no position to start an attack or uprising of any kind.

"Where are you wanting these firearms delivered?" he asked.

"Wheatland."

"Well, I'm not sure I can help you. I've mostly been running between Astoria and Portland. Heading south to Wheatland would require I go through the locks at Oregon City. That will be an added expense."

"But you can take it all the way to Wheatland for a price, I presume."

Andrew shrugged. "It may not be a price you're willing to pay."

Gerome pressed his fingers together and leaned his elbows on the table. "I think you'll find that I'm every bit as generous as my friend, Captain. Now, are you interested in doing business, or shall I go elsewhere?"

"When do they need to be delivered to Wheatland?"

"By the end of March. No later."

"Let me ask around and see if I can find some additional loads bound for Wheatland or towns along the way. I can hardly afford to take a few crates of guns and nothing else."

"Good. Send me word at this address as soon as you know." Berkshire pushed a card across the table. "And say nothing to anyone about this."

Andrew picked up the ornate calling card. "I'll be in touch."

Faith returned home feeling frustrated. The candy store wasn't open but promised to be in two days, and the ivory thread she needed was nowhere to be found. Fearing she'd have to give up, Faith had finally found it in a small dressmaker's shop that was just closing when she arrived. Thankfully, the woman managing the place was eager for a sale and allowed Faith the after-hours purchase. Feeling bad because of the candy store disappointment, Faith then stopped by another store as it was closing and bought half a pound of peanut brittle. She had no idea if Mrs. Weaver and Alma would like it.

Nothing had gone right. At the meeting with her fellow students, she explained Lakewood's threats. None of them wanted to cancel or even change the venue at first. Instead, Faith's comments only served to drive the students forward in increased determination.

"How dare that old man dictate to us what we can and cannot do regarding charity," Malcolm had declared. "I won't have it, even if we should come to blows."

Violet too had been livid. The others had agreed as well. Faith suggested that perhaps it might be wise to speak to a local pastor or two about holding the event at a church. She didn't trust Lakewood and didn't put it past him to make trouble. There was no sense in securing a venue at the college, only to be told at the last minute after all the flyers had been printed that they couldn't hold their event on campus.

When she returned home, it was almost seven, and a light rain had begun to fall, leaving her drenched to the bone. She slipped into the house, grateful that everyone seemed occupied elsewhere. Taking refuge in her room, Faith quickly stripped out of her clothes and pulled on a warm cotton nightgown. Taking up a towel, she sat by the fire someone had thoughtfully lit in her hearth.

She pulled the pins from her hair and let the dark brown mass fall to her waist before drying it with the towel. She gazed into the flames and steadily massaged her hair.

Lakewood was a problem, and she knew it was probably best that she get some advice on the matter. Nancy had indicated he was dangerous, and Faith knew the time had come that she further investigate the matter. All she had hoped to accomplish before graduation in April were some charitable acts of kindness. She hoped that by helping fulfill the reservations' medical needs, she could also introduce her abilities to the local authorities and thus be allowed to work with the Indians. It assuaged her guilt to remind herself that one day she would take all that had been allowed her because of her white heritage and use it to better life for the Indians. But Lakewood clearly wanted to stop her from helping the reservations.

She went to her dressing table to get her brush. As she maneuvered her hair back into a manageable plait, Faith contemplated how she might accomplish all she desired in spite of Lakewood. She'd had to deal with powerful men before. There was always a way, if one was smart about it.

Faith finished braiding her hair, then pulled on her heavy wool dressing gown. A cup of tea sounded like just the thing to warm her. Perhaps there would be a few cookies as well. Her light supper was nothing more than a memory at this point. She took up the bag of candy and made her way to the kitchen.

For the life of her, Faith couldn't stop thinking about Lakewood and how quickly he'd turned on her. He was used to having everyone obey his directives. He wouldn't be happy that she had defied him. In fact, she was almost certain he was even now plotting against her.

"I wondered if you'd ever made it home," Seth said as she came into the kitchen.

"Just a little while ago. I thought a cup of tea would help me thaw." Faith went to the teakettle and lifted it. "I see I wasn't the only one who had that idea." She nodded toward the mug he was stirring.

"We just finished supper, but there's plenty left if you're hungry. Bedelia insisted we leave a plate warming for you."

"How considerate. I'm starved." She grabbed a potholder and opened the warmer. "Mmm, fried chicken. It smells wonderful." She placed the dish on the counter. "Are you working late?"

"No, Nancy and I decided a quiet evening together would be nice. This tea is for her."

Faith considered this. "I wonder if I might come and speak to you both. I have an issue that must be dealt with, and I'm in need of advice."

"Of course. I'll take this to her, and we'll anticipate you in a few minutes."

Faith grabbed a fork and a glass of water, deciding to forgo the tea. She headed down the hall to Nancy and Seth's bedroom, hoping they'd be understanding. She found them both by the fire, with Seth just pulling up another chair.

"Come sit and tell us what troubles you," he said.

"Well, it's not like you haven't warned me about Samuel Lakewood."

Seth frowned. "What has he done?"

Faith sat and balanced the plate on her lap while she took a long, needed drink of water. "He wants us to stop our plans to raise money for the reservations. We have a fundraiser scheduled so that we can speak about the poor reservation conditions. With the money we raise, we hope to buy additional medical and cleaning supplies." She put the glass to one side and picked up her fork. "I believe he will insist that the college ban us from using the lecture hall. He made clear his intentions this afternoon as I was on my way to meet my friends."

"Why were you with him?" Nancy asked.

"He offered me a ride, and since we'd had a pleasant enough time together earlier this morning, I thought nothing of it. He immediately made it clear that he didn't approve of what we were doing. He told me there were consequences for sticking my nose into matters that weren't mine to worry about."

Seth heaved a sigh. "Look, you need to understand that Lakewood is just as corrupt as Gerome Berkshire. Berkshire at least pretends to be working for the government, which allows them to keep an eye on him, but I'm sure he's told Lakewood what he's doing. Lakewood is part of all this scheming to get the Indians to rise up and cause a war. Once they do that, the whites will have their excuse to take charge and demand the tribes be moved to a smaller reservation far away, where they can cause no harm. Lakewood and his friends will sell the reservation land to their cronies."

"Listen to Seth, Faith," Nancy pleaded. "He knows what he's talking about. These men are dangerous and will stop at nothing to have what they want. They once snuck into my house and stole a book with Albert's confidential maps. I wouldn't put it past them to do most anything to see their plan succeed. The government and the army are our only hope of keeping them under control."

"I won't be bullied into walking away from a good cause." Faith took a bite of chicken.

"Lakewood isn't going to walk away from a challenge either."

Faith shrugged. "There is more than just me involved in this. He can't fight all of us."

"He can and he will," Seth replied without hesitation. "He doesn't care how many of you there are. He has powerful friends, and together they made this town. They can certainly stop a few students."

"I'm sure this storm caused a lot of damage to the reservations, even if no one is talking about it. Grand Ronde is sure to have suffered, since they're not far from the coast. I want to help them."

"As do we, but Lakewood is ruthless. I don't want you to get hurt," Seth replied, looking grave.

Faith sat back and put her plate on the small side table. "I think the time has come for you to explain everything to me. I know bits and pieces of what's going on, but I think I need a clearer picture in order to better understand how to deal with this matter."

Nancy and Seth exchanged a look, and Nancy shrugged. "I think you should tell her everything. Faith can keep a secret."

"It's imperative that you say nothing about this to anyone. Secrecy is still very much needed in order to get to the bottom of who is actually controlling this situation." Seth crossed his legs as he stretched them toward the fire. "And there is still so much we don't know."

"I promise I will say nothing."

Seth nodded and began to explain. "As you know, Nancy's husband Albert was involved in secreting shipments of weapons and whiskey to the Indians. I was approached by the government to come to Portland and investigate. Of course, by the time I did, Albert was dead. He had fallen or was pushed into the Willamette. We now believe he was murdered before he reached the water, but we have no way of knowing who killed him. We suspect Berkshire or one of his rowdies but are still uncertain and have no proof whatsoever."

"Right. That much I already understood."

Seth continued. "We didn't know if Nancy was involved, so when I realized she was my old childhood friend, I managed to get her lawyer to let me come onboard and help with her late husband's estate."

"But you didn't tell Nancy what you were really doing."

Nancy answered before Seth could. "No, he didn't."

Seth smiled. "It didn't take long before I confided in her." He reached over and squeezed his wife's hand. "However, we had Berkshire to contend with, and he wouldn't leave Nancy alone. We've since learned that he wanted to convince her to marry him so that he might have access to her money. Berkshire plays at being well off, but in fact he has very little, and Nancy's money would have allowed him to step into the society of his cronies like Lakewood without fear of being realized for what he really was."

"Do you honestly think Lakewood doesn't know about Berkshire's lack of money?" Faith asked. "I mean, it seems to me that Lakewood is the kind of man who knows the details of every man's fortune—or lack thereof."

"I'm sure you're right," Seth agreed. "The thing is, Lakewood and his associates have been helping fund the weapons and whiskey and probably a lot of other things, but the government knows there are other men who are in charge of all this."

Faith nodded. "They suspect Uncle Adam and Aunt Mercy as being at the top of the plot."

Nancy shook her head. "Can you even imagine?"

"They can't be serious." Faith looked at Seth. "How can they possibly believe that two people who have spent their lives among the Indians and working with them as advocates could be responsible for pushing for insurrection?"

"I suppose the thought is that because the tribes have been treated unfairly, your aunt and uncle are encouraging them to rise up to demand fair treatment. And while they could be suggesting this for the betterment of the tribes, someone else may well have it in mind to cause them harm. The government believes that whoever is involved is also a part of the plot to see the reservation lands decreased and given over or sold to white settlers who have come to this state demanding farmland."

"If they took a good look at the bulk of those reservation lands, they wouldn't be quite so eager." Faith picked up her plate. "This is madness."

"Yes, but we cannot say anything about it to our family," Nancy declared. Her expression was grave. "The only reason we're telling you is so you won't be harmed by Lakewood. Steer away from him and don't allow your actions at school to enrage him."

"I won't stop our plans. He won't scare us off. We already discussed that this evening. We're going to move the fundraiser to one of the churches and proceed. There's very little he can do to any of us."

"Don't say that." Nancy looked to Seth. "Convince her."

Seth nodded. "Faith, these men have worked a long time at this. It's not the first plot they've had, and it won't be the last. Don't put yourself in harm's way. Maybe delay your gathering for a few months. Let things calm down, and see if the government can't get to the bottom of their investigation first. Then you can do all you want to benefit the Indians."

"By then they may have died from lack of proper medical supplies. The government doesn't provide them with what they need. You know that. Aunt Mercy and Uncle Adam have tried for years to get the government to do better. You know they would never harm the Indians or work against them."

"I do," Nancy replied. "But I also know these men are dangerous. I believe, as Seth does, that they killed Albert. God alone knows who else they might have killed. I don't want them to have any reason to put you on that list."

"Looks like you've got enough wood here to build a log cabin," Andrew said as he came upon Seth chopping wood behind the boardinghouse.

Seth took a break from chopping. "We might as well. We aren't lacking for firewood."

Andrew smiled. "We've got more than enough for the *Morning Star* too. This storm provided plenty of fuel to get us through, at least. I have stockpiles here, in Vancouver, Astoria, and all points in between."

Seth smiled and pulled a handkerchief from his pocket. "It's been a lot of work, to be sure. I'm not sure how all this wood will ever be processed, but it's employed quite an army of men."

"To be sure."

"So what brings you here? As if I didn't already suspect."

"I wanted to check on Faith, but I wasn't sure she'd be completely honest with me. I'm just as glad to question you. How's she been feeling?"

"Good. She told me she had to accept that the injury was worse than she'd originally thought. Thankfully, with all the cleanup needed for the town, they cancelled classes for two weeks. She used the time to rest and recover. I think it's fair to say that she's back on her feet and doing just fine."

Andrew smiled. "That's good to hear. Very good. I figured, given her spirit, she'd be out on the streets, trying to help."

Seth stopped and fixed Andrew with a serious look. "Are you familiar at all with what she's been doing with the other students regarding fundraising for the Indians?"

"Not really. Why do you ask?"

It looked as if Seth were about to say something, but then he shook his head. "It's nothing. You mentioned her being out on the streets, trying to help, and it brought that to mind. Faith would be hauling supplies out to the reservations herself but for the women in the house. They were adamant that she take it easy. And with Nancy getting closer to her delivery, they want Faith to be here as much as possible." Seth wiped his brow. "Say, would you like to stay for dinner? I know the plan is for a large Yankee pot roast."

"Sounds wonderful." Andrew glanced at the back of the house and smiled. "Do you suppose Faith would mind?"

"That you've come to check up on her, or that I've invited you to supper?"

"Both." Andrew laughed. "I wouldn't want to upset her on either count."

Seth chuckled and stuffed the handkerchief back into his coat pocket. "Let me put away my things, and we'll go see. My gut tells me she'll be happy for your company."

Andrew smiled and picked up several cut logs. "I'll help you get this stacked."

It only took the two of them a few minutes to see to the wood and tools. Before he knew it, Andrew was being shown to his place at the dinner table while the rest of the Carpenter boardinghouse joined them. Faith seemed genuinely happy to see him and sat beside him before anyone could suggest otherwise.

"I think you'll be pleased with the food here, Captain. It might not be the same as Remli's, but I'm betting it will taste just as good."

He threw her a smile. "I'm betting it'll be better, but don't tell him I said so."

Faith grinned and nodded. "I promise I won't."

"Captain, how is it that you've come to be with us this evening?"

He looked at the pale, thin woman who asked this and smiled. "I came to check on Miss Kenner. I wanted to see for myself that her head wound had healed properly, since one of the men on my boat was the one to stitch her up."

"Is he a doctor?"

"Not exactly. He's just had some experience."

She gave a huff. "That's hardly any reason to go sewing on someone."

"Miss Bedelia, the cut healed quite nicely," Faith said, doing her best to keep the peace.

She huffed again, making sure they knew she disapproved. Andrew might have laughed out loud, but she was obviously miffed.

"It seems irresponsible to allow such a thing, Captain Gratton," Miss Bedelia said, reaching for a dinner roll.

"You may call me Andrew if you like. Most of my friends do."

Miss Bedelia raised her head and considered him for a moment, then chose a roll. "I shall call you Captain Gratton."

Andrew nodded and caught the amused expression on Faith's face.

"Welcome to the family," she said.

CHAPTER 15

Bedelia and her sister served up a tasty breakfast of pancakes and warm syrup, sausage links, and hot coffee. They were turning out to be quite useful and more than earned their keep. Nancy had confided in Faith that she had considered asking if they'd like to hire on full-time but didn't want to offend the prideful Bedelia.

"Your husband has already left for work. That seems terribly early," Bedelia commented as she poured Nancy a glass of milk.

"He likes to go early to spend time in Bible study with his boss, John Lincoln."

Faith had just come into the room for this exchange and could see the effect Nancy's answer had on the older woman. "That is a very wise thing to do. Sister and I study the Word every morning before we start the day."

Cornelia bobbed her head. "We do indeed. This morning's reading was from the Psalms."

Faith suppressed a yawn and took her place at the table. She longed for another couple of hours of sleep but knew that wasn't going to happen. She had way too much to do. She poured a cup of coffee, then inhaled deeply and smiled. Bedelia's coffee was stronger than Nancy's, and Faith needed all the help she could get to stay awake.

"Mmm, what a heavenly aroma," she said.

Bedelia smiled. "I do not believe my coffee is even remotely related to the heavenly realms, my dear, but I am happy that you think so."

Everyone gathered at the table save Mrs. Weaver and Alma. Faith couldn't help casting a glance at the two empty chairs at the end of the table. She and Nancy had talked about the situation only the night before.

"Let's pray," Nancy said, taking her seat. "Father, we thank you for this meal and all the bounty you have given. We know there are some who have nothing, and we ask that you make us mindful of them so that we might share a portion. We ask that you guide us throughout this day and make us mindful of the needs of others. In Jesus' name, amen."

"Amen," Bedelia and Cornelia murmured in unison. Mimi and Clementine seemed to be just as reflective as Faith and said nothing.

"I have something to speak to you about, Mrs. Carpenter," Bedelia said as she passed the platter of sausages to her sister. "Cornelia and I have discussed it, and we would like to remain here permanently. We were hasty to believe that the presence of Mr. Carpenter would somehow compromise us, and now with you expecting a wee one . . . well, Sister and I believe we could be of use. We once worked at an orphanage and are quite capable with children."

Everyone looked to Nancy, wondering what she might say. Nancy lifted her coffee cup. "Mimi, I wonder if you might go upstairs and ask Mrs. Weaver to come down—and bring Alma."

Faith was surprised by her announcement but said nothing. Instead, she served herself two pancakes and passed the platter to Clementine.

"I would be very happy to have you and Cornelia remain with us," Nancy said after taking a sip of coffee. "You were both delightful boarders, and I had no complaints with your living here. However, there is something that might change your mind. I've been trying to figure out how to tell you about it, but it seems that just being forthright is the best way."

"It generally is," Bedelia agreed soberly.

Faith could hear the older women coming down the back stairs. She slathered butter on her pancakes and then looked around the table for the syrup. Clementine seemed to understand what she wanted and passed the ornate porcelain pitcher without being asked.

"We've returned," Mimi declared, taking her seat.

Nancy waited until Mrs. Weaver stepped into the doorway to speak. "Something came to our attention after you and Cornelia ceased living at our house. Mrs. Weaver has a friend who has been staying with her. Alma."

Mrs. Weaver came into the dining room, eyes wide and full of fear. "I didn't know you planned to do this." Her voice was barely audible.

"Neither did I, but Bedelia has asked that she and her sister be allowed to stay. It's only right that we share the truth with them and hope for their silence. I must ask that of you, Bedelia. You too, Cornelia. This woman's life depends on your secrecy."

Bedelia frowned while Cornelia began to eat. "I cannot imagine anything so grave."

Alma stepped into the room. She was, as usual, clean and neat. Her graying black hair was braided tight against her head, and her clothes were freshly pressed. Her dark eyes were just as wide as Mrs. Weaver's.

"Mrs. Weaver has had Alma with her since birth. Alma was once a slave but has long been Mrs. Weaver's bosom companion and dearest friend. When they moved to Oregon, only then did they learn the laws were against them. Alma could be beaten and forced to depart against her will if she were discovered. Mrs. Weaver and her husband lived quietly in the country and hid Alma's presence from the world. When Mr. Weaver died and Mrs. Weaver moved here, she hid Alma so that she wouldn't be forced to live without her. I will not see them separated, and if you are to live here, you must agree to say nothing of Alma's existence and protect her as we have all agreed to do."

The two women took their seats at the table and stared at the Cliftons as if their life or death would be decided by the sisters.

Bedelia's stern expression remained as she sized up the matter. She looked at Nancy. "Why would anyone feel the need to separate two such dear friends? Sister and I have no complaint in the matter, nor will we. The very thought of this woman receiving a beating sickens my heart." She turned back to Alma. "I am Bedelia Clifton, and this is my sister, Cornelia. We will keep your secret."

Faith had liked Bedelia since their first meeting, but at this moment she could honestly say she felt love for the spinster. Bedelia was so matter-of-fact with her conclusion, so willing to accept Alma and protect her, that Faith wanted to hug her. It took all her restraint to keep from doing exactly that.

"Thank you both," Nancy said, smiling. "We weren't sure how you would feel, and since we thought you were only staying a short time, we didn't think it necessary to tell you about the situation."

"Well, it certainly explains how Virginia knew there had been a thief in the house that day we were all in church and your book was taken," Bedelia said.

Nancy nodded. "I hadn't even thought of that, but of course you're right."

"I remember that. Alma was scared half out of her mind," Virginia said, taking up her napkin.

The black woman nodded. "I sure was. A man just came into the house, bold as you please. He didn't seem to think anybody was home, 'cause he was makin' enough noise to wake the dead. I knew I needed to hide, but could hear him tearin' through things. I figured he'd look in the blanket box, so I hid behind the drapes. Sure enough, he come into the room and went first thing to the box. I was shakin' so hard, I figured he could see the drapes movin', but if he did, he never paid it any attention. It was terrifyin'."

"I can well imagine," Bedelia replied. "Just the thought of what might have happened is most alarming."

"Well, we're glad it's behind us now." Nancy shifted in her seat and put a hand atop her abdomen. "I'm glad you accept Alma. She is a dear woman and has become our friend, just as you and Cornelia are."

Bedelia began slicing her pancakes, and the conversation moved from the continued repairs of storm damage and to spring planting.

"I believe a garden would be a good thing to have," Mimi began. "Since the yard has been damaged anyway, why not go ahead and plow up a large portion in the back, and we can plant vegetables and berries. It will help feed us, and frankly, I find gardening relaxing."

"As do I," Mrs. Weaver said, nodding. "Alma and I both enjoy it. However, we could hardly allow Alma outside."

The Way of Love

Nancy considered this for a moment. "I think a garden would be perfect. I'll speak to Seth about plowing up a nice big plot. If he agrees, then we'll do it."

They were nearly finished with breakfast when a knock sounded at the front door. Nancy rose and excused herself despite Bedelia's protest that she could answer on her behalf. While Nancy headed to the front door, Alma hurried to the back stairs and made her way to her room.

When Nancy returned, Gerome Berkshire trailed behind her like a well-trained puppy.

"Faith, Mr. Berkshire would like to speak with you." Nancy reclaimed her place at the table.

Faith dabbed her napkin to her lips. "I can't believe you allowed him in the house after all his threats."

"I've also come to beg your forgiveness, Nancy. I've turned over a new leaf. I am not the man I once was," Berkshire declared. "I am even working with the government to help secure information against my former associates." He looked contrite. "I tell you this to prove myself. Should word get out, my former associates would see me dead. So you can see that I have put my life into your hands, ladies. Surely this proves my sincerity."

"The Bible does say we are to forgive others," Mrs. Weaver murmured.

Faith pushed away from the table. "Why do you want to speak to me, Mr. Berkshire?"

"In my desire to prove myself, I thought I would offer you a ride to the college. It's quite cold, and I must go that way myself. It came to mind that perhaps I could be of some use to this family."

"Thank you, Mr. Berkshire. That was thoughtful." Faith got to her feet. She didn't really believe him, knowing there was probably some other reason for his actions. Perhaps he'd been instructed by Lakewood to speak to her. "I suppose it would be prudent of me to accept."

"Unchaperoned?" Bedelia questioned.

"I assure you, Miss Kenner will be quite all right in my company," Berkshire countered. "After all, even if I were the man I used to be, I should not dream of causing trouble." He smiled. "You would all know that I would be the one to blame."

Again, Bedelia gave a huff and focused on her food. "People today care nothing for the respectful behavior of their parents and the rules that were put in place to preserve proper society."

Faith smiled to herself as she went to her room to collect her things. Miss Bedelia would be more than a little alarmed if she knew some of the dangerous situations Faith had allowed herself to get into. Why, her visiting the *Morning Star* without a proper escort was itself enough to render Faith guilty of the most egregious of behaviors.

As she buttoned her coat, Faith wondered what Gerome Berkshire's real purpose in coming was. No doubt it had to do with Samuel Lakewood. The older man had probably asked Berkshire to speak to her, but why, she couldn't imagine. He had to know that she held no great esteem for Berkshire. For a moment she considered rescinding her acceptance of his offer, but there was always the slim chance Berkshire might say or do something that she could share with Seth. Something that might help the investigation.

She grabbed her satchel and headed for the front foyer. Berkshire was waiting for her and smiled as she arrived.

"You look lovely, Miss Kenner."

Faith returned his smile. "It's the same uniform and coat I've worn all winter." She set her satchel on the table and took up her dark blue felt hat. She continued to speak as she pinned it carefully atop her knotted hair. "I was just pondering what your true purpose might be in coming here today."

"My true purpose? You wound me, Miss Kenner. Can a man not do a simple act of kindness without his motives being called into question?"

"Perhaps some might." Finished with the hat, Faith pulled on her gloves. "I'm ready to go."

Berkshire reached out to take her satchel. "My word, what are you carrying? Rocks?"

"Books. Very thick and heavy books." She smiled. "I can manage them on my own, if you'd like."

He frowned. "No. I wouldn't dream of it." He opened the door and held it for her. "After you."

For a while Faith thought their ride to the college would pass in silence. Berkshire seemed to want to speak, but he appeared confused or perplexed about it. Finally, Faith could take no more.

"What is it that you are supposed to tell me, Mr. Berkshire?"

He looked at her oddly for a moment, and then his brows drew together. "I didn't realize my appearance was so predictable."

"As I said earlier, I presumed that you had come with a purpose. After all, you aren't on good terms with my cousin, and our residence is hardly on a direct road from yours, if the college is the final destination."

"Well, the fact of the matter is that Mr. Lakewood is concerned about you and your friends. He fears that your plans are going to give people a negative opinion of the college. He wanted me to speak to you because, well, he thought perhaps you didn't appreciate his position."

"In what way?"

"He is considerably older, and I am closer to your own age." He smiled and shrugged. "He thought perhaps you would appreciate my thoughts on the matter. He said he worried that you looked upon him as nothing more than a worried father figure."

Faith couldn't suppress a laugh. "No, I saw him as an unfeeling bigot."

Berkshire's eyes widened, and he began to cough. Faith waited until the shock passed.

"You see, Mr. Berkshire, I grew up with Native people, as my parents were missionaries to the Tututni tribe of the Rogue River Indians. They were good people, Mr. Berkshire, and I learned a great deal while with them. Then the whites came and killed many of them and rounded the rest up to take to the Grand Ronde Reservation. Many died during the forced march, and many others died because there were never enough medical supplies or medicine. When the Storm King came through our land and stripped away people's possessions up and down the coast of Oregon and Washington, Grand Ronde suffered too. My friends and I only desire to ease the discomfort of those who have nothing. We want to honor the Bible's admonishment that we consider others as better than ourselves and love others as Christ loved us. We seek only to raise money to provide medicine and supplies for a people who have no chance to acquire those things for themselves."

Berkshire looked at her for several long moments before speaking. "You must know that those people have no regard for you except a desire to see you dead. They might have called you friend once, but given all that has happened to them, they have grown to hate all whites—yourself included. The Indian men would see you as nothing more than a woman to be used.

They would—excuse my bluntness—rape you and then most likely scalp you. They would not care at all that you wanted to love them as Christ loved others, because they have no understanding of who Christ is. They are heathens."

"That is not true. Many of them accepted Jesus when my parents shared the gospel message. Many are accepting Him every day. My aunt and uncle are missionaries to the Indians. They have told me that many are willing to receive Jesus. They crave the truth and listen to the Bible eagerly. And even the ones who don't accept Christ . . . it doesn't mean they're all violent."

"Your aunt and uncle would of course say that. Their livelihood depends on it."

Faith laughed. "Their livelihood? You think they are paid by the government or a particular church? They receive most of their support from our family. Too many men who think exactly as you do populate the churches and refuse to see the ministry as one called for by the Lord. Although, when the Bible says that we are to go and make disciples of all men—that we are to preach the gospel to all nations—I hardly see how they figure that excludes the Indians. But raising money amongst white churches for people of color is often frowned upon."

"And well it should be. There are enough white people who have need that we should focus our attention on them first. We need to take care of our own people before worrying about theirs."

The carriage came to a stop, and Faith shook her head and gathered her things. "You may tell Mr. Lakewood that we students plan to move ahead with our fundraiser even if we have to stand atop a soapbox on the street corner to do so."

She climbed out of the carriage, shaking with anger. The audacity of these men to try to force her to walk away from something she believed in. It wasn't right, and she wasn't going to stand for their interference.

"Just understand that you have been warned," Berkshire said, following her out of the carriage. "Samuel Lakewood isn't a man to suffer fools."

She stopped and looked at him for a moment. She started to make a snide comment about that not being true, or Berkshire wouldn't be in his company, but she held her tongue.

"You may tell Mr. Lakewood whatever you deem necessary, but I won't be bullied. I don't need his permission, and my friends and I have already changed the venue, so he needn't fear his dear college's reputation will be damaged because of our lecture."

"This is madness, Miss Kenner. Lakewood, once driven to a thing, will not simply drop the matter without making an example of someone. In this case, it will most likely be you who suffers."

"Then that's the way I suppose it will be." She smiled. "I trust that God is able to keep that which I have committed to Him. Mr. Lakewood will merely be a thorn in my flesh. Nothing more. And, as with Paul in the Bible, God's grace for me shall be sufficient."

CHAPTER 16

I just wanted you all to be fully aware of the threats against us," Faith told her gathering of friends.

"Well, we have changed the location of the lecture, and our speaker, Mr. Peabody, has been informed. Mr. Singleton wasn't able to come after all. We've got just two days left, and surely in that time we can persuade Mr. Lakewood to change his mind," Malcolm declared. "I will go and speak to him myself. Maybe a man-to-man discussion will help him see reason."

"You are welcome to try, but I have my doubts." Faith knew enough about Lakewood to know that he wouldn't allow a group of ragtag students to best him.

After classes that day, Faith handed out flyers downtown and encouraged people to join them for Mr. Peabody's lecture.

"He is quite knowledgeable about the Pacific Northwest Indians, in particular the Chinook, Alsea, and Haida. He lived and worked with them for over twenty years," she told a group of men as she thrust a flyer into the closest man's hands.

"The lecture is also a fundraiser for the Indians at the Grand Ronde Reservation. They suffered greatly from the storm."

"Pity it didn't kill them all," one of the men declared.

Faith frowned. "Would you say such things if our Lord were here to hear you? Because I assure you that He does hear and knows your heart."

The man looked momentarily embarrassed but did nothing more than shrug. Faith found it discouraging that so many people shared his opinion. At one point, she handed an older woman one of the announcements and was stunned when the woman dropped it to the walkway and ground her foot atop it.

"Filthy heathens killed most of my family. I will never help them."

"I'm sorry for your loss." Faith didn't know what else to say.

Obviously, some people had been hurt by the Indians and still held a grudge toward them. Even some of those who hadn't had a personal encounter were so blinded by the hate they'd learned that they were unwilling to consider helping the reservation tribes. History and extravagant tales did the Indians no favors.

Friday night arrived, and Faith held her breath, wondering whether anyone would show up for the lecture. She was grateful that the ladies from the boardinghouse had agreed to come— minus Alma, of course. Seth had rented a large carriage to transport them to the Methodist church, which had agreed to allow Mr. Peabody to speak.

The problem came when, just minutes before the lecture was to begin, Malcolm appeared to declare that Mr. Peabody had cancelled.

Faith knew it was the work of Lakewood and his cronies, but she was determined not to let that ruin the event. There was a nice crowd gathered, and she felt certain they could be convinced to donate to the cause of the reservation Indians.

"I'll do it myself. I have plenty of experience and can speak to the problems on the reservations. After all, I spent more than one summer helping my aunt and uncle."

At exactly seven o'clock, Faith took to the podium and smiled out on the audience. "Good evening and thank you for coming. I must tell you that this event was hard to bring together, and at the last minute our speaker, Mr. Peabody, was unable to come. However, I have lived among the Indians and worked on the reservation lands with my aunt and uncle, and I can speak to the problems they face. I might not be as informed in some areas as Mr. Peabody, with his government position, but I can vouch for many of the hardships experienced by the various reservation tribes, so I ask you to bear with me."

Faith began by speaking of how Grand Ronde came about. "I was living with the Tututni Indians along the Rogue River when the Rogue River Indian wars broke out in 1855. My father was a missionary to the Tututni and some of the other tribes along the river. He was killed by whites who hated the Indians. My mother was expecting a baby and died shortly after that because of her fragile health. My aunt and uncle and I had to escape the village and get to safety. Not because the Indians sought to harm us, but because the whites had declared war on anyone in the villages." Faith explained the war and the mass killings on both sides.

"In the end, the Southern Oregon tribes were forced to march from their homelands to Grand Ronde. Many died on the two-hundred-sixty-three-mile trip. Some from exposure, some from the arduous journey itself, and still others from disease and starvation. Many of my friends never reached the reservation."

After detailing the conditions of the journey, Faith then described the poor living conditions at Grand Ronde. Finally, she explained that one of the biggest problems was the forced blending of various tribes.

"I know that many of you consider Indians to be one people, but they aren't. They consider themselves to be tribal members. Their tribe is an important part of who they are. As I mentioned earlier, when I was a child, I lived among the Tututni people. Outsiders referred to them as the Rogue River Indians, but dozens of tribes lived in the area of the Rogue River, and all were very much individual groups with varying cultures and traditions. It was no different from a city neighborhood that holds Swedish families, as well as Irish, German, and French. All might appear white, but their backgrounds, cultures, and languages are all different. It is the same with the Indian tribes.

"When the government rounded up the various tribes and forced them to the reservations, it was a difficult time for all. The government couldn't understand why many would rather die than leave their homeland, but surely you can imagine the heartache of being driven from the place you cherished. In the case of the Tututni, they were river people. The river was an important and critical element in their lives. The river was their transportation system, and much of their food came from the river. Their livelihood depended on it. Many of the tribes caught fish and sold them to coastal citizens who owned stores.

"Grand Ronde has river access, but it's not the same. The weather isn't the same, the climate and growing seasons aren't the same. Add to this the fact that more than just the Tututni people were rounded up to live at Grand Ronde. Some of their enemies were there as well. They forced a great many Indians to come together in a small area after they had lived free, wandering the land at will, moving if necessary to hunt or collect food for their families. Now they have become prisoners."

Faith paused to take a sip of water before continuing. "But today we have come together to speak of other issues. The

Storm King left many of you with vast amounts of cleanup. It caused all manner of damage to your houses and felled more trees than can be counted. Grand Ronde and other reservations suffered too. Grand Ronde took a heavy hit. It was in the direct line of the storm system, and the Army Signal Corps told us that the lowest barometric pressure—the center of the storm, if you will—was directly over Grand Ronde as it made its way inland to Portland. This caused them to experience some of the heaviest damage, just as we did, and that's why we're here today. It is my hope that we can raise enough money to take medical supplies to the people at Grand Ronde so they can receive proper care. Along with medical supplies, we hope to include blankets and common household items—perhaps even lumber to rebuild damaged areas. My aunt and uncle are determined to do whatever they can, and my family has already pledged their assistance, but we need your help as well."

There were murmurings in the crowd, and Faith waited a moment before continuing. The people seemed completely caught up in her stories of her time with the Indians. Faith felt a sense of pride in being able to speak with some authority about the Tututni and other tribes. By the time she finished and allowed the audience to ask questions, Faith was certain she had done the right thing in speaking in Mr. Peabody's place. She sensed God with her and His pleasure in her willingness to defend a people so maligned.

"Do the Indian people continue to live as tribes on the reservations, or do they all live mingled together?" an older woman asked.

"Most still work to keep their tribes together, although they live in separate houses. Some of the tribes, however, have very few members left. In fact, there are tribes that have disappeared altogether due to epidemics."

"And are there still enemy groups after all these years?" a man asked.

"There will always be problems between people, but I'm happy to say that most of the tribes are working together. They see the benefit of coming together. And because of this, they have their own legislature and police force."

"Isn't it possible," the same man asked, "that this will only lead them to join together against the white man?"

Faith considered his question for a moment. "I suppose anything is possible. I know some white people would love nothing more than a war with the Indians—a war that would end the conflict between whites and Indians once and for all by eliminating the Indian tribes completely."

"If the Indians are inclined to fight against the white man, then why should we help them? Aren't we in fact only encouraging their animosity?"

Faith hadn't seen Samuel Lakewood come into the church and join the audience, but there he was.

"No!" Her reply was almost a shout, which caused everyone to look first at her and then at the man who had asked the question. "I believe the Indians are being encouraged to maintain hatred and anger toward white people. I believe a great many people deny them their basic needs, then condemn them when they complain. I believe there are even those white men who would stir up this hornet's nest in order to have an excuse to kill each and every Indian man, woman, and child. We students, however, suggest that the men in power—the people who have plenty and are able to help—should help. We should come together to recognize that people are people no matter the color of their skin, their language, or their culture. As a doctor, I can tell you that if I operate on a person of color, their insides look no different from those of a white man or woman. We are all human beings made by God's good hand. He loves the Indian no less than He loves the white man, and any idea that suggests otherwise is wrong. It most assuredly isn't biblical."

She paused and calmed her spirit with a quick prayer and a deep breath. She hadn't expected Lakewood to invade her lecture, and just the sight of him left her feeling off balance.

"Are there other questions?" she forced herself to ask.

There were enough questions from other people that Faith did not have to address Samuel Lakewood again. By the time they concluded the evening and Faith was mingling with the attendees, she was relieved to see that Lakewood had gone. She was thankful she wouldn't have to discuss anything further with him. At least not for the time being.

"You did an amazing job, Faith," Malcolm said, grinning from ear to ear. "We've raised several hundred dollars. Violet is working on the final count, as there are a few people still writing out their checks."

"How exciting. I know it will make a big difference on the reservation. Hopefully hearts have been changed and people will come to see that the Indians are just as human as the white man."

"I think this will definitely help. I'll get right to work on securing us additional speakers. I don't know why Mr. Peabody was unable to come, but hopefully we can acquire some new lecturers."

Faith felt encouraged. "I wrote to Mr. Singleton, who works with my uncle at the reservation, as well as Mrs. Jackson. I know we could fill the entire church with people if she were to come speak to us."

"No doubt. That would be quite the thing if you were able

to talk her into coming here." Malcolm tugged at his navy blue coat. "I feel like celebrating. Why don't we all plan to meet at Brickerson's? I know they're open until ten tonight."

"I can't." Faith glanced over to where Nancy and Seth stood talking with several people. "My family expects me to return with them. Maybe we can celebrate another time."

A man approached her. "Miss Kenner, I'm with *The Oregonian* and wondered if you would answer a few questions for an article I plan to write regarding your purpose here tonight." He was stocky in build and several inches shorter than Faith.

She smiled and nodded. "I will be happy to answer your questions, Mr. . . . ."

"Stanley. Robert Stanley." He stuck out his hand.

Faith nodded. "Mr. Stanley. What questions do you have?"

"Isn't it true that your mother and her sisters were a part of the Whitman Massacre of November 1847?"

Faith hadn't expected this and couldn't keep the surprise from her face. She forced her composure to return. "I . . . well, I suppose I wasn't expecting that question." She looked at Malcolm and shrugged. "But yes. My mother and her younger sister were taken hostage during the massacre. Their elder sister was away from the mission at the time and escaped harm."

"So your aunt and mother did not escape harm. What exactly happened to them?"

Faith had no intention of betraying her mother's situation during that time period. "Mr. Stanley, I am curious as to why you are asking these questions. We are seeking to join hearts and minds together, not remind people of past hostilities."

"Be that as it may, the thirty-year anniversary of the trial of the Cayuse warriors who were responsible is this year, and the newspaper intends to do a series of articles on what happened and how that affected the community. That, coupled with your family's desire to help the Indians now, is rather fascinating, don't you think? I believe readers will want to know more about this and better understand why women who were held captive and forced to endure God only knows what would now desire to help their captors."

"While I believe the love of God is what compels my mother and aunt to help those who did them wrong, I hardly see this as a time to bring up the ugliness of the past. I would prefer you write nothing about us. We want to put aside those bitter events and focus instead on how we might all live together in peace and harmony."

"Peace and harmony don't sell papers," he replied, grinning. "Now, will you tell me what you know about the attack?"

Faith looked at him for a moment, then shook her head. "No, Mr. Stanley. I won't."

The final tally showed that they had raised three hundred and eighty-six dollars to aid the Indians. Faith was pleased with the amount and immediately penned a letter to her aunt Mercy. In it, she asked for a list of anything and everything that was most needed. She also asked what particular illnesses were most prevalent at the moment. The college gave medication to the poor on occasion, and Faith had suggested Malcolm speak to President Parrish about whether the college might donate some for the reservation. Otherwise, she was going to speak to Andrew about where they might be able to secure medication and blankets at a wholesale price.

By the time Monday rolled around and Faith headed off to school, she was all but floating on air. Many people had spoken to her at church, promising to add to the funds, while others were hoping Faith would again lecture and speak of her time with the Tututni in even more detail.

She thought about her life on the Rogue River as she walked to the trolley stop. Every day the cleanup and restoration brought life a little closer to the way it had been before the storm, but it would still be a long while before the residential neighborhoods got much attention. Downtown and its businesses were of the utmost importance, and the massive number of downed trees still commanded everyone's focus.

When she finally reached the trolley stop, Faith could hardly feel her toes for the cold. She was grateful that her wait was less than five minutes and even happier when they made it to the college in record time.

"The president is looking for you," Malcolm said as she made her way to the table where they usually gathered before lectures.

"Did he say why?" Faith pulled off her gloves and tucked them into her coat pockets.

"No, just that you were to come see him first thing before classes."

Faith nodded. "Maybe he heard about our success and is willing to let us host the lectures here. Wouldn't that be nice?" She hoisted her satchel on her shoulder. "Take notes for me if I don't get to class before the lecture starts."

"I will."

Faith made her way to President Parrish's office. She smiled at the secretary. "I'm Faith Kenner."

"Yes, I know that," the man answered, seeming rather irritated by the interruption. "Take a seat, and I'll let Mr. Parrish know you're here."

Faith did as he instructed and began unbuttoning her coat.

Everything seemed to be so rushed this morning. She hoped it wasn't the way the entire day would go. She glanced at a copy of *The Oregonian* newspaper on the reception table and noticed her name.

Picking up the paper, she began to read Mr. Stanley's story about her lecture. He embellished several of her comments, making her life among the Tututni sound far more harrowing than it really had been.

"Mr. Parrish will see you now."

Faith had no choice but to put the paper aside and see what the president wanted. She hoped he wasn't dismayed about the article. Not having read the entire thing, she could hardly defend or deny the details.

She gathered her things and made her way into the large office. Mr. Parrish sat behind a massive oak desk. It was strikingly bare for a man who was in charge of an entire college.

Faith smiled. "Good morning, Mr. Parrish."

His expression was stern. "Please be seated, Miss Kenner."

She did as he asked and did her best to sound cheery. "How may I be of service?"

"I'm afraid this isn't a pleasant meeting, Miss Kenner. In fact . . . well, that is to say . . ." His voice faded, and he got up from his chair. "This is the most unpleasant meeting I've ever had to hold."

She felt her stomach clench. "I'm sorry. What's going on?"

"I'm afraid that you have upset a great number of our donors."

"Upset them? How?" She presumed this was about the lecture she'd given. She was even more certain that it had been instigated by Samuel Lakewood, but she wasn't going to let Parrish off easy.

"You spoke to a group of people Friday evening."

"Yes. We had arranged another speaker, but he had to cancel at the last minute, so I took the podium."

"I believe your topic had to do with the Native people and raising money to provide them with medicine and other supplies."

"Yes." She hoped her one-word answers would give him no additional ammunition to use against her.

"Our donors believe this is uncalled for. It gives the supposition that the college is in support of the matter. They are threatening to withdraw their support for the medical college unless drastic measures are taken."

"I suppose they hope to silence me, but I won't be silenced. The reservations were hard hit by the storm, and the Native people there have a great need for help that the government will not supply. My fellow students and I believe it is our Christian responsibility to help those who cannot help themselves. What can your donors possibly take offense at, when we are following the Bible and caring for the poor and needy?"

"Miss Kenner, I personally have no argument against what you've done, but without donors, this college cannot continue to function."

Faith saw the futility of arguing. "I presume your donors want my promise that I will never again lecture on such matters, but I cannot give them that promise. I believe in what I'm doing, Mr. Parrish. I also believe that this protest is mostly stirred up by Samuel Lakewood, who is a bigot and desires for only white people to live in Oregon."

"They are not asking for your promise, Miss Kenner. The truth is, you are being expelled from the medical college."

"For how long?" Faith was glad that most of her work had

already been completed, including her required lecture attendance.

"I'm afraid for good."

"What?" She hadn't meant to raise her voice, but she couldn't help it. "I'm to graduate in April. I've had perfect grades and positive comments from my professors. You cannot do this."

"I'm sorry, Miss Kenner. I have no choice. You are dismissed, effective immediately." He looked truly sorry, but that didn't help Faith's state of mind. This was Samuel Lakewood's fault, and she had never been angrier at one particular person in all her life.

"This is not fair. Have I no recourse, no means of protesting this decision?"

"No, I'm sorry. You were a good student, but this is too big a matter to ignore."

Faith got to her feet. "This isn't the last you've heard from me, Mr. Parrish. You may have yielded to Mr. Lakewood and his friends, but I doubt very seriously they will be pleased when I next speak to a group of people and tell them of the unfairness of this college and of the donors' prejudices in particular. Not only that, but my family has been a substantial donor to this university. Let's see what happens when they withdraw their yearly support."

"Miss Kenner, as I said, this isn't my desire."

"Then maybe you should have stood up to Samuel Lakewood instead of letting him scare you into expelling me." She could see by the look on Parrish's face that she'd hit upon the truth. "Good day, Mr. Parrish. My father—the lawyer and donor—will no doubt be in touch."

She stormed from the room and away from the outer office. She was halfway down the block before she realized she hadn't bothered to put her coat back on. Part of her wanted to scream and throw things, while another part wanted to curl up in bed and have a long cry. She would have been a certified surgeon in less than three months. All of her hard work had been for nothing.

She looked up at the cloudy sky. "Why, God? Why has this happened? I've tried only to do what was right. I've tried only to serve you and others, and look what it has gotten me. I do not understand this at all!"

A Bible verse came to mind. Proverbs three, verse five. *Trust in the Lord with all thine heart; and lean not unto thine own understanding.*

She tried to quiet her spirit. Her own understanding was failing her once again, and the Scripture said she needed to trust in the Lord . . . with all her heart.

"God, I do trust you, but I do not understand this. Not even in part." She felt tears come to her eyes. "Help me, please."

CHAPTER 17

Faith found the house quiet when she returned. The Clifton sisters had gone out on some mission, and Mimi and Clementine were at the school, teaching. Faith had no idea where Nancy might be, but it was just as well. She didn't want to talk to anyone just now.

She deposited her satchel in her room and wondered what to do. Her thoughts were completely fixed on Samuel Lakewood's being responsible for her dismissal from the college. Part of her wondered how she might get back at him for what he'd done. She was angry and hurt, and the idea of hurting him in return was at the forefront of her mind. However, she knew that wasn't what God would want. God would call her to give it over to Him—to let go of the wrongs done to her by man and trust that He could make all things work together for good.

"But how can any good come of this?" She sighed and stretched out on her bed. "What am I to do, Lord?"

She heard the knocker sound at the front door. The last thing she wanted was to entertain someone coming to call. Perhaps Mrs. Weaver would hear it from upstairs and take care of it herself. When the knock came again, however, Faith knew no one else would save her from the task.

She took her time but finally opened the door to find a young man, probably no more than sixteen. He held out a piece of paper.

"This here is for Miss Faith Kenner," he said. "No money needed. The captain already paid me."

Faith took the folded paper and smiled. The only captain who would be writing to her was Andrew. "Thank you." She opened the note as the boy made his way back down the walk.

We're in Portland, and Remli demanded I invite you for lunch. He's making beef pasties.

Smiling, Faith felt a sense of calm. She could go to lunch and explain everything that had happened to Andrew. He might have some good ideas as to how she could fight the situation. And if all else failed, she'd arrange a trip home to see her father and get his legal advice.

She went back to her room and began to plan what she would wear. Andrew was used to seeing her in her uniform. It might be nice to put on one of her better outfits and do up her hair in a more fashionable style.

Faith studied herself in the mirror. Her reflection served as a reminder of all that she kept hidden. Her Cayuse heritage was disguised by the way she dressed as well as the icy blue eyes she'd inherited from her mother. In the summer, Faith's skin tanned to brown, making her look more like her Indian ancestors, but she always did her best to stay out of the sun, lest someone question her. It wasn't so much to keep people from hurting her as it was to protect her mother. While family knew the truth, no one else did. Not even her mother's closest friends were privy to the story of Faith's conception, and Faith intended to keep it that way. If the truth leaked out, her mother would suffer.

Even though it was only nine o'clock, Faith went to work readying herself for her visit to the *Morning Star*. She found Nancy's curling iron and started it heating, then went to figure out what she would wear. Faith only had a couple of winter outfits to choose from and settled on a dusty rose wool suit with a high-collared white blouse. Once she'd donned this, she let down her hair and brushed it out until it gleamed. Next, she began to curl it, and finally she pinned it up, doing her best to keep it simple yet stylish. When this was complete, she fastened a cameo her parents had given her for her thirtieth birthday to her collar and then pulled on the outfit's matching jacket.

She looked again at her reflection. There wasn't even a hint of an Indian staring back at her, yet Faith couldn't help but frown. The lie was getting harder and harder to stomach, especially in light of all she'd said in her lecture. How could she convince others to see Indians and whites as the same when she didn't see it that way herself? Yet to confess the truth would ruin her mother's reputation as well. After all, while people may have surmised that the women of the Whitman Mission were raped, no one spoke of it. The gentler phrase *were forced to be wives to the Indians* was always used when speaking of what had happened, and of course no one mentioned any children conceived from that ordeal. Faith had to believe other women had gotten pregnant, and yet no one ever admitted as much. Had they sought out a midwife and gotten rid of their babies? Had they had them as her mother had and given them up—sent them away? Perhaps they had miscarried from the stress, but the fact was that no one mentioned any child being born out of that situation. If Faith were to speak openly of her ancestry, what might the repercussions be?

Finishing with her toilette, Faith dabbed a bit of perfume behind each ear. She so seldom wore the expensive scent that she felt almost ridiculous using it now. Perhaps Andrew would think her silly for her manner of dress and hair arrangement, not to mention the perfume. She hesitated, wondering if she should just change back to her uniform.

"Hello?" Mrs. Weaver's voice called from the hall.

"Hello, Mrs. Weaver." Faith opened her bedroom door. "I'm going to have lunch with Captain Andrew on his boat. What do you think?" She gave a twirl.

The old woman smiled. "You look lovely. I believe your captain will be pleased."

Faith started to correct Mrs. Weaver that the captain was hardly hers, but she knew it would do little good. "What can I do for you?"

"I heard you speak to someone at the door."

"It was just a delivery boy bringing me a message from the captain."

"Oh, well, that's fine. I'm sorry to bother you when you're all dressed up, but it's Alma. She has a sore throat that's gotten much worse, and now she's running a fever."

Faith nodded. "Let me come and examine her."

"I was hoping you might do exactly that."

Retrieving her black bag, Faith followed Mrs. Weaver upstairs and found Alma resting in bed. The tiny black woman looked worn out.

"I'm sorry to hear that you're unwell, Alma. I will try to

determine what's wrong and see if we can find a treatment. How long has your throat been sore?"

"Started last night. I thought maybe I just needed to drink more water. It didn't help, and then came the fever after breakfast."

Faith quickly looked at Alma's throat and then checked her glands, as well as her ears and nose. Lastly, Faith listened to her heart. It had been recently discussed in class that several cases of measles had been reported in the city, but Faith saw no sign of this.

"It's hard to tell at this point, but we'll treat it as best we can." Faith reached into her bag and pulled out a small bottle. "Gargle this solution at least five times a day. Then drink willow bark tea. I know Nancy keeps some in the kitchen cupboard. Make it strong at first and add honey. Above all else, stay in bed and rest. I'll check on you again when I return home and see how you're feeling."

"Thank you," Alma said, her voice scratchy and weak.

"I'll see that she does as you've instructed." Mrs. Weaver looked worried. "I couldn't bear for anything to happen to her."

"Well, hopefully we have caught it soon enough, and it won't develop into anything else. However, keep an eye open for a rash, just in case it's measles or scarlet fever."

"I will. I promise," Mrs. Weaver replied, going to Alma's side. "You must get well, Alma dear. I will fix you some toast and tea this very minute."

Faith smiled and gathered her things. It was more than a little touching to see how the two women took care of each other. Their loyalty was inspirational.

Faith made her way down the back stairs with Mrs. Weaver following close behind her. "I can't thank you enough," the older woman declared as they entered the kitchen. "If anything were to happen to Alma, I don't think I could bear it. I could never live alone."

"I doubt you will ever have to, Mrs. Weaver. You've become such a part of our family that I can't imagine you not being with us always." Faith patted the old woman's shoulder. "Don't fret. I'm sure that with your tender care, Alma will recover soon enough. Now, if you'll excuse me, I should be on my way. The walk to the trolley will take me a bit of time. I don't know what time lunch is served, but I don't want to be late."

Mrs. Weaver smiled. "No, of course not. Although I doubt your young man would even care. You will make someone a wonderful wife—it might as well be him. You'll see. The clock will not interest him at all, except to make him wish the hours would pass sooner until you two can be together."

Faith allowed herself to pretend the older woman was right and that their friendship might become something more. It was a dangerous pretense, but sometimes she couldn't help herself.

"I'm glad you could make it. I wasn't sure your classes would allow it," Andrew said.

"Yes, well, it seems that isn't going to be a problem any-more," Faith replied, taking off her coat.

"Ah, yes. You're soon to graduate."

"That's hardly the case."

Her expression was so dismayed that Andrew's muscles tightened with concern. "What's wrong? What are you talk-ing about?"

She placed her long coat over the back of one of the saloon chairs, and Andrew motioned for her to sit by the large stove.

"It's warmer over here."

Faith took a seat. It was obvious she was upset. She looked so sad, and it made him anxious. What was wrong? Could he make it right?

"Please tell me what has happened to make you so glum."

Faith took a deep breath. "I was expelled from school for supporting Indian affairs. I helped with a fundraiser and spoke about my time growing up with the Rogue River Indians and how awful their life on the reservation is. This morning I was called into President Parrish's office, and he told me I was expelled—permanently."

"Permanently? But graduation is in April."

"It is," Faith admitted. "I have all of my requirements completed for the most part, and my grades are perfect. I'm at the top of my class, but this is about politics."

"Politics?" Andrew took the seat beside her. "What are you talking about?"

"Men like Samuel Lakewood and Gerome Berkshire. Men so lost in their hatred of people different from themselves that they would impose this punishment upon me for daring to oppose them. They are ruthless and underhanded. It's no wonder they're under investigation." She put her hand to her mouth.

"What's wrong?"

Faith lowered her hand. "I wasn't supposed to mention that, but I can't help myself. I need to talk this out or I'll go mad. Would you please pledge to keep what I've said—what I'm about to say—to yourself? To tell no one else?"

"Of course. I'm not one to gossip." He smiled. "I would, however, like to comment on how pretty you are today. Although I rather miss the uniform."

She laughed. "I thought dressing up for lunch would be fun.

I wanted to take my mind off what happened, but at the same time I wanted to talk about it with someone . . . with you. I need counsel, and my father is miles away in Oregon City."

"What are you seeking counsel in regard to? The expulsion?"

Faith nodded and settled in to explain everything. She spoke for over ten minutes, then eased back in her chair. "I don't know what to do."

Andrew took a minute to ponder the tricky situation. "You mentioned them being under investigation. Can you explain that part?"

"I'm not supposed to, but I don't see that it's any real harm, since you've pledged to keep my secrets." She started into the story of her cousin's deceased husband and his gun sales to the Indians.

"Whiskey is forbidden because of the Indian's low tolerance, and of course guns are very limited—hunting only, and the government keeps a strict accounting. Berkshire and these men see no reason to adhere to the law, however. They want to get the Native people riled up, and the whiskey helps—especially when you have men sitting around with nothing to do."

"I heard the Indians were helping with the tree removal."

Faith nodded. "Some are. They're paid pennies compared to what the whites receive though. And many have no desire to help the white man and refuse to lend a hand, even for pay. I honestly can't say that I blame them."

"No, nor can I." He looked away and thought of his past business transactions. "I have a confession to make."

Faith smiled. "I've shared all of my secrets, so you might as well reciprocate."

He didn't so much as move. "I've done business with Lakewood and Berkshire. I did a great deal of business with Albert Pritchard."

"You did?" She leaned forward, clearly excited at the possibility of gaining knowledge that could reveal Lakewood's wrongdoing.

"Yes. I delivered a great deal of freight to various locations up and down the Willamette for Pritchard. I remember it well, because while I always have the occasional farmer who wants his supplies offloaded on the riverbank near his farm, they aren't storing their goods in hidden shacks along the way."

"Do you remember all of the places you delivered to?"

"I do. And if there were any problem with my memory, I have everything recorded in my logs."

"You should speak to Seth. He's helping in this—at least he was. It's all quite complicated, and as I said, I wasn't supposed to say anything."

"And as I promised, your secrets are safe with me."

"Miss Faith!"

It was Remli, carrying a tray of food, and Andrew was glad for the interruption. The things Faith had told him were worrisome. If Berkshire and his cronies were trying to stir up an Indian war, then Andrew had delivered more than enough weapons and ammunition to see the matter through to completion. It had never dawned on him that these men might be arming the Indians on the reservations.

"I've made you some of my specialties," Remli declared. "I got beef pasties and gravy, greens and bacon, and for dessert, a berry cobbler good enough to turn your grandma's head."

"I never knew either of my grandmothers, but I'm certain your food would impress anyone who tried it. Andrew thinks I came here to enjoy his conversation and company, but in fact I came for your food."

Remli laughed heartily, and Andrew grinned. He couldn't

help it. Since he'd met Faith Kenner, he'd smiled more than he had in his entire lifetime before meeting her.

"I've put the table just over here. We can move it to be by the stove, if you like."

Faith nodded. "I would like that. I spend so much time out walking in the cold and damp that I never feel quite warm enough."

"Well then, let us do the lady's bidding." Andrew got to his feet and stretched out his arm to assist Faith from her seat. "First, we must make way."

Once she was standing to the side, he and Remli made short work of moving the table and chairs. Remli had thought of everything, even bringing fine linen napkins for them to use. Once Remli had the table set and the hot food uncovered, Andrew was more than ready to eat.

"Allow me to help you to your seat," he said in a formal manner. Taking Faith's elbow, he led her to her chair and seated her before taking his own seat. The setting was intimate—perhaps too intimate—but Andrew couldn't bring himself to change the situation. He offered a blessing for the food and then asked Remli to serve them.

They ate in silence for several minutes, sampling each of the things Remli had brought. Faith seemed more than pleased, and when Remli returned to see how they were doing, she lost little time in praising his efforts.

"This is wonderful, Remli. I want the recipe for the pasties. I am not much of a cook, but my cousin who runs a boardinghouse is, and I am going to suggest she make these at least once a week."

He laughed. "Ain't nothin' needin' a recipe, Miss Faith. Just cut up some cabbage and onion and cook it together with left-over roast beef. I use rosemary to season it, and salt and pepper too. Then I chop it all up real fine. Roll out some pie crust. I make mine with buttermilk, and I think that makes all the difference. Make yourself some small circles of dough. Put in a generous scoop of the meat mixture and fold over the crust and pinch it closed. Then you bake 'em till they're golden brown. Ain't nothin' to it."

"Sounds delightful. I might even be able to manage it on my own." Faith beamed at him.

Andrew marveled at how open she was with the black man. Most women wouldn't even speak to his crew, but Faith made a point of it. He could well imagine her calling Remli one of her friends. And yet she sat there very prim and proper, looking every bit the lady of society.

After lunch, Faith seemed far less agitated, and Andrew decided against asking her anything more about Berkshire and Lakewood's doings. Instead, he would go see Seth and let him know what had transpired in the past and what Berkshire had just asked of him regarding supplies in Astoria that he wanted delivered to Wheatland. Wheatland would put them in a perfect location to take on to Grand Ronde, and Andrew figured that, as large as the order was, they might very well be ready to push for their hostilities.

"Thank you for the lunch," Faith said as she prepared to leave.

He wanted to encourage her to stay but knew he had plenty of work to do. "You're welcome. I'm glad you could make it, but I'm sorry for the circumstances of your open schedule."

She sighed and looked so sad that Andrew wished he could take her in his arms. "I know God has a plan even in this, but I'm afraid I can't see it. I'm trying hard not to lean on my own understanding, but honestly . . . my heart is broken. I've planned for my surgeon's certificate for a long time. I wanted to have it so people would take me seriously as a physician."

He smiled. "I think when they see your work, they'll take you plenty seriously."

"Yes," she murmured, "but they have to be willing to let me perform first in order to see what I can do. Without the certificate, I doubt that will happen."

Andrew again fought the urge to embrace her and assure her that everything would be all right—that he would see to it. He cared for her more than he could ever admit, but that didn't mean he couldn't try to right some of the wrongs done to her.

Faith noted the time as she caught the trolley. It wouldn't be long before her friends gathered for their afternoon study period. Hopefully they would go to one of their regular places, and she could meet with them and explain what happened. She would start with Brickerson's, and if they weren't there, she'd go to one of their other favorites.

Thankfully, Brickerson's was the restaurant of choice. Faith was once again frozen to the bone and wanted no part of a citywide search. Malcolm was already seated and sipping hot coffee when Faith made her way to his table. He put the cup aside and jumped to his feet to help her with a chair. "At last. Where have you been? You never came to class."

"I was expelled." She said it so matter-of-factly that it sounded as though it was nothing of importance. She sat and began to remove her gloves.

"Expelled? For how long and why?" Malcolm's tone was

disbelieving, and his gaze searched her as if waiting for her to tell him it was all a joke.

"Permanently. They were livid at my having spoken on behalf of Indians. Well, let me restate that. Lakewood was livid. He made them dismiss me."

"But graduation is just weeks away, and you hold the highest marks."

"I know." Malcolm sank to his chair, and Faith continued. "I wanted to come and let you know what happened. I'm not sure what I'm going to do regarding school. I'll speak to my father. As a lawyer, he may know recourses that elude me. As for our lectures, I plan for them to go on. In fact, I'm more devoted to them than ever before and plan to let everyone know what has happened to me. I'm going to get in touch with Mrs. Jackson and implore her to come. I'm sure once she hears what happened, she'll be more than willing."

Malcolm had grown quiet, and for a minute Faith thought he was going to suggest they cancel the lectures.

"I can't bear that they've done this to you. It's not fair. I intend to go speak to the president on your behalf. I'm sure we'll all be willing to do that."

"I don't want you to risk your own well-being. As you said, graduation is just a few weeks away. I suggest you focus on that, and I'll take care of the lectures. Distance yourself so that the school will have no reason to expel you as well."

"No. You don't understand, Faith." He paused a moment and looked away. "I care for you."

She was touched. It had been evident for some time that Malcolm had feelings for her. "Malcolm, it's important that you finish your college studies and get your certificate. Your family is counting on you. I cherish you as a dear friend, but I have no other feelings for you. My heart, unfortunately, belongs to another."

"That riverboat captain?" he asked, lifting his gaze. He looked so unhappy.

Faith smiled and nodded. "Yes, but nothing is going to come of that either. I am devoted to doing what I can to help the Indians, and I doubt being involved with Captain Gratton will allow for that. So you see, I am called of God to remain single so that I can do His work."

"It hardly seems fair of God to demand you be alone."

"But I'm not alone." She did her best to convince her heart of this truth. "I'll always have God, and I have my friends and family. Nothing else matters."

CHAPTER 18

Andrew approached the boardinghouse with several ship logs tucked under his arm. Since learning the truth about Pritchard and the other men, he wanted to do whatever he could to keep the worst from happening. If only he'd known what they were up to. Pritchard had told him they were selling weapons to those living well away from any town or city. He insisted that storing them along the river made it easier for his drummers to pick up their supplies and get packed for their routine selling expeditions. Pritchard was smart too. He didn't just buy guns and ammunition, he purchased traps and tools, whiskey and tins of crackers and meat. For all intents and purposes, he appeared to be doing nothing out of the ordinary—just a merchant supplying his customers with what they needed. Now, however, Andrew knew the truth.

Seth's sister opened the door, and Andrew smiled. "Miss Carpenter."

"Good evening, Captain Gratton. Faith said you'd be stopping by. Won't you come in? I'll take your coat."

"It was just starting to rain, so beware. I wouldn't want to damage the fine furnishings."

She smiled. "There are rumors that it will turn to snow before midnight. Wouldn't that be something?" She hung his coat on the coat tree and motioned toward the open archway. "The others are gathered just through here in the front room. You'll find Faith there as well. We've been working on my wedding gown."

"When's the big day?"

"May thirtieth. Nancy insisted that I had to wait until after the baby is born." Clementine stepped into the room. "Look who's here," she said to everyone, then crossed the room to take her seat.

"Captain Gratton. What a pleasant surprise," Nancy said, looking up from the lace she was tacking onto a bodice. "How are you this evening?"

"Doing well, thank you. I apologize for barging in uninvited. I would have waited, but the *Morning Star* will depart quite early in the morning, and I'll be gone for a while."

"It's no problem. We're always happy to have friends here. We have been working on Clementine's wedding dress."

"Yes, she mentioned that."

"I found the rest of that lace," Faith said, coming into the room. She noticed Andrew immediately and beamed a smile. "What a pleasant surprise."

Nancy laughed. "That's exactly what I said."

Faith deposited the lace on the small table between Nancy and Clementine. "If you recall, this is Mrs. Weaver."

He nodded at the older woman who sat close to the fireplace.

"And the dark-haired woman over there reading is Mrs. Bryant. She is the other lady you and Seth went to rescue the day of the storm."

"We finally meet, Captain Gratton. I appreciate that you came with Seth to look for me," Mrs. Bryant said, looking up from her book.

"They had taken you to the hospital, as I recall."

"Yes. I was rendered unconscious by flying debris but only mildly injured. I'm pleased to report I am doing much better."

"I'm glad to hear it." Andrew gave her a nod, then looked at Faith, who had taken a seat by Clementine. She was already deep in conversation, pointing to the piece of material in Clementine's lap.

"As I remember, you met the Clifton sisters. They are still upstairs but will soon join us. Now, might I get you a cup of coffee or tea?" Nancy asked, getting to her feet.

"You needn't bother."

"It's no bother, I assure you."

Andrew could see that one way or another, she was determined to serve him. "Coffee would be just fine. Black, please."

She nodded and moved away without another word. Andrew tried to imagine her married to Albert Pritchard, but the image wouldn't come together. She seemed nothing at all like the kind of woman who would have married the hard-living storekeeper. Maybe she had been attracted to men who emitted danger, because that was how Pritchard had struck him. The man he had known was always up for a thrill or adventure and had told Andrew many a tale of his wild expeditions. Did Nancy know about them too?

"I'll show you down the hall to the office. That's where you'll find Seth," Faith said, getting back to her feet.

"I don't want to interrupt the sewing. It looks important." He smiled.

"It is," Faith agreed, "but I am only advising at this point. Oh, and running for supplies. I'm very good at sewing sutures but less talented with fabrics and lace."

Nancy reappeared with his coffee. "I thought you'd prefer a mug rather than fine china."

"Yes, thank you." He took the mug and let it warm his hands.

"We eat at six. Would you care to stay for supper?"

"Of course he would," Faith replied for him.

Andrew laughed. "I guess that's settled, then."

"We're having chicken and dumplings as the main course. There will be vegetables and bread, as well as dessert. We make certain no one goes hungry here," Nancy said.

"That sounds delicious. I shall look forward to it."

"I was just about to show him to the office. I know he and Seth will have a lot to discuss." Faith reached for his arm. "This way."

Andrew worried about spilling the coffee as they made their way down the hall. The hardwood floors were covered with lovely carpet runners, and he had no desire to mar them with splashes of coffee.

"Slow down, or I'll make a mess of things."

Faith chuckled and slowed her step. "You are perfectly capable onboard the *Morning Star*, but less so on land, is that it?"

"Something like that." He fought to keep the journals snug under his arm.

Faith knocked on the first door to the right, and Seth bid them enter.

Andrew shrugged as he approached the desk. "I've got my hands full, or I'd offer to shake yours in greeting."

"No need. You're a friend now, and we have no use for formalities," Seth said, moving some papers from his desk. "Feel free to put your coffee here."

"As I told you, Andrew has proof of his business dealings with Albert Pritchard," Faith explained. "He's hoping it will help in the investigation."

"As Faith must have also told *you*, this is of the utmost secrecy," Seth stressed. "We cannot let it get out. I chided her for confiding in you, but I know you have proven yourself to be a man of honor."

"I am that, and I know the value of keeping my mouth shut."

Seth looked at Faith. "Why don't you give us some time alone? We can go through the logs faster on our own."

Faith's expression betrayed her disappointment, but she nodded. "I'll go help with supper. Andrew has agreed to join us."

"Good. Then you'll have time to visit with him later. In the meantime, we have much to discuss." Seth got up and led her to the door.

After closing the door, Seth locked it, to Andrew's surprise. He wasn't about to question the other man, but his look must have betrayed his curiosity.

"I figure we'll have fewer interruptions this way. The women here have a way of bringing you things they think you might need in order to figure out what's going on. I've had sweaters and blankets brought to me, as well as various drinks and food." He smiled as he crossed the room to put more wood on the fire. "They know now that I lock the door when speaking with others, so hopefully they won't attempt it this time." Seth rubbed his hands together and held them out to the fire. "I'll be glad when this cold weather concludes. It seems nothing has been right since the big storm."

"Indeed. The river is still full of obstacles despite the logging companies claiming all they can." Andrew put the ship journals on the desk. "First of all, I want to assure you that I will guard this information and the secrecy of the investigation. I don't think Faith would have ever said anything had she not been so upset."

"I don't really blame her," Seth replied. He took a seat at the desk. "She has great trust in you. But a lot of lives depend on

215

this, and you know what Benjamin Franklin said about secrets. 'Three may keep a secret, if two of them are dead.'"

Andrew picked up his coffee. "I think you'll find I'm quite capable of keeping secrets. I have no intention of doing anything that helps Berkshire and Lakewood after the way they've treated Faith."

"It is troubling. I plan to speak to John Lincoln, my law partner, and see if there is something we can do to help her."

"I feel so bad for her. She loves medicine, and she's good at it. I hate to think she would be refused her certificate just because someone like Lakewood forced the school to expel her."

Seth crossed his arms. "This entire business of riling the Indians to war has caused men to forget themselves."

"Is that the complete plan? Get the Indians and white people fighting one another? Then what?"

"I believe most of the men involved think it will be a short-lived war. Despite the fact that they are giving the Indians weapons and ammunition, I think they're convinced that the government soldiers will be better warriors and therefore able to put an end to the Indians. On the other hand, they don't realize the desperation of the tribes. There are people there who have never known anything but captivity on a reservation. They hear their grandparents and parents tell stories of the days when the tribes roamed free, and they want that for themselves. And frankly, I would want it too."

Andrew couldn't agree more. He thought of the stories his grandfather had told him. "White people won't be happy until the Indians are dead and completely wiped off the earth."

Seth gazed at him, the frown on his face making Andrew nervous that he had said too much, but then Seth nodded. "I know you're right. I wish it weren't that way, but even seeing what happened a few years ago with Chief Joseph and his Nez Perce proved that. The white settlers couldn't have the land, so they felt compelled to just start killing—even pushing the Nez Perce off reservation land that should have been theirs."

"If these men want Grand Ronde and Warm Springs, then they'll no doubt find a way to get those reservation lands as well. They'll find a way. I've no doubt about that."

"Nor do I, but I intend to keep a war from starting—if at all possible. Men like Pritchard and Berkshire, however, are being controlled by someone much more powerful. Someone who has the money and ability to sway the government officials. We have to find him. It might even be a consortium of men."

"I'm sure that's possible. Starting wars isn't cheap. Faith said that her aunt and uncle are missionaries to the Indians. Can they help?"

"They're being accused of being at the very top of the conspiracy. They don't realize this yet. It's been kept quiet, because the people investigating are sure there is someone over them—someone who has instigated the entire thing. They're afraid that Adam Browning, Faith and Nancy's uncle, is in cahoots with this person. Frankly, like the girls, I don't believe the Brownings are involved. I doubt they know anything about it. My money is on a government official being to blame. It's impossible to know who to trust. When I was recruited to help, it was clear there were divisions even in the same department."

Andrew put his coffee aside. "I hope these journals will help. They record each trip I made, what I was carrying, and where it was taken. It shows the individuals who owned the shipments as well, although I know that can be falsified."

"Do you recall how long it's been going on? With Pritchard, for example."

"It goes back quite a ways, but I only brought the last three years of logs. Pritchard was a big customer, given his riverfront store. He served a lot of the ship captains with repair parts and other ship needs, but he was also supplying goods to men up and down the river. I may not have been the only one he was using for shipping. He could have used other firms as well, and I'd have no knowledge of it. And as for delivery, like I explained to Faith, his orders were more often than not delivered to locations along the Willamette."

Seth rubbed his chin. "We know about some of those places. I'm hoping you can help me by marking spots on this map of the river where you know there to be hidden storage sheds." Seth pulled a rolled paper from his desk drawer and spread it atop his desk. "You'll see there are already some places marked. Nancy's brother Gabe and I were able to locate several by following Berkshire's men from place to place. This also resulted in Berkshire being forced to help the government. He thinks they believe him true to helping dissolve this affair, but the men in charge know Berkshire is a liar. They realize he's been giving just enough information to keep them interested but that he's not sharing what he really knows."

"And who does Berkshire report to on the other side?"

"Lakewood. At least that's how it appears. Lakewood is a wealthy man in his own right, but he doesn't have the kind of money that has been used to buy officials in addition to the goods."

"Are there no inspections on the reservations? I thought the Indians were closely policed regarding guns and alcohol."

"They are to a point, but before I left the investigation, we learned that most of the supplies were moved in at night and then hidden on the reservation, not kept in the homes. We know that not all of the Indians have any desire to rebel. They're tired. Weary from the mistreatment and abuse. They don't have it in them to fight. However, once a war is started, I believe most will rise up to fight alongside their relatives." Seth shook his head and sighed. "I honestly can't say that I would blame them. We've made a real mess of their treatment."

Andrew knew this as well as anyone. It was the reason he'd removed his grandfather from the Nez Perce reservation to live with him on the *Morning Star*. Of course, that hadn't come with the approval of anyone, but rather a stealthy raid in the middle of the night.

"I've worked with representatives from Lakewood as well as Berkshire himself. In fact, Berkshire just came to me. He wants a big shipment of weapons taken from Astoria to Wheatland. It wouldn't be difficult to get them from Wheatland to Grand Ronde. I figure it's less than forty miles by land."

"When will the delivery take place?"

"I'm supposed to pick up the guns at Astoria in two weeks. They're coming up from California. Berkshire wants them in Wheatland by the end of March."

"Well, that should give us time to speak to the army and see what, if anything, they want to do about it. The logs should be a great help and will maybe even give them additional names. I'll need to get them to Major Wells in Fort Vancouver, and they'll probably want to talk to you."

"I'm taking a load of flour to the fort tomorrow. I could take the logs as well."

Seth grinned. "Your timing is perfect. I'll write a letter to Major Wells after supper and explain the situation. I have a feeling your help is going to be a boon to this investigation."

"I'm glad. I'll do whatever I can to help stop these men. The last thing we need is another Indian war."

After supper, Faith, with help from the Clifton sisters, finished cleaning the kitchen while Seth and Andrew completed the last of their business. She'd heard Seth mention a letter he needed to write but had no idea what the two had discussed or what solutions they might have come up with. She had mixed feelings on the entire matter, wanting desperately to help keep the peace between the Indians and whites, as well as being consumed by her own issues.

"Thank you for your assistance," Bedelia said, taking up the dishcloths. "I shall hang these to dry, and then Sister and I will head upstairs for our evening Bible reading."

Faith put the last of the dishes in the cupboard, then glanced around the room to see if anything else needed to be dealt with. Everything was in order. They'd sent Nancy to rest as soon as supper concluded, and Mimi and Clementine had papers to grade. Since there was a stranger in the house, Mrs. Weaver had taken her meal upstairs so that she and Alma could eat together, and once the Clifton sisters had gone up, that would be the last of the boarders and family. At least Faith hoped it would be. Seth might want to stick around until Andrew departed, but hopefully he'd see that Faith wanted a little time alone with the captain.

She went to the front room and found there wasn't much left of the earlier blaze in the fireplace. Since everyone would soon retire to their rooms, there didn't seem much sense in building up a big fire. Unless, of course, Andrew was of a mind to stay and visit. Hoping to encourage him, Faith placed another log on the fire and smiled as the dry wood easily caught.

It seemed to take forever for Seth and Andrew to conclude their business. Faith paced back and forth, remembering the frustration of the day and wondering what her next plan should be. She really needed to see her father. Lance Kenner was an authority on the law, and she had no doubt he'd have some ideas. However, Seth was a good lawyer, and John Lincoln was well known in Portland for his legal mind. Surely the two of them could come up with some ideas on what she could do next.

She heard the men coming down the hall and struck a pose by the side of the fireplace. When Seth entered the room first, she hesitated, not knowing what to say.

"I was going to show Andrew to the door," Seth said, giving her a knowing look. "Instead, I think I'll check on Nancy and let you show him out. Thank you for coming tonight, Andrew. As I said before, I believe this will be most useful."

Andrew was still holding the books he'd brought. Faith wondered why he wasn't leaving them with Seth. Could they have held nothing that would help the investigation?

Faith waited until Seth had left the room to offer her thoughts on the matter. "I know your information will be helpful. It can't help but fill in some of the missing pieces."

Andrew nodded. "I think it very well might, but you can't pin all your hopes to this. Those men have been very good at sneaking around and conspiring against the government. They are wolves posing as sheep—or worse still, maybe even white men posing as Indians. It will be hard, if not nearly impossible, to know who can be trusted."

She thought of the accusations against her aunt and uncle. No one who knew them as she did could ever believe them capable of doing anything to cause the Indians harm. But there were very few white people, outside of family, who knew them that well. Mercy and Adam Browning had spent most of the last twenty-five years with the Indians.

"I should get back to the *Morning Star*. We leave early."

Disappointed, Faith walked with him to the door. "Why are you taking the logs back with you? Were they not as useful as we hoped?"

"Just the opposite. Seth wants to get them to one of the army men at Fort Vancouver. I have to make a trip there tomorrow to drop off flour and then head out to Astoria. I'll be gone for quite some time."

The thought of Andrew leaving again left Faith feeling empty inside. Something desperate rose up inside her. She wanted him to stay, or else she wanted to go with him. She needed him, just as she needed air.

"I wish we had a carriage so I could drive you back to the *Morning Star*." She forced her voice to remain calm and clasped her hands to keep from reaching out to touch him.

He turned and smiled. "I wouldn't allow you to do so even if you did. It's far too dangerous out there. Always some hoodlum or ruffian out to prove himself. No one is going to bother a rough old river captain."

"You're hardly old," she murmured, and he laughed.

Faith reached for the door handle at the same time as Andrew. His hand closed over hers, and for a moment all she could do was gaze into his eyes. He was so handsome, and she fell completely under his spell. Did he know how much her heart ached with love for him?

When he pressed his lips against hers, it seemed the most natural thing in the world. It seemed even more natural when Faith stepped closer and felt his arms go around her. She knew

222

nothing could come of this, and yet she couldn't bring herself to stop. At least she'd have this moment. This kiss.

Andrew pulled back. His eyes seemed to have darkened, but whether from passion or anger, Faith couldn't be sure. He frowned and pushed her away in a gentle but firm manner.

"I have to go."

And then, without another word, he bounded out the door and down the porch steps.

Faith stood watching him, wishing she had some reason to call him back. The cold permeated her wool skirt and stockings and caused her to shiver, yet even then she couldn't seem to stop watching as Andrew's figure moved farther and farther away.

Words left unspoken stuck in her throat. She wanted to shout after him that she loved him—that she knew she shouldn't and that she didn't expect him to return her feelings, but that it was nevertheless true.

She bit her lip and leaned against the doorjamb. "I love you," she whispered, knowing that no one but God would hear her confession.

CHAPTER 19

F aith prayed as she accompanied her father to their appointment with President Parrish. There was no telling what might or might not be said, but she begged God to intercede on her behalf. Thankfully, her father wasn't given to losing his temper. The last thing she wanted was for the men to come to blows.

Faith had dressed in a new outfit her mother had made for her. It was supposed to be her graduation outfit, but now it would help her persuade the college just to allow her to graduate. Faith thought she looked very smart and fashionable. The burgundy suit was fashioned with the narrow skirt of the day and a small back bustle. The accompanying jacket was long and overlaid with copper and gold designs that had been cut and sewn along the edges. Mother had even arranged for the milliner to fashion a matching hat.

Faith had immediately loved the outfit and loved that her mother had taken time to make it for her. Especially given Oregon City and the Armistead farm itself had suffered just as much damage from the storm as Portland had. Faith hadn't wanted to wear the outfit to the appointment, but her mother felt confident that she should.

"Look your best. Be pleasant and show your strength. Don't give them any thought of being able to defeat you," Hope Kenner had told Faith before they'd parted company.

Father gave her gloved hand a squeeze. "Don't be so nervous. I'm sure that once we make our position clear, the president will rethink the matter. He won't want to see the college caught up in litigation."

"Oh, Father, I just don't know if this is the right way to handle it. I mean, I don't want anything to cause problems for the other medical students. I'm sure this is all Mr. Lakewood's fault and that President Parrish was just following his instruction."

Lance Kenner frowned. "A better man would not be put into such a position. President Parrish knows the importance of this program. His own wife attended and graduated. As I hear it, she is now actively practicing medicine in Portland."

"Yes, that's true, but I worry that anything we do will cause problems for my friends. They are supposed to graduate this year, just as I was. If they should be expelled because of me, I would never be able to bear it."

"Don't worry. Let's just go see him. It might have all blown over by now, and we'll find that he's willing to work something out."

"I doubt that." Faith bit her lip and fell silent. She had to trust that God and her father would know how to handle the matter. She might have her own ideas of what she'd like to happen to Lakewood, but as a Christian, she needed to calm her spirit and let God lead. After all, Lakewood had already done what he could to hurt her. There was really nothing left that he could do.

They waited nearly half an hour before the secretary showed them into President Parrish's office. Faith was glad that her father took charge almost immediately. Lance Kenner had served in the army before going into law full-time. Men all over Oregon came to him for help, especially with government problems, and Faith greatly admired his ability to command almost any situation.

"Mr. Parrish, I want to thank you for seeing us today."

"You left me little choice, Mr. Kenner."

Faith's father smiled. "You hardly needed to admit that. I would have allowed you your pride in front of my daughter."

Parrish looked embarrassed. "I'm sorry that this situation has caused your family grief, but I'm afraid the college is quite firm about its students not participating in political demonstrations."

"Yes, about that. I've reviewed all of the charters, organizational papers, and records from each and every official meeting, and nowhere have I found evidence that a student—especially a student who is at the top of her class—can or should be dismissed for participating in off-campus events that are not related to the university."

The door behind Faith opened. She thought perhaps it was President Parrish's secretary, but instead, Samuel Lakewood walked past her to take a chair beside the president's desk. He smiled and gave Faith a nod.

"Mr. Lakewood insisted on joining us today, as he is one of our larger donors and the person who made the original complaint," President Parrish said.

"I would have expected nothing less," Faith's father responded.

Lakewood didn't so much as acknowledge Father. Instead,

he looked at Parrish. "This man has something of a reputation. But given his family, that isn't surprising."

Faith could hear an underlying tone of accusation. She wasn't sure what Lakewood was implying, but he apparently thought he had the upper hand.

"As I was just telling President Parrish before you interrupted us," her father continued, "I studied the university's rules and regulations for students and found nothing that allows you the right to dismiss a student for practicing his or her beliefs away from university property. Therefore, I want my daughter to be reinstated."

Lakewood smiled. "That, my good sir, is quite impossible. You see, we became aware of other matters related to Miss Kenner. Things that I doubt you would want to become public knowledge."

Faith stiffened. What was he talking about? Did he know about her dealings with Captain Gratton? She supposed many would condemn her for her trips to the *Morning Star* without a proper escort. She frowned. Why should it matter to him or anyone else? She'd done nothing wrong.

"What threat are you making, sir?" her father asked before she could pose the question herself.

Lakewood pretended to study his fingernails. "I'm making no threat, but rather suggesting that if the truth were known about your daughter—your *adopted* daughter—it would cause a great many problems not only for her but for your family."

Faith's stomach clenched. She looked at Lakewood just as he met her gaze. There was a hint of a smile on his lips. He knew. She didn't know how, but somehow he knew about her birth.

"What are you implying, Mr. Lakewood?"

Faith heard her father ask the question but wished he hadn't.

A feeling of helplessness washed over her, and her cheeks heated up as her breath quickened.

"I'm not implying anything, Mr. Kenner. I have proof that your daughter Faith Kenner is part Indian."

Her stomach dropped, leaving Faith queasy. How could he know? How could Samuel Lakewood have found out the truth?

Faith hardly heard anything else the men had to say. There was a loud whooshing in her head that left her dizzy and confused. After years of carefully concealing the truth of her conception, these men were now discussing it as if it were nothing more important than the weather. She tried to steady her breathing. Maybe she'd just misunderstood him. Maybe in her guilt, she'd only imagined Lakewood had said those things.

It was her father's voice that restored her concentration. "I fail to see your point in this matter. We're talking about a dismissal just weeks away from graduation for my daughter's having participated in a lecture event. I would remind you that she is at the very top of the graduating class in grades and performance."

"Yes, but none of that really matters, since we do not allow Indians to attend the university. There is really nothing more to discuss."

"She's a qualified student who has paid her tuition and has received honors for her work."

"Your money will be returned," Lakewood said. "Although we are under no obligation to do so. She entered this university under false pretenses. But perhaps you'd prefer to sue the college. A public lawsuit would, however, reveal your daughter's shame."

"My daughter has nothing to be ashamed of, Mr. Lakewood, and you would do well to carefully consider saying anything against her. I do not suffer fools."

Faith realized that her father had neither admitted nor denied Lakewood's accusations, but if he wanted to press this situation, Faith knew the truth would come out and her mother would be the center of attention.

"I'm sorry," she blurted. "I feel overheated. This room is quite stuffy. Perhaps we could continue this meeting at a later time. I fear I may be sick."

"Of course, Miss Kenner," the president said, getting to his feet. "We can resume this at a later date. Just make an appointment with my secretary."

"There's no need for that, Josiah," Lakewood said. "I think Mr. Kenner understands perfectly well the consequences of pressing this matter. I think we've already dealt with all the particulars."

Faith got up and moved to the door. She couldn't bear to hear anything more. She had wondered for a long time what the price of her deception might be. Now it was coming clear. She would be refused her certification to practice surgery, and if they were lucky, that would be all. But Faith didn't believe in luck, nor the goodwill of men like Lakewood. Somehow, he had found out the truth about her conception, and he was the type of man who would do whatever he deemed necessary to humiliate them all.

She didn't remember the walk to the carriage, but once inside, she burst into tears and sought her father's arms. She felt as if she were a small child again as he held her and reassured her that it wasn't the end of the world.

"Faith, the truth is what it is. We've always known it would come out one day. You mustn't grieve yourself over this."

"But Mother. Poor Mother. She will face such ridicule. People will be cruel." She struggled to get her breath. "I . . . I don't care . . . what they think of me."

"Shhh, it's going to be all right. Your mother and I talked about this in detail. We've always known that this might happen one day. Few people know that you are your mother's natural child. Most people think you're adopted—that you were Isaac and Eletta's child. It's very possible that Lakewood learned of Isaac's Cherokee blood. Remember, he stressed that you were our adopted daughter."

Faith sat up and nodded. "Yes. Yes, that must be what this is about. I hadn't thought of that. Oh, it would be such a relief if that was all that Mr. Lakewood knew. I could bear that. I've always known I could bear whatever came my way regarding the past, but I didn't want Mother hurt. She doesn't deserve to go through that. It would be as if she were raped all over again."

Her father nodded. "I know."

"I'm sorry. I shouldn't have been so blunt."

He shook his head. "You owe me no apology. It is the truth. Like you, I don't want her to suffer, and if it goes in that direction, we may well move away to save her from further embarrassment. Still, I don't think Lakewood knows anything beyond believing you are part Cherokee. Isaac's past would have been easy enough to learn, and Lakewood has plenty of resources."

It was such a relief just to imagine that her mother might be spared. Faith fell back against the carriage seat. Her father handed her a handkerchief.

"God has a plan even in this, Faith. Even in what happened to your mother. No matter what, we have to trust in the Lord."

"And lean not unto our own understanding." Faith wiped her eyes. "God's been speaking that verse in Proverbs to me over and over. But my own understanding has no patience for this, no belief that good can come from it."

Father put his arm around her and hugged her close. "I know,

231

but no matter what, we have Him and we have each other. Your mother is a strong woman, and she will get through this, but she'll be worried about you. I need to be able to tell her that you're doing just fine—that they haven't defeated you."

She nodded and squared her shoulders, pulling slightly away from his hold. "I will be fine. They won't defeat me."

"That's my girl." He smiled. "Besides, we're not done with them yet. Lakewood is facing more than he realizes. He'll be sorry he ever got involved in his scheming to see you ruined and the Indians at war."

Faith's eyes widened. "You know about that?"

"I do, but it's probably best we leave it at that."

"Yes. I'm sure it is." She leaned back against her father's shoulder and sighed. "Thank you for always loving me despite, well, everything."

"You're easy to love, Faith. You always have been."

Samuel Lakewood got up to leave Parrish's office. He'd accomplished his purpose and defeated the great Lance Kenner. His day was going just as he'd hoped.

"Samuel, is it true?"

Lakewood turned to look at Josiah Parrish. "Is what true?"

He knew what Parrish was referencing. He wanted to know if Faith Kenner was really part savage. Lakewood had paid a lot to have the matter investigated in detail and knew it was true, but he wasn't sure he wanted Parrish to know that. At least not yet.

"The part about her being Indian. Faith Kenner has blue eyes and looks nothing like an Indian."

"Did you hear Mr. Kenner admit to her being of Indian blood?"

"No. He never did."

Samuel smiled. "I simply said that as a ruse. I figured it would give them pause to rethink their threat of a lawsuit. It would be easy enough to get someone to testify against her birth parents. Remember, she is adopted by the Kenners."

Parrish nodded and then just as quickly shook his head. "You could ruin the girl's life by claiming such a terrible thing."

"That was the point of my threat, Josiah. It'll save the college a considerable amount of time and money if they back away from suing us. If they insist on moving ahead, we can present the idea of Faith's heritage. By the time it's dealt with in court, she'll be ruined. But somehow I don't think it will come to that. Now, I presume you will keep all of this to yourself."

"Of course."

"Then good day."

Lakewood was finished with his business at the college, but not with his dealings with Faith and her family. He ordered his driver to take him to Gerome Berkshire's office and was glad to find him alone. Not a single one of his lackeys was anywhere in sight.

"Where are your rowdies?" Lakewood asked as he took the chair opposite Gerome's desk.

"I've got them working on the various things you ordered me to do. Why?"

"I want to make certain we aren't overheard."

"No one else is here," Gerome assured him.

"Good. I want you to kill Seth Carpenter."

A smile came to Gerome's lips. "I'd be happy to. Do you want him to go the same way Pritchard did?"

Lakewood shook his head. "No, I want him to suffer. I want you to beat him nearly to death and then stop. We'll let him recover a bit—just enough to have hope of living—and then we'll finish him."

"Why such hatred toward Carpenter?"

"I hate them all. Every one of those Indian-lovers. Everyone who has interfered in our plans for an Indian-free Oregon."

"Well, a whole lot more than just Carpenter have interfered in that."

"Yes, but we'll start with him and make him an example. Once we let it be known that such interference will not be tolerated, I'm sure our plans will be easily managed."

"When do you want it done?"

Lakewood considered a moment. "When is his wife due to deliver?"

"April or May. I don't exactly remember."

Again, Lakewood mulled it over. "We don't have to rush. Let's set the attack closer to when the child is due. The complications it will create might lend themselves to our plans to kill him." He smiled. "There's nothing quite so cruel as giving a man false hope, eh?"

"And what of Mr. Smith?"

Lakewood frowned. "What of him? You know better than to think you can bring him up and be privy to his plans."

"I don't even know his real name," Gerome said, shrugging. "How can my asking about his plans possibly cause you trouble?"

"You're informing the government about our plans. At least the plans we want them to know about. You don't need to know anything about Mr. Smith, lest you accidentally say something you shouldn't."

"Well, it's not like I've never met him. He and I have talked many times," Gerome boasted.

"Shut up." Lakewood fixed him with a hard look. "As far as you are concerned, he doesn't exist. If I thought for one minute you were sharing information about him with the army, I'd kill you myself."

"I'd never do anything of the sort." Gerome looked wounded. "I've been nothing but faithful, and yet you treat me like a traitor."

Lakewood rolled his gaze heavenward. "Honestly, you are as difficult as one of my children. No one believes you to be a traitor." If they did, he'd already be dead. "Now, I've given you your instructions, and I intend for you to carry them out." Lakewood got to his feet. "Oh, and if the situation arises to put the fear of God into Faith Kenner, feel free to use your imagination and do that as well."

"Faith? What has she done to rile you?"

"Again, it's none of your concern, but don't hurt her. I have plans for her."

"I just don't understand why. It makes no sense."

"Are you going to follow my orders, or should I seek out someone else? You know what happened to Pritchard when I lost confidence in him. I'd hate for the same thing to happen to you."

He saw fear wash over Gerome. It gave him a sense of strength he'd not felt in some time.

"I'm glad we understand each other."

"I still can't believe they kicked you out of school with graduation just weeks away," Nancy said at breakfast the next day. Everyone at the table shook their heads in agreement. "And all because of your charity work. That hardly seems right."

Faith tried to smile. "I must admit, I'm still in shock. I was so close to getting my certificate and seeing all of my hard work pay off."

"Well, I'm glad your father is helping you." Nancy passed a bowl of oatmeal to Faith. "If anyone can get this straightened out, he can."

Faith hadn't told Nancy the details of the dismissal. Had she done so, she was pretty sure Nancy would change her tune.

Mrs. Weaver shook her head. "This world is just falling to pieces. So much hatred. But don't despair, Faith, dear. You will overcome. I just feel certain of this."

"We must pray that God will let wiser thinking prevail," Bedelia declared. "After all, you were working for His glory and in His name. He won't leave you orphaned now."

Faith appreciated all the encouragement but knew they were unaware of the real reason she'd been dismissed. "How is Alma?" she asked, trying to change the subject.

"All but healed," Mrs. Weaver said. "She was impressed by how quickly the illness faded after your healing touch. See there? You don't even need a certificate. God has given you a natural ability."

Again, the topic had been brought back to Faith's situation. She supposed there was no hope of getting the women onto another topic. This was understandably a concern to each of them. They cared about her and wanted good things for her. She had spent many a night in study only to have one of the ladies slip into her room with a cup of hot tea and cookies. They always asked how her classes were progressing—especially Clementine and Mimi. They were all so good to her, and she couldn't blame them for wanting to figure out a way to help. However, she just didn't feel up to the conversation.

"You have all been so kind, but I need to be alone." Faith pushed back from the table and stood. "I appreciate you all more than I can say."

With that, she left for the solitude of her room. She couldn't bear to discuss her lost dreams. She wasn't even sure she could pray.

Andrew gave his men the order to secure the load before making his way from the ship with Major Wells.

"My men removed all of the firing pins, as you clearly saw," Major Wells said, "with exception to those rifles on top. That way if someone insists on checking the quality and firing ability of the weapons, they won't be disappointed."

"I feel better knowing the pins are missing. I'd hate to think of a real war breaking out." His grandfather had told him many times of the terrible wars of days gone by. Andrew knew war took its toll on both sides, but inevitably it would be the Indians who lost the most.

"We've got all the information we need from you. We'll wire ahead to have the boat under observation via various ports and checkpoints. Don't fear, you'll be under constant monitoring."

"I understand."

Wells paused when they reached the end of the dock and extended his hand. "Good sailing, Captain. Our prayers and best thoughts go with you."

Andrew nodded. "Thank you. I'm hopeful we can put an end to the threat of an uprising."

Wells looked grave. "As am I. Many of the soldiers under my command are just boys. They aren't old enough to have seen the Rogue River Wars. Some were even too young for the Nez Perce

Wars." He shook his head. "They're all fired up and anxious to confront what might come, but they don't understand what they're facing. I'd rather they never know."

Andrew couldn't agree more. Grandfather always said there was nothing like war to alter the heart of a young man.

He left the major and signaled for his men to cast off. Next stop, Portland. It seemed like forever since he'd seen Faith. The last time he was with her, he'd done the unthinkable.

How could he have kissed her? He knew there could never be anything between them. Not legally, and he wouldn't have a more intimate relationship with Faith unless it was legal. He loved her too much. He would never shame her by lying to her.

He frowned and made his way to the wheelhouse. No matter how much he wanted her for his own, Andrew knew he would have to forget her. It would be best never to see her again, but now that he was entangled in this mess, it was inevitable that they would encounter each other at some point. When they did meet again, Andrew couldn't imagine what he'd say to her.

"You all right, Captain?" Denny asked, looking up from his paperwork.

"I'm fine," Andrew growled. "Just head us toward Portland."

Denny's eyes narrowed, but he did as Andrew ordered while Andrew released his clenched fists. He wouldn't go see Faith. He would deliver what was ordered for Portland and leave. Leave before she could learn that the *Morning Star* was even in port. Leave before he could make a fool of himself . . . again.

CHAPTER 20

By mid-April the rains had tapered off and the temperature had warmed. Faith tried not to think of Andrew's long absence or the kiss he'd given her on that night so long ago. It was useless to pretend it never happened, even if she knew nothing could ever come of it. Instead, she tried to keep her thoughts on the medical college's graduation, which was taking place on the twenty-seventh, despite her inability to participate. She had met with her friends on several occasions, usually in secret. No longer did they feel they had the luxury of public gatherings, and because of Lakewood's threats, they had decided to postpone their lecture series until after graduation. Still, each one assured Faith that they were committed to helping the Indians. She was glad for that and for the fact that their lecture had made it possible to send a large supply of medicines to the reservation. Added to this, Mrs. Jackson and Mr. Singleton had both responded to her letters with assurances that they would do what they could to help. With the aid of a celebrity such as Mrs. Jackson and a government official, Faith felt confident they could put Mr. Lakewood in his place. She would just have to be patient.

Faith was the one who had driven home to her friends that nothing was going to change overnight and it was important that they do nothing to interfere with their own graduation. She could see the relief in their eyes at the understanding that they could move toward graduation without fear. She didn't blame them at all. She only wished it had been true for herself.

As her cousin grew larger and her pregnancy progressed, Faith felt a certain degree of responsibility to watch over her and be available should she go into labor. Nancy's mother was slated to come in May and stay with them until the baby was born, and Faith knew once Grace Armistead arrived, she would have far less responsibility. But until then, Faith was in charge, and the women of the boardinghouse were very protective of both her and Nancy. They didn't want Faith leaving the house for any reason.

It amused Faith that the ladies were all growing more and more anxious. None of them had children, and they were nervous about Nancy's condition and whether she might give birth at any moment. Faith tried to reassure them that first babies generally took their time being born and that they needn't worry. But worry they did. Even Clementine was more focused on the birth of the baby than her upcoming wedding.

But then on the sixteenth of April, Grace and Alex Armistead appeared at the front door of the boardinghouse, suitcases in hand.

Faith was nearest the door at the sound of the knocker and had opened it to the joyful expressions of her aunt and uncle. She couldn't help but be excited by their arrival.

"I didn't know you were coming so soon. How wonderful!" She embraced them both.

"I asked them to come early," Seth said behind her. "I was

beginning to worry that the ladies were going to chain you up so you couldn't leave the house."

Faith laughed and pulled back from her aunt's embrace. "I feared the same thing myself. I thought maybe Nancy had taken pity on me."

"Well, now there will be two of us, and everyone can relax," Grace declared.

"I'll show you to your room," Seth said, reaching out to help Alex with the suitcases. "I hope you like it. We sent all the way to California for the mattress on the bed."

"Goodness, you needn't have done that," Grace replied.

"Speak for yourself," Alex countered, laughing. "I'm excited about the new mattress. If it suits us, we may have to order one for the farm."

Faith laughed, as did the others. "It's so good to have you both here."

Nancy came waddling out of the front room. She looked miserable but still smiled. "Mama. Papa. I'm so glad you've come."

Grace went to her daughter and hugged her. "We wouldn't have missed this for the world. Just look at you. You look wonderful."

"I look fat, like an overstuffed sausage casing. Did Meg come with you?" Nancy looked around for her younger sister.

"No, she still has classes. She wanted to come, but we promised she could spend some time helping you this summer. The thought of getting to spend time in Portland without her mother and father's watchful eye ever upon her softened being left behind," Nancy's mother explained.

"It will be good to have her here. I'll definitely put her to work. We're going to plant a big garden. Since the storm destroyed the grounds, we've been reworking things and trying to figure out what we want and where. We all decided that since I intend to keep up with the boardinghouse, we should have a sizeable garden to help feed everyone."

"I think that's wise," her mother said.

"It's even wiser to show your parents where they're going to be staying these next few weeks," Seth said, pretending to be overburdened by the weight of the suitcases.

"Yes, by all means." Nancy grinned. "We turned another of the empty downstairs rooms into a bedroom. It's just down the hall from the bath we added last year, so while you'll share it with us and Faith, at least it will be close."

"It's nice not worrying about outhouses," her father called over his shoulder.

Once he had his in-laws settled, Seth excused himself. "I have a lot of work to contend with today. Don't wait supper for me. I'll be at the courthouse a good part of the day and then back at the office until late, working on yet another project."

"But tomorrow's Saturday." Nancy was less than delighted at the news.

"I can't help it. This matter will be resolved first thing Monday morning. I'll work all day Saturday if need be."

"Do you want me to send someone down with your supper?" Nancy asked.

Seth shook his head. "No. I'll have the secretary go out and bring something back." He kissed her forehead and gave her belly a pat. "Take good care of our baby."

The tenderness between them stirred Faith's heart and desire for such a life. She knew the threats Lakewood had made caused more problems than ever before, but they didn't put an end to her longing. She was grateful that he'd said nothing more on the matter, but she knew her father was still trying to resolve the issue, and what might come out of that was unknown. Mama had written a beautiful letter reminding Faith that she was blessed of God and that He would continue to oversee her entire existence just as He always had. She told Faith to be strong and not fear what man could do. And she assured Faith that she wasn't afraid of what man could do to her. If the truth was told, then it was told.

Without classes to attend, Faith did what she could around the house. Since the day was dry and quite warm, she went out to the large plot of ground that they planned to plant. David, the young Irishman who worked for Nancy and Seth, had helped mark it off and plowed it up. Each of the ladies had been working the soil to ready it for planting, and Faith found churning and hoeing the dirt to be therapeutic.

She pondered how Andrew might be. A part of her wondered if she'd ever see him again. She had acted quite wanton in her response to his touch. She couldn't blame him at all if he'd been offended. He seemed upset when he'd left. Maybe he somehow knew of her Indian blood. Faith reached down, plucked out a large tuft of grass, and threw it beyond the garden plot.

"The kiss meant nothing." It could mean nothing. Faith continued to remind herself of this truth over and over. She had thought it would help if she told herself this enough times, but it made it no easier. The truth was still the truth. That kiss had meant everything.

Faith lost track of time as she worked in the garden. She was surprised to see how much ground she'd covered when Bedelia showed up to announce that supper would be soon.

"I'm sorry. I should have been in there helping you." Faith pushed loose strands of hair away from her forehead.

"You were doing some good work out here," Bedelia said, looking at the garden plot. "It looks nearly ready to plant."

"We always had big gardens at home." Faith glanced over the turned earth. "Much bigger than this, but then, we were feeding a lot more people. I think this will give us a great bounty to put up for the winter."

"It should cut the cost of the food budget considerably," Bedelia replied. "I am more than pleased to help, but for now I need to get back to the stove. I left Cornelia to oversee the casserole in the oven, and there's no telling what might happen."

Faith began to walk toward the house, and Bedelia fell in step beside her. "Have you always watched over your sister?"

"Oh yes. Our mother insisted. Cornelia is rather . . . well, she isn't quite capable of taking care of herself."

Faith frowned. Her medical experience made her curious. "What's wrong with her? If you don't mind my asking."

"I seldom speak to anyone about it lest I cause Cornelia embarrassment. When she was born, the cord was wrapped around her neck several times. She was without air for a long time. Mother said it made her simple."

"Oh. How terrible there wasn't a proper midwife to see that didn't happen. Even then, they can't always prevent such things from happening."

Bedelia nodded. "We were poor, and my mother relied upon the help of a neighbor who knew very little. She made me promise from the time I was quite young that I would always look out for Cornelia. It's the reason I've never married."

"You sacrificed your life for hers."

"I made a promise."

"She seems mostly capable."

"She is. She is not by any means unable to function. But she has difficulties with many things. I read to her because she was never quite able to master it. She can read a little, but it becomes so burdensome to her that she easily gives up."

Faith could better understand the stern, almost harsh personality of Bedelia Clifton considering what she'd just confessed. Here she and the others had presumed Bedelia to be overbearing and demanding. "She is very fortunate to have you. What a tender, giving heart you have."

Bedelia blushed and looked away. "Thank you."

"I promise to say nothing about this," Faith added, "but thank you for the trust you have placed in me by telling me your story."

Looking up, Bedelia met Faith's gaze. "I knew that, as a medical woman—a physician—you would understand."

Faith realized the honor Bedelia was bestowing on her and nodded. "I do."

Supper came and went, and there was no sign of Seth. Nancy knew he planned to be late, but she was restless and unable to relax, and when the clock chimed nine o'clock and he'd still not returned, she began to fret.

"He's never been this late."

Her mother sat knitting. "Yes, but he told you he would be quite late. I think you should make your way to bed. Maybe by the time you get ready, he'll be home."

Nancy did her best to pace in front of the fireplace. The baby's weight was slowing her down more each day. "I just can't shake the feeling that something isn't right."

"Even if there is a problem, what can we do?" Faith hadn't really meant to ask the question out loud, but now that she had, there was nothing to do but anticipate Nancy's answer.

"Well, we could send someone to check on him. Father could

go down to the office and make sure he's all right." Nancy gave her mother a hopeful look.

"And what if Seth is already on his way home? Your father would never know, and he'd get there and then be worried about whether Seth had met with harm."

"Yes, but once he came home and found Seth here, then he'd know. And if he came home and Seth wasn't here, then we'd all know for certain that something was wrong."

Grace Armistead put her knitting back into her bag. "Do you honestly want me to go wake up your father?"

Nancy frowned. "No, I suppose not. I just don't know what to do. Seth would never stay away this long."

"The time could have gotten away from him." Faith knew the suggestion wasn't at all helpful, but she was trying to think of possibilities for Nancy to focus on.

Clementine had been waiting for her brother's return as well. "I could go. Faith and I could go together."

"Absolutely not!" Grace declared. "If anyone is going to go, it will be Alex." She got up from the chair. "I'll go wake him."

Nancy looked uncertain. "I don't want to wake him up. I just want to know if Seth is all right. I'm worried that with everything that's been going on, something has happened. I just have a bad feeling. Oh, I wish I'd put in a telephone."

Grace came to her and put her arm around her daughter. "It's all right. Sometimes we have those feelings for a reason. That's why I'm going to wake up your father."

The sound of someone on the front porch brought a smile to Faith's lips. "Ah, here he is. I'll let him in and give him a good piece of my mind for making us worry." She went to the door and flung it wide. "Seth Carpenter, how dare—" She stopped.

The man facing her wasn't Seth. He was a uniformed policeman.

"Good evening, is this the residence of Seth Carpenter?"

"It is. Is something wrong?"

"Are you his wife?"

Faith shook her head. "Nancy is." She backed away from the door and toward the front room. "Nancy, you need to come here."

Nancy appeared with Grace close beside her. Clementine followed. "What is it? What's happened to Seth?"

"Are you Mrs. Carpenter?" the officer asked Nancy.

"I am. Is my husband all right?"

"No, ma'am. He's been hurt pretty badly. He's in the hospital, and they sent me to tell you he's gravely injured."

"I must go to him." Nancy looked at her mother.

The policeman shook his head. "Ma'am, the visiting hours are done for the day. The doctor told me to tell you that if Mr. Carpenter lives through the night, you can visit him in the morning. They won't be allowing anyone any sooner, because he's unconscious."

Nancy looked as though she might faint. Faith decided to pull rank. "I'm a physician. I'll go to the hospital and learn what I can." She looked at Grace, who nodded.

"You're in no condition to go, Nancy," her mother said. "Let Faith go. She'll be able to tell you what's going on."

"But if he dies . . ." Nancy's voice broke, and she sobbed against her mother's shoulder.

"Try not to worry." Faith went to the coat tree and took up her jacket. "Officer, do you have a horse?"

"I do."

"Might I ride double with you back to the hospital? That will save me some time."

He looked uncertain for a moment, then nodded. "Of course. I'm sorry to have brought you such bad news."

"We needed to know," Grace replied, holding her daughter tight. "Faith, come back to us as soon as you can."

Faith nodded. "I will."

She followed the officer outside. He climbed atop his horse, then held his hand down for Faith. She hiked up her skirt and barely managed to place her foot in the stirrup. Thankfully the officer had a powerful arm and easily lifted her up, and she sat behind him.

"Hold on tight."

The sound of the horse's hooves against the brick echoed in Faith's ears. "What happened to Seth?" she asked.

"He was beaten. We found him in the street. His injuries are the worst I've ever seen, and I'm surprised he's still alive. *If* he's still alive."

Faith swallowed hard. "Was most of the trauma to his head?"

"Yes. It's like somebody laid into him with a club. They may have busted his arms too. They looked to be in pretty bad shape, and if he was trying to defend himself, they would have taken bad blows."

Faith pictured Seth's body in her mind. She tried to prepare herself for what she would see. When they reached the hospital, she slid off the side of the horse.

"Thank you. I can make my way from here."

She entered the hospital through the same doors she had used when doing her training. This was where the nurses and doctors generally entered, and no one would pay much attention to her at this hour, since most of the doctors would be gone and the nurses would be on their rounds.

There was no one at the nurse's desk, so Faith just acted as though she belonged there. She looked through the various record files and found where they had taken Seth. Without even trying to hide her presence, Faith made her way to his room and walked in like she owned the place. There was no one else in the room.

The lamp offered her ample light to see that Seth was still breathing as she approached the bed. The patient lying in front of her looked nothing like her cousin's husband. Had it not been for his blood-caked red hair, Faith might have questioned whether she had the right room.

For a moment her medical training failed her. "Oh, Seth. Who did this to you?"

She checked him over as best she could. She'd never in all her years of assisting Grace and Hope or helping people on her own seen a man in such bad shape. There was a time when a lumberjack had fallen from high in the trees. He'd hit every branch on the way down, or at least that was what his buddies said. He'd looked very similar to Seth and had died a few hours later.

"You can't die, Seth. You have a baby coming and a wife who needs you."

Faith finished looking him over, then read the chart at the end of his bed. The doctor's examination and thoughts matched her own, but where the doctor noted that the injuries were most likely terminal, Faith couldn't bring herself to agree.

Hurrying from the room, she made her way outside. She hadn't considered how she might get home once at the hospital. She glanced around, but there were very few carriages out and about. She tried to find a cab, but even that seemed impossible. There was no choice but to walk.

The clock in the hall was just chiming the half hour after

eleven when Faith finally made it back to the boardinghouse. Grace, Nancy, and Clementine were waiting in the front room. Each woman looked at Faith. The hope in their expressions was almost more than she could bear.

"It's bad." She could barely force out the words.

"I'm going to him. I won't let him be there alone," Nancy said. "I don't care what any of you say."

"We've already talked about this, Nancy. You must be reasonable," Grace said, taking hold of her daughter's arm.

"He's my husband. I need to be with him."

"And tomorrow you can be," Faith promised. "The hospital won't allow you in at this hour, so you might as well get some rest so you can deal with what you see tomorrow. Someone clearly wanted him dead. They beat him with a club or a bat or even just a plank board. It's hard to tell, but he's . . . he's hardly recognizable. I'm sorry to be so blunt, but you need to prepare yourself for the worst."

Nancy burst into tears, as did Clementine.

Faith went to Clementine and put her arm around the younger woman.

"What is your honest opinion of this, Faith?" Grace asked.

Faith shook her head. "We need to pray."

Grace somehow managed to get Nancy to her room and into bed. Faith wasn't sure what had been said between mother and daughter, but when Grace reappeared, she seemed at peace. "I'm going to bed. I want to be able to help her in the morning."

Faith nodded. Clementine clung to her and sobbed. She doubted either of them would be going to bed anytime soon.

"He didn't deserve this," Clementine murmured. "Who would do such a thing?"

"I don't know. It seemed far more deliberate than a mere robbery."

"It's probably because of that investigation. They'd never tell me much, because they said it was dangerous and better that I not know."

Faith stared across the room as she held Clementine. She was right. It was probably something to do with Berkshire and Lakewood's plans. It might even be related to her own defiance.

Dear Lord, would they really have tried to kill Seth because of my speaking out on behalf of the Indians?

"I can't bear the thought of him dying," Clementine said, seeming to regain control of her emotions. "It's even worse to imagine him dying alone."

"That's why I'm not going to let it happen," Nancy said, surprising them both. She was fully dressed and ready to leave the house.

Faith knew there was no sense in trying to persuade her otherwise. "It's a long walk."

"We'll borrow a carriage from the Taylors. They'll understand," Nancy replied matter-of-factly. "Just don't try to talk me out of it."

Shaking her head, Faith got to her feet. "I have no intention of doing so."

CHAPTER 21

Faith made certain the way was clear before taking Nancy and Clementine down the hall to Seth's room. She knew there was no way to ready the ladies for what they would see. She had hardly been able to bear it herself, and she was professionally trained. Nevertheless, Faith wasn't going to convince either woman to abandon this visit.

They stood outside the door for a moment as Faith held fast to the handle. "Look, I can't stress enough that he is in very bad shape. He's barely holding on to life. Are you sure you want to see him this way?"

"Get out of my way, Faith." Nancy closed her hand over her cousin's. "I have to see him. It doesn't matter what he looks like. I have to be here."

"Me too," Clementine whispered.

Faith let go of the handle. "Very well. Just prepare yourselves."

She pushed open the door and stepped inside to make sure Seth was still alone and still alive. She motioned for the other two women to join her, then closed the door.

Nancy went immediately to her husband's side. She was stoic

and gazed down at him without grimacing. She took hold of his bandaged hand. "Seth, it's Nancy. I'm here."

Clementine did her best to control her tears, but they made a steady stream down her face. Faith put her arm around Seth's sister as she buried her face in her hands.

"Seth, I know you can hear me. I need you to fight. I need you to live," Nancy said, still showing no sign of emotion. "Seth, I love you so much. You cannot die. I will not let you."

The puffiness in his face was even worse than when Faith had been there earlier. She worried about the brain swelling that must be going on but said nothing. There was nothing to say. If she mentioned the things that worried her, it would only make matters more painful for Nancy and Clementine.

"Who could do such a thing?" Clementine asked yet again, looking up at Faith. "Why would anyone treat another human being like this?"

"I don't know." Faith gave her shoulder a squeeze. "But God does, and hopefully He will bring Seth justice by leading the police to the man or men responsible."

"Do you think this was random?" Clementine asked.

Faith got no chance to reply.

"No. This was personal," Nancy said, her gaze never leaving Seth's face. "No one would take the time needed to beat a man this badly if it wasn't personal."

"I had the same thought." Faith let go of Clementine and went to the opposite side of the bed. "If it was a robbery, they would have knocked him unconscious and taken his money. They wouldn't have stuck around to do this. Even if he had fought back."

"Someone tried to kill him." Nancy looked at Faith and then Clementine. "That much is clear. They wanted him dead."

Clementine's face hardened. "I hope they die."

Faith shook her head. "Our rage won't help. We have to give this to God and focus on doing whatever we can to help Seth. I suggest we spend a few minutes praying—here at his side."

The other two women nodded. They prayed silently for several minutes, and then Nancy spoke aloud.

"Father, Seth is a good man and He loves you. I know it is appointed unto everyone to die, but I'm asking that you delay that time for my husband. He has so much to live for, and we need him, Father."

The door behind them opened, and all three women turned to find a startled nurse looking back at them. "What in the world are you doing here at this hour?" she asked.

Nancy was not chastened by the woman's question. "This is my husband. The police came a few hours ago to tell me he was here, near death. I wasn't going to wait until morning." She let go of Seth's hand.

"You're in no condition for this." The nurse nodded at Nancy's abdomen. "Not only that, but it's against the rules."

Faith stepped forward. "You look familiar. Have we met? I've been here with the students from the medical college."

The nurse seemed to relax. "I thought you looked familiar too. I'm Caroline Harmon."

Faith went to her and extended her hand. "Dr. Faith Kenner—or soon to be." She saw no reason to mention her college dismissal. It was clear the distraction was helping their cause. "We were just leaving. My cousin, as you can see, is going to have a baby soon, but she was so worried about her husband, I felt I had to bring her."

The nurse bit her lower lip and nodded. "The doctor doesn't have much hope," she whispered.

Faith nodded. "I read his notes. However, we are women of prayer and believe that the God who created this man to begin with can also knit him back together."

"I hope so," the nurse replied. "But now you need to go."

Nancy leaned down and placed a kiss on Seth's swollen face. "I'll be back in the morning. Make sure you're here to greet me."

The trio made their way home in silence. What could they say to one another? How could they begin to express their thoughts without giving way to their fears? Faith secured the carriage brake and decided to see Nancy inside before returning the rig and horse to the Taylors.

They had no sooner walked into the front room, however, than they came face to face with Grace Armistead. Her expression made it clear that she wasn't in any mood for nonsense.

"How could you have taken her to the hospital in the middle of the night?" she asked Faith.

"She was going to go there with or without me."

"I would have too, Mama. I had to see him," Nancy countered. "It's very bad. The nurse said the doctor hasn't much hope. We need to pray like we've never prayed before."

Grace's expression softened. "I'm so sorry, sweetheart, but having this baby early isn't going to help matters. Your father and I will be happy to take you there when it's time for proper visiting hours. First, however, you must get some sleep."

"I doubt I can sleep. Not until he's out of danger."

"He wouldn't want you putting yourself and the baby in danger," her mother scolded.

Faith suppressed a yawn. "Your mother is right. We all need to rest."

Grace got up. "Come on, Nancy. I'll help you get ready for bed, and I'll stay with you like I did when you were little. Remember when you were afraid, and I would lie down beside you and tell you stories?"

Tears came to Nancy's eyes. "Yes. I remember. Nothing could hurt me so long as you were there."

Knowing Nancy was cared for and Clementine was already headed upstairs, Faith returned the carriage, then made her way to bed. She didn't even bother to undress but fell across the bed and closed her eyes.

I'll just rest for a minute and then change my clothes.

When she opened her eyes, it was light again, and there was an irritating sound coming from her door. She stretched and sat up only to realize the sound was knocking.

"Come in."

"Sorry to wake you," Mimi said, coming into the room, "but the delivery man said this was urgent." She brought Faith an envelope.

"Who is it from?"

"The man said it was from Mrs. Lakewood."

"What could be urgent from her?" Faith opened the envelope and pulled out a notecard.

Come to tea at two this afternoon. It's most important I speak to you regarding the college.

It was signed Deborah Lakewood.

Faith tossed the invitation onto the bed. "What time is it?"

"Noon." Mimi smiled. "Grace said to let you sleep as long as possible."

"Is Nancy still sleeping too?"

"No. She and Clementine went with Grace and Alex to the hospital. They left earlier this morning."

Faith nodded. "I'm glad. I knew Nancy would be difficult to keep here."

"Is it really as bad as they were saying?"

"It is. It will take God's mercy to bring Seth through. He's in a very bad way. Clementine is going to need your love and support in the days ahead."

Mimi lowered her face. "We've been praying all day. Bedelia and her sister even left to meet up with some of their church ladies who are having a sewing circle this afternoon. They plan to get them to pray instead."

"Good. Prayer is what will see us through." Faith glanced down at the invitation. She might as well go and find out what Mrs. Lakewood wanted. Then she'd make her way to the hospital and see if Seth was still holding on to life. "I must look a fright." She got up and began to pull out hairpins. "I'll have to take a bath and rearrange my hair."

"I'll start the water for you while you get ready," Mimi said, heading for the door. "Oh, there's also some lunch warming on the back of the stove. Bedelia left it for you."

Faith smiled. "Thanks."

She hurried at her tasks, knowing that to be late would be socially unforgivable. But Mrs. Lakewood would just have to understand. After all, her last-minute invitation could be considered just as rude. Faith chose her green walking-out dress. Made of a lightweight tussore, the outfit was perfect for tea. She hurried through her bath and then dressed her hair in a simple knot at the back of her neck. She found a ribbon-trimmed snood and carefully attached it before checking her image in the mirror. It was good enough for afternoon tea.

Mimi had the lunch plate ready for her, but Faith found she

had no appetite. She took a piece of buttered toast and sampled it. It sat like a rock in her stomach. "I'm not hungry."

"I'll take care of it. Don't worry." Mimi put a cloth back over the plate.

"I should go," Faith said when the clock began to chime.

The Lakewood estate was not close enough for a comfortable walk, and without a carriage at their disposal, Faith knew she would have to walk to the trolley and perhaps go all the way downtown, where she could hire a cab. It seemed a terrible waste of time and money, but at the moment she had no other idea how to get there.

In the foyer, she took up her umbrella. It looked like rain. "I'll head to the hospital after I see Mrs. Lakewood," she told Mimi.

"I'll let them know if they return. I think the Armisteads will be hard-pressed to get Nancy away from her husband."

"I'm sure you're right."

Faith had no sooner stepped onto the sidewalk than a carriage drove up alongside her.

"Are you Miss Kenner?" the driver asked.

"I am." She looked at the man and then at the carriage. There was a large *L* on the door.

"Mrs. Lakewood sent me to bring you to tea," he said, halting the team of matched bays.

"How fortunate for me." Faith waited as the driver climbed down and opened the door to assist her.

The carriage ride was much appreciated and gave Faith time to consider what this meeting might be about. She hoped that Mrs. Lakewood had found out about the college situation and had forced her husband to have pity on Faith. It was doubtful, however. Maybe Mrs. Lakewood wanted to discuss Faith's opinions on the Indians. The summons made little sense, and by the time Faith reached the Lakewood estate, she was quite perplexed.

The butler showed her to the library and told her to wait there. Faith looked around the large room at the walls of books and thought it strange that a woman would entertain her here. This was more of a man's domain, with its polished oak paneling and shelves. Even the draperies and furniture were more masculine than feminine.

A young uniformed woman appeared with a tea cart. Still there was no sign of Mrs. Lakewood.

"I'm to offer you refreshment," the girl said, pouring a cup of tea. "Would you care for cream or lemon?"

"Cream, please."

The serving girl added the cream, then handed Faith the beautiful china cup and saucer. The tea smelled of flowers and spices.

"May I prepare you a plate?" the maid asked, motioning to a three-tiered arrangement of food.

Faith looked at the delicacies and shook her head. "Maybe I'll try something later."

The girl took that as her cue to leave. Faith sipped the tea but felt too restless to sit. She took her cup and walked along the shelves, reading various titles and wondering if anyone in the Lakewood house had read each and every book.

"I'm glad you could come, Miss Kenner."

Faith turned so quickly that she nearly spilled her tea. "Mr. Lakewood. I wasn't expecting to see you." She steadied the cup.

"I know, and I apologize for giving you a fright. In fact, I apologize for my duplicity in its entirety."

"What are you talking about?" Faith stood frozen in place as Lakewood crossed the room to join her.

"The invitation you received today wasn't from my wife. She just left about fifteen minutes ago with our children to attend a birthday party across town. I wanted to see you myself but knew you would never agree to come."

"It's hardly appropriate for a single woman to meet a married man in private." Faith sipped the tea, desperate to appear unconcerned. Her brain warned her to put the cup down and leave, but her stubbornness wouldn't allow it.

"It's true, but once you hear me out, you'll understand why that hardly concerns me." Lakewood smiled and motioned to the chairs. "Please sit."

Faith frowned. What was he up to? She remained standing.

"I know we last parted under less than comfortable circumstances, but I wanted you to come here today so that I might explain," he said.

"Explain why you had me expelled from college just weeks before my graduation?"

"Yes, well, once it was learned that you were part Indian, that certification would have been rescinded anyway. Now, please sit."

Faith didn't want to argue about chairs and tea when she had her heritage and college degree to focus on. She took her seat on a silk upholstered throne chair and fixed him with a stern gaze.

He smiled. "You look like Queen Victoria holding court."

"But Queen Victoria isn't part Indian." Faith saw no reason to avoid the truth.

He chuckled and sat on the settee. "I thought you might deny it."

"Why should I? I am curious how you know anything about me."

"Well, it wasn't that difficult." He crossed his legs and folded his arms. "Your father's family made no secret of your grandmother being half Cherokee."

Faith sighed. He thought she was Indian because of Isaac Browning, just as her father had suggested. She could manage that well enough.

"Now, I understand that makes you only one-eighth Indian, but blood is blood. It's a wonder, however, that you have those beautiful blue eyes."

"A gift from my mother's side," she said, then drank the last of her tea.

"Now that the truth is out, I asked you here to tell you what I want to do about it. I know you're dismayed over losing your chance to play doctor, but I have a much better future in mind. I want you to help me with the Indians. And to become my mistress."

Faith nearly dropped her cup. She steadied her hand and looked at Lakewood. "You cannot be serious."

"But I am. You see, I find you to be the most exotic and intelligent of creatures. I suppose that's why I looked into your background and family. I longed to know more about you."

"You mean you hoped to find something you could use against me. Something that would silence me. Well, I won't be silenced, and I won't be your mistress."

Lakewood shook his head. "You aren't thinking this through. If you did, you would see how your cooperation will ultimately help the Indians." He leaned over and poured himself a cup of tea. Holding the pot aloft, he asked, "More?"

"No." She put down her cup and started to rise. "This conversation is over."

"Sit down, Miss Kenner. You really have no choice in this."

She sank back onto the chair. "I have plenty of choices. You can tell the world about my Indian heritage. I don't care. As for helping the Indians, I don't believe you would lift a finger to aid them, given your feelings on people of color."

"Do you care about your cousin's husband?" He stirred sugar into his tea.

Faith felt as if he'd kicked the wind out of her. She could say nothing for several moments. What was he getting at?

"I see I have your full attention. You are surprised by my knowing about Mr. Carpenter. The simple fact is that I arranged his beating and fully planned to see him killed, but then I got another idea. Perhaps if I allowed him to live, you might be grateful and do my bidding." He put the teaspoon aside and sampled his tea. "Perfect."

Faith felt sick as the truth began to wash over her. This man was cruel and heinous. He didn't care at all who he hurt.

"Simply put, my dear Faith, if you do as you're told, your cousin's husband will be allowed to live."

"He's in a bad way," Faith said, shaking her head. "The doctors aren't holding out much hope for him. I saw him myself last night, and it will take a miracle—an act of God—for him to pull through."

"Yes, well, Berkshire's lackeys were a little too enthusiastic. If he doesn't make it, then there are always others with whom to contend. Your cousin, for instance. She's expecting a baby. It would be such a pity if something were to happen to her . . . or to the baby."

"Stop it! You have no right to threaten the lives of innocent people."

"Ah, but they aren't so innocent. You may or may not realize what Mr. Carpenter has been up to, but he has caused me a lot of grief. And before that, his wife interfered with my plans."

Faith didn't want to give away what she knew. Seth and Nancy had told her over and over that the investigation was secret, so she played dumb. "What are you talking about? How has Seth caused you grief?" She hoped her look of confusion convinced him.

Lakewood frowned. "He didn't tell you? I suppose that's understandable. What is important is that you know I will stop at nothing to rid myself of trouble and those who delay what I want to accomplish. Including you." He finished his tea and set the cup and saucer back on the serving cart. "I am giving you a few days to think this over and accustom yourself to the idea. My wife and children are leaving for California the day after tomorrow. It will free me up to spend a great deal of time with you—initiating you, so to speak, in being my mistress and helping me with my affairs." He grinned. "I have a lovely place where I intend to put you up. I will lavish you with every comfort. I think you'll be quite pleased."

"I won't be, and I won't do it."

"Now, my dear, you really must think this through." His eyes narrowed. "I wasn't making an idle threat in regard to Mrs. Carpenter. Perhaps you would feel more inclined to say yes if I told you that I have a man watching your young brother."

She jumped to her feet. "Leave my family alone. You have no right!"

"I have whatever right I decide to have," he replied. "I simply take what I want when I want it. And, my dear, I have decided that I want you. In fact, I feel rather daring, what with you being Indian and all. Perhaps you'll convince me of a reason that Indians should be allowed to live." He laughed, leaving Faith quite ill.

What in the world was she supposed to do about this? How could she fight such evil?

CHAPTER 22

It was easy for Samuel Lakewood to see that he had the upper hand where Faith Kenner was concerned. Her weakness in the situation made him feel strong, and that power was absolutely intoxicating. He wanted her, that was true enough, but it was so much more. It was the power that came from her knowing that she had no choice but to do whatever he wanted. It was all about supremacy.

"So you see, my dear, this is how it will be." He eased back in his chair. "We have a war to plan."

"A war?"

She was clearly clueless. He smiled. "Yes. What your Mr. Carpenter has kept from you all this time is that he's helping the government interfere in some very important plans of mine. Plans that surprisingly include your aunt and uncle."

"What are you talking about?"

"Your uncle, Adam Browning, knows how important it is to cooperate. We approached him, hoping for his assistance. At first he wasn't keen on the idea, but we were able to convince him. After all, he has a wife and children to think about."

"I don't believe you."

Lakewood chuckled. "I can be very persuasive, as can my friends. You see, I belong to an association that desires to see the Indian eliminated from Oregon."

Faith watched him with those icy blue eyes he found so intriguing. She had a captured-prey expression that made him feel all the more empowered, yet at the same time her gaze held raging hatred. It stimulated his thoughts.

"As you've pointed out, Uncle Adam is part Cherokee," Faith said. "Why would he help you do anything against the Indians?"

"Well, at first he refused to help me. Not only that, but he reported my offer to the Indian Affairs Regulator, Mr. Singleton. But, as you might understand, I'm not easily dissuaded, and I know that the nature of most men is to desire power and money for themselves. It wasn't that difficult to convince him."

"I don't believe you. My aunt and uncle would never do anything to cause the Indian tribes harm."

Lakewood seethed, but he remained composed. "Your family has caused me plenty of trouble, and that has given me a powerful grudge against them all. Add to this the trouble Mr. Carpenter has caused and . . . well, let's say that you owe me, Miss Kenner."

"I owe you nothing. You've nearly killed Seth, and you've seen to it that I cannot graduate. If anyone owes anyone anything—you owe me and my family."

He laughed. He had to admire her spirit. After all, it was that spirit that made her so deliciously appealing to him.

"Faith, the sooner you realize your situation, the better. We can accomplish a great deal together. I believe that with your help, I can get what I need from your aunt and uncle."

"You don't know them at all if you think that. They are both passionate about their work. I was hoping to join them as a fully certified medical doctor. Now, I'll simply go as an educated healer. I don't need your piece of paper to help others. It would have been nice, but it's certainly not necessary. I was acting as a doctor to people long before I attended school, and I'll go on doing the same."

"Hardly. I won't have my mistress involved in such matters."

"And I won't be your mistress." She got to her feet, and Lakewood felt her slipping away.

"Then you will be responsible for a great many deaths. I'll start with Mr. Carpenter, and just as his wife's grief makes her life unbearable, I'll see to her infant's death . . . and then hers, but not until the pain is so great that she's ready to end her own life. Perhaps I'll even allow her to do so. Next I'll start on your family in Oregon City."

"Stop!" Faith pointed her finger at him. "I will kill you myself before I'd allow that to happen. You may think you have me backed into a corner, but I am not easily commanded. And as you would say, I'm part 'savage.'"

She seemed strangely at ease, and for a moment a ripple of fear coursed through Lakewood. She stormed for the door.

"Faith, I wouldn't underestimate what I can do. I've had people watching your loved ones for well over a year."

She stopped at the door and turned. Her confidence seemed to wane. She opened her mouth to speak, then closed it again as if she'd thought better of crossing him.

"Take a day to consider everything," he said. "Think it through carefully. You have in your hands the power to cause a great deal of heartache."

She shook her head. "It won't be me causing the heartache. You've already done plenty of that."

"Nevertheless, think carefully. I'll be in touch soon."

267

She huffed and left the library, soundly slamming the door behind her.

Lakewood walked to the window. It was raining, and the light appeared muted. Everything had a dream-like quality, like it wasn't quite real. He was sure Faith was hoping his threats weren't real—that he was just an old man grasping for things he could never achieve. But if she thought that, she was wrong. He had always acquired what he wanted. He had always been successful. No man, and certainly no woman, was going to stop him.

After a few minutes, Faith appeared with her umbrella raised. He had known she would walk rather than take his carriage. She was very predictable, and that was why he knew she would yield to his demands rather than see her family suffer greater harm. She would help him accomplish what he needed with the Indians, and she would be his mistress. It was all too simple.

Faith hadn't planned to go to the docks to see if the *Morning Star* was in port. She had intended to visit the hospital to be with her family and see what Seth's condition might be. However, after what she'd gone through with Lakewood, seeing Andrew was all she could think about.

She knew she would do whatever was required to keep her family safe, but becoming Lakewood's mistress and helping him cause an Indian war was asking too much. Instead of pondering how she could bear those things, Faith was given to an entirely different direction of thought. She had to find a way to stop Lakewood—even if it meant killing him herself.

She'd never before thought about killing someone. Murder was illegal, but it also went against God. How could she take the life of another just because they were threatening to harm her? But Lakewood wasn't only threatening to harm her. He had already harmed Seth by ordering it to be done. He'd made it clear that he had no problem killing others in her family. Grief, the man had no trouble planning an entire war that would no doubt kill hundreds. He had to be stopped.

Faith tried to imagine shooting Samuel Lakewood. She remembered a story her father had told her of when he first met her mother. Hope Flanagan had gone to the jail where the Cayuse man who'd raped her was being kept. He was on trial as one of the main perpetrators of the Whitman Massacre.

"Your mother somehow snuck in there with a Colt revolver," her father had said. "She was there to kill the man who'd hurt her."

"My father?" she had asked.

"I'm your father," Lance Kenner had insisted. "He was just an inconvenience. Tomahas was his name, and it was already well known that he had been involved in the massacre, but his lawyers were suggesting otherwise. Your mother was afraid he would get off and then kill more people. I convinced her that the law would deal with him."

Her father had thought her mother admirable in her bravery, but even more so in her willingness to back away and let the law deal with Tomahas. Her mother said that she was always glad Father had stopped her—that she could never have lived with the knowledge that she'd taken a life. Even the life of a worthless miscreant like Tomahas.

Faith had asked her if she would have really killed Tomahas, and to her surprise, Mother had answered without reservation— yes. At the time, it had stunned Faith, but not now. Now she finally thought she understood. It wasn't about revenge; it was about keeping him from harming anyone else. Her mother was afraid the government wouldn't hang him—that he and his friends would get away with what they'd done. She wanted to stop him before he could hurt another person.

The situation with Lakewood was even more distressing. No one was ever going to put Lakewood on trial. He was a pillar of the community. Like her mother, Faith thought of the pain and suffering he had caused, the misery he still planned to cause. Stopping him was of the utmost importance.

As she neared the docks, the rain let up. She saw no sign of the *Morning Star* and thought she might burst into tears. She needed to talk to Andrew. She needed to explain to him what had happened and what was going to happen. She was only fooling herself. She would become whatever Lakewood demanded she be. She couldn't allow him to hurt her family.

"Hey there, Miss Kenner."

She looked up and found Remli—his arms wrapped around a crate of goods. "What are you doing here? I was looking for the *Morning Star*, and it's not here."

"She's due anytime. Captain left me here to go huntin' for supplies I needed while he took on cargo upstream. How've you been? Ain't seen you in a while."

"My life has been very complicated. I was just coming to speak to Andrew in order to avoid buying a gun so that I can kill a man."

If her comment surprised Remli, he said nothing. He gave her a nod and shifted the load in his muscular arms.

She couldn't help but smile at his response. "I can see I haven't shocked you."

He gave a deep, throaty chuckle. "Everyone has those times, Miss Kenner."

"Faith. Please call me Faith."

Several blasts of a riverboat whistle could be heard. "That'd be the *Morning Star*, Miss Faith. You come along with me, and we'll make sure you get to see the captain first thing."

She followed Remli to the docks. The *Morning Star* was approaching from the south, and she could see Andrew up in the wheelhouse, shouting orders to the deck crew below. It took nearly half an hour to see the boat properly docked and tied off. The procedure was one Faith had never really paid attention to. Another time, she might have had plenty of questions, but this time all she could think about was confessing to Andrew that she was part Indian and that she wanted Samuel Lakewood dead.

"Looky what I found wanderin' the streets," Remli said as he came up the gangplank. "Miss Faith says she needs to talk to you before she goes and shoots a man."

Andrew had been focused on his work until the last comment. His head snapped up from the log he was showing to Denny. "What did you say?"

"Thought that might get your attention." Remli laughed and passed on by. "I'll let you two figure it out."

"Denny, go take care of our paperwork and get the loading started," Andrew ordered. The younger man didn't say a word but took the log and headed off. Andrew held Faith's gaze. "I hope I'm not the man you plan to shoot."

She smiled. "Not this time. Although I am rather upset that you've made yourself so scarce. I must have offended you."

He shook his head. "I believe the offense should be yours. Nevertheless, come aboard and tell me what has you so vexed." He led the way to the saloon. "Have a seat. You look done in."

"I walked all the way here, and these shoes are hardly made

for it." She sat on the nearest chair and reached down to rub her ankle.

Andrew pulled up a chair and waited for her to speak. She wasn't quite sure where to start. She wanted to discuss their kiss, but Remli had made the comment about her shooting someone, so she supposed it was best to start there.

She straightened. "I'm in trouble. There's nothing you can do about it, but I know you're going to hear about it—hear terrible things about me—and I wanted to explain."

"So you really plan to kill someone?"

She shook her head. "I can't. As much as I think it might resolve my problem, I don't have it in me to kill. At least I don't think I do. When I actually try to plan it out in my mind, I get all sick inside."

"That's good. I wouldn't want you to become a killer." He was perfectly serious, but there was a hint of humor in his voice.

"How would you feel about me being someone's mistress?" She couldn't believe she'd just said such a thing.

"I doubt you have it in you to do that anymore than to kill," he said matter-of-factly.

"I don't have much of a choice." She went on to explain what had happened to Seth and then Lakewood's threats. She told him everything except the details of what Lakewood had on her personally, but as the conversation continued, Faith knew she had to be honest about that as well. It would explain why even though she'd loved their kiss, nothing could come of it.

"I know I can trust you, Andrew. And because of that, I need to tell you the whole truth, but I beg you to promise me you'll tell no one."

Andrew nodded. "I promise."

"And promise you'll hear me out—even if the truth offends you."

He frowned but nodded again. "I promise."

Faith licked her dry lips. She had never in her life told another person what she was about to tell Andrew. "Lakewood had me dismissed from the college because . . . he found out something about me. About my family background. He thinks he knows . . . but while the facts are not quite right, the result is the same."

"And what result is that?"

She felt her face grow hot. "I'm part Indian."

Andrew stared at her and said nothing. Faith felt sick to her stomach but knew she had to continue.

"My mother was forced. It was during the Whitman Mission attack. Only family knows this, and I beg you to say nothing."

"I won't, but I thought you said Lakewood already knew."

"He believes me to be part Cherokee because the family I was given to at birth had Cherokee blood. My adoptive father was a quarter Native, and it was well known back east where he grew up, so it was easy enough to find out. Lakewood apparently investigated me, hoping to find information he could use against me and my family, and that's what he dug up. I don't really care if he tells everyone that Isaac Browning was a quarter Cherokee. Isaac and his wife are dead. Most important, if people believe that I am Indian because of Isaac, then it saves my mother from being publicly humiliated. I've lived with the guilt of passing as white all these years, so perhaps it's only right that the truth comes out, but I don't want anything to hurt her. She did nothing wrong."

Andrew remained silent. He just stared at Faith, leaving her feeling even more exposed. Would he demand she leave the ship once she finished explaining?

She hurried on. "Lakewood threatened to reveal my blood-line and harm my family if I don't help him with the Indian war he wants. He intends to see the reservation Indians make war on the surrounding settlers. If Seth weren't near death, I might have gone to him and asked for counsel, but he can't help me now." Her vision blurred as her eyes welled with tears. "Lakewood admitted to having Seth beaten, and he said he'll kill Nancy's baby and Nancy and my family if I don't obey him."

Her voice broke, and she stopped trying to speak. She looked at the carpeted floor and shook her head.

Andrew got to his feet, and Faith braced herself for the command that she leave. Instead, he came to her and pulled her to her feet. Was he going to physically throw her out?

She raised her head to look at him, and when she did, Andrew lowered his mouth to hers and kissed her. He pulled her so close and held her so tightly that when Faith's knees gave way, he simply held her in place. When he finally pulled back to speak, Faith could hardly breathe.

"There's nothing to stop us now," he murmured against her face. He kissed her cheek and then her temple.

"Stop us? Stop us from what?"

"Marrying. I want you to marry me, Faith Kenner. I've wanted you to marry me since you sewed up my arm."

She shook her head. "Didn't you hear what I said? I'm not the person you think I am."

He chuckled and kissed her cheek again. "And I'm probably not the man you think I am. Only I didn't have the courage to explain after our kiss. Instead, I stayed away, trying to convince myself it would never work out—we could never be together. But the truth is that Benjamin Littlefoot is my grandfather. He is my mother's father."

The truth dawned on Faith. "So you're Nez Perce?"

"Among other things that add up to about half Indian, half white. Just like you. So now I can marry you and love you freely for the rest of my life, and no one can threaten us or force us apart."

Faith could hardly comprehend what he was saying. She looked into his dark eyes and tried to figure out if he might be lying—telling her this just to make her feel better—but Andrew didn't strike her as the kind of man who would do such a thing.

"I love you, Faith, and I feel quite certain you love me."

"I do," she barely whispered.

He grinned. "Then marry me. Nothing else matters."

"But it does. There's so much going on—Lakewood and poor Seth."

Andrew's eyes darkened. "You'll never be Lakewood's mistress. I guarantee you that. I'll take care of him myself. I'll make him understand the repercussions that will come his way if he should dare to pursue this. I won't let him hurt you, nor will I let him hurt Seth again. I'm not without my friends."

A sense of peace washed over her. She touched his cheek. "I don't know what to say."

"Say yes to my proposal. We don't have to wed this moment, but promise you will marry me. We can deal with the rest of these problems after we settle this one thing. I will help you figure it all out. Just say you'll marry me."

Faith nodded. Even if it never came about because of Lakewood, she at least wanted to promise herself to Andrew. "I will."

He kissed her again, this time quick and to the point. When he released her, Faith felt a little unsteady on her feet. She reached for the chair and stared after Andrew as he crossed the room and called for his grandfather.

She sat down, not sure what was going to happen. There was still no answer to her problems. In fact, instead of simplifying things, they had gotten much more complicated.

But Andrew loves me, and he's part Indian. We can be together and legally marry.

The thought chipped away at her sorrow and fears. She was in love with a man who loved her in return, despite her Cayuse blood. She could perhaps even say because of it.

"Grandfather," Andrew said as Ben came into the saloon, "I want you to meet the woman I'm going to marry."

The old man didn't ask questions but instead laughed out loud. "That is good. She is a good woman and will make you a good wife."

Faith shook her head. Ben didn't seem the least bit worried or concerned about the details. She had no idea how all of this could possibly work out, but because no one else seemed to care, she was determined she wouldn't worry about it either.

At least not for the moment. This moment was hers.

Andrew seethed at the thought of Lakewood's threat to Faith. How dare he try to impose himself on the innocent? There were more than enough soiled doves to be had. He didn't need to degrade a decent woman.

As he lay in his bunk, sleep eluded him. His anger wouldn't allow for even the slightest peace. Lakewood was evil, and he deserved to be taken to task for what he'd done. Not only did he desire to force Faith into a lascivious relationship, but he'd nearly killed Seth Carpenter. These were good people, and Andrew wanted to be useful to them.

"Lord, show me what to do. Help me not to act out of rage."

A knock sounded on his cabin door.

He sat up in the dark. "Enter."

When the door opened, light flooded the room. His grandfather smiled. "I knew you were awake," he said in Nez Perce.

"'*Eehé*—Yes. I can't sleep."

"Because you asked Faith to marry you?"

"No, there's something else—a problem she's facing. Wrongs done to other people. Wrongs threatened to be done to her. I just don't know how best to help."

The old man squeezed Andrew's shoulder. "Sometimes our hands are not big enough."

"You're trying to tell me that only God can manage this, and I suppose I know you're right, but I also feel compelled to do something myself."

Andrew's grandfather shook his head. "Even Jesus said He did nothing without the Father."

Andrew exhaled a heavy breath. "You're right, of course. It just seems like I should do something."

"Let God show you what to do. Don't be like the foolish man who rushes about from place to place, accomplishing nothing, creating chaos. You love her, and she loves you. God has brought you together for a purpose. He won't forget to let you know what that purpose is. Trust Him, Andrew."

Andrew eased back into his bunk. "I will. Thank you for speaking truth."

CHAPTER 23

Seth is doing much better," Nancy told Faith. "The doctors relieved the pressure on his brain by operating. Since then he has woken up twice, and both times he recognized me."

Faith smiled. "I'm so glad." She knew it was a very good sign. "How are you feeling?"

Nancy patted her belly. "I'm just fine. Mother will hardly let me do anything, so I'm at no risk of causing myself or the baby harm."

"She doesn't like the idea, but she has agreed to return home this afternoon for some much needed rest," Grace Armistead announced.

Nancy gazed heavenward. "I don't like leaving him alone."

"Well, you might not realize this," Faith said, "but Seth needs rest too. With us here, he might feel obligated to try to remain conscious, when sleep is what will help his healing."

Frowning, Nancy looked to her mother. "Is that true?"

Grace nodded. "Quiet and rest are sometimes the most important things for the body in order to heal. Seth has been awake, and he knows how much you love him. He knows you're close by and will come to him if he needs you. But he also knows you are carrying his child and need rest yourself. He may be unable to sleep because he knows you aren't."

"Fine. I'll return home, but I don't intend to stay there."

"Of course not," her mother replied.

"I want Papa to buy me another horse and carriage. A nice big carriage for a family. That way we'll have what we need to get around, and I can even transport the ladies to church on Sunday. I'll need a team of horses, not just one."

"Has the repair on the carriage house been completed?" her mother asked.

"Yes. David told me he has only to finish some painting."

"There's a good livery at the corner of Southwest Park and Jefferson Street," Faith offered. "I know because the medical school rents rooms above it for dissection work. The last I knew, the owner had several good horses for sale, and carriages as well."

"Good. We'll send Papa there first thing tomorrow."

The light was starting to fade outside. "Tomorrow is Sunday," Grace reminded her daughter.

Nancy's chin had a stubborn set to it. "All right, then I'll send Papa there on Monday."

"Send me where?" Alex asked, coming into the hospital room.

"I'll explain it on the ride home," Nancy said, getting to her feet.

Faith could see it took more and more effort for Nancy to move. Not only that, but it appeared the baby had lowered. The delivery couldn't be too far now, probably no more than a couple of weeks.

Nancy kissed her husband's bruised and swollen face. "Seth,

I'm going home, but I will be back soon. Please rest and get well. I love you so." She lowered her voice to a whisper. "I need you, and our baby needs you."

Grace leaned close to Faith. "They gave him something to help him sleep, but the doctor was encouraged by how stable his heart rate and breathing are."

"That is good news. Are his arms broken?"

"The left is. The right is badly bruised and strained, but no breaks that the doctor could discern."

Faith thought of all she'd gone through that day. "I need to speak to you and Uncle Alex after Nancy goes to sleep." She whispered this as Nancy continued fussing over her husband.

Grace gave her a questioning look, but Faith just shook her head. "Later."

"There's a rented carriage waiting at the front entrance," Alex said. "If you want to go ahead, I can make sure Nancy gets there safely."

Grace looped her arm through Faith's. "That sounds good. I'm quite tired."

They left the room and headed toward the exit. Faith knew Grace would expect to hear the details right away.

"I know who beat Seth."

Grace stopped mid-step. "Then we must speak with the police."

"No. This man is very rich and probably owns most of the police department. He arranged it with Gerome Berkshire."

"That terrible man who constantly pesters Nancy?"

"Yes. Samuel Lakewood hired him to beat Seth nearly to death. He is going to kill him and . . . others if I don't help him with his Indian war and. . . ." Faith couldn't bring herself to admit the rest. "He threatened Nancy and the baby as well as my brother and all of you. If I refuse to do what he expects of me, he will order his men to kill. Apparently, he's had people watching us for over a year."

"How terrible. What a horrible man." Grace shook her head. "You must not help him."

"I know." Faith started walking again, and Grace fell into step with her. "I'm only telling you this so that you and Alex can do whatever is necessary to see to Nancy's safety and that of the boardinghouse ladies. I wouldn't put it past Lakewood to hurt them as well."

"We should tell the police and at least try to get help."

"Like I said, he probably has the police department sewn up in his pocket. I think the army may be a better bet."

"Is there anything else?"

"He knows I'm Indian," she said. "He thinks I'm Isaac Browning's natural daughter and knows that he was a quarter Cherokee. He got me kicked out of college by telling the president that, and now he's hoping to use that and the threats of harm to my loved ones in order to force my hand. I told him I didn't care if he exposes my Indian heritage. And I don't. If he tells the world about Isaac's ancestry, that will at least save Mother from anyone knowing what happened to her."

"Your mother can handle whatever comes, but she won't be very happy if you allow that man to harm you. What does he want you to do, Faith?"

She let out a heavy breath. "He wants me to help him with his Indian war. He said they want to see the reservations dissolved and the Indians killed. I'm not sure yet what he wants me to do to help with this. I told Andrew about it, and he suggested we speak to Major Wells at the fort in Vancouver. I plan to leave with him this evening on the *Morning Star*. He's headed to Astoria, and we'll stop to see Major Wells first. I'll be gone for a while. I just wanted to make sure that you knew what was going on so you could keep Nancy safe. I didn't want to burden her with the details when she already has enough to worry about."

Grace nodded and squeezed Faith's arm. "Thank you. I'll explain it all to Alex. We'll get some people we can trust and have them nearby to protect Nancy if need be. Will Andrew keep you safe?"

"Yes. He and the crew of the *Morning Star*. I'll be fine. Try to keep everyone out of sight. I don't know what Lakewood would do if he knew I was telling you all of this. He feels so confident of having me over a barrel. I just let him think what he would, even though I was vocal about having nothing to do with him. He intends me to give him an answer in a day or so, but I'll be gone, and that will no doubt infuriate him. We need to make sure Seth and Nancy—and the family—are guarded. We'll need to get a telegram to my folks."

"We'll figure it out, Faith. Don't worry about us. I'll get word to your father about the situation and see that your family are safe and that they watch out for Meg as well. I wish now that we'd brought her, but she had to finish school."

"It's just as well. I'm sure she's safer there than here. Lakewood's initial threats are against Seth and Nancy, so I figure we start there."

"He's obviously threatened you too."

Faith gave a solemn nod. "Yes, but I believe with Andrew's help I can handle it."

"Let me get this straight," Major Wells said, signaling the sergeant to bring the notes he'd been writing as Faith told her story. "Lakewood gave the order to attack Seth Carpenter, and now Carpenter lies near death."

"Yes. He was responsive today, which was better than last night, but he's still gravely ill, and the doctors will probably have to operate again to relieve more pressure on the brain. Frankly, he may never be the same, even if he recovers."

"I understand." Wells scanned the notes.

"We need men who can guard Carpenter and his family. We don't trust the police," Andrew added.

Wells nodded. "And Lakewood is insistent that you help him with the Indian wars but didn't say exactly how."

"Yes. I got the impression he wanted me to go to the reservation on the pretense of my medical work. There's someone there he's working with. He said my uncle Adam was part of it, but at the same time said he wouldn't cooperate. Major, if you knew my uncle, you would never believe that he has anything to do with what's going on there. He has lived with the Indians and broken bread with them. He has prayed at the beds of their sick and has stood alongside them as their advocate. I don't think he could change so much that he would now want to harm them."

"Still, we've had others mention him as well. We can't overlook what part he may be playing. None of us wants to think badly of our loved ones. What about his children?"

"My cousin Isaac was named after Uncle Adam's brother. The man who was my father." She didn't feel the need to explain further. "Isaac attended college back east but lost interest. He came back to the reservation and has been helping my folks and the Indian Affairs agent. His sister, Constance, is in Washington, D.C., finishing her education at a female seminary there. I'm not sure what she has planned for the future."

Wells made notes on the paper. "Did Lakewood say who he answered to?"

"No. As I said, he implied that there was a connection with Uncle Adam but also others."

Wells leaned forward. "Do you feel Lakewood would do you harm if you were to pretend to help him with his plans?"

"She's not going to work with him," Andrew said.

"But she might be able to give us the name of the man in charge. She might be able to overhear their plans."

Andrew slammed his fist on the table. "He wants her to be his mistress. She's going to be my wife, so don't even think of asking her to work with him."

Well's eyes widened for a moment, and then he smiled. "I wouldn't dream of it."

Lakewood summoned Gerome to meet him that evening at the house where they often conducted business. It was the same house in which he intended to install Faith. He sat down and wrote a short letter to Faith, instructing her to meet him the following day for lunch. He would expect her answer to his demands at that time. He sealed the letter in an envelope, then instructed the houseboy to see it delivered immediately. Everything was coming together nicely.

He was dressing for his meeting with Berkshire when the butler interrupted.

"Young Enoch has returned. He needs to see you."

The valet finished tying Lakewood's tie, then stepped back. Lakewood pointed to one of two coats before speaking.

"Bring him to me."

"Yes, sir." The butler left the dressing room.

The boy appeared just as Lakewood's valet helped him into his coat. Enoch held up the sealed envelope.

"What's this? Why didn't you deliver it as I told you to do?"

"The ladies at the boardinghouse said Miss Kenner is gone. She won't be back for at least two weeks."

Lakewood took the letter and struggled to hold his temper in check. How dare she try to disappear or escape his hold! He tucked the letter in his coat pocket.

"Get out of here," he yelled.

The wide-eyed boy turned and ran from the house.

"Leave me, Prescott," Lakewood told the valet. Prescott made a quick dash from the room, and Lakewood slammed the door behind him.

Rage coursed through every fiber of his being. Faith Kenner had defied him, and no one did that and got away with it. He would give Berkshire the word to move forward with Carpenter's killing. That would show her that he meant what he said. Once Carpenter was dead, he would see that something awful happened to Mrs. Carpenter. Faith would no doubt hear about it and return, knowing that Lakewood was carrying out his threat.

Before going downstairs, he looked in on his children. The younger ones were taking their supper in the nursery. They seemed excited to see him.

"Come eat with us, Papa," his daughter Ellen begged.

"No, I'm afraid I'm dining out tonight. But you be sure and eat all of your vegetables and meat. They will make you beautiful, and you must be beautiful in order to catch a wealthy husband."

The ten-year-old screwed up her face. "I don't want to marry anybody."

"That will change soon enough," he said, laughing. "Now, get back to eating so that you can go to bed early. Your trip starts tomorrow, and you'll need your rest."

He made his way downstairs, where he knew Deborah and their older children would be gathered in the music room, awaiting the dinner announcement. His wife wouldn't be happy that he was leaving for dinner elsewhere, but she knew better than to question him. She was an obedient, boring little thing, but she served him well.

"How nice you look," Deborah said as she swept across the room to join her husband.

"Thank you, but I won't be staying to join you for supper. I have a business supper to attend."

"Oh, how regretful," she said, her expression proving her disappointment. "Especially with us leaving in the morning."

"Yes, it is, as you are as lovely as a summer day." And she was. Deborah always looked beautifully gowned because he paid for her to be that way.

"Papa, can you stay long enough to hear me play my harp?" sixteen-year-old Caroline asked.

He kissed her forehead. "Why don't you begin the piece now, and I'll hear at least part of it as I go."

The other children said nothing, knowing that he would not appreciate their delaying him further. Caroline only dared it because she knew he favored her more than the others.

"Will you be very late, my dear?" Deborah asked.

"Possibly. Don't wait up for me. As I told Ellen, you need your rest for the trip."

He signaled the butler to have the carriage brought around and enjoyed the musical talents of his daughter as he waited. She would make someone a good wife. He really needed to start considering who that young man would be. He had it narrowed to three contenders but hadn't given it much thought beyond that, what with his more pressing plans to arrange the Indian war.

The carriage ride across town seemed to take forever. Maybe it was just that he was anxious to see Carpenter's life ended. When the driver finally stopped in front of their destination, Lakewood didn't even wait for him to open the carriage door.

"Should I wait or return for you, sir?" the driver asked.

"Come back for me around ten. I should have concluded everything by then."

He walked to the front door and went inside. He'd already arranged for a tasty supper to be made. It smelled heavenly.

He heard noise coming from the dining room. He'd clearly instructed the staff to prepare the meal, then take the evening off and stay away from the house until after ten. He felt for the small pistol he carried in his coat pocket.

"Hello?" He stepped toward the dining room.

Seated at the table was an unwelcome surprise. Lakewood's mouth went dry, and his throat felt as if it were full of sawdust.

He hadn't expected to see the tall, muscular man. He was usually content to remain in the shadows and control all of his puppets from a distance. If he'd bothered to come to Portland, something was very wrong.

"Mr. Smith," Lakewood said, moving into the dining room. "What a surprise."

Mr. Smith looked up at him, a piece of filet halfway to his mouth. He had helped himself to a hearty portion of Lakewood's meal. "Yes, well, circumstances have changed, and we must reconsider some of our plans." He popped the beef into his mouth.

Lakewood went to the sideboard and helped himself to dinner. He saw the wine was already at Mr. Smith's right hand and grabbed an empty goblet as well. "I hope you are well." He started for the end of the table.

"Sit here at my left. We have a lot to discuss, and we can't risk being overheard."

"Of course." Lakewood knew there was no sense in trying to make small talk. Smith wasn't interested in anything other than business.

Lakewood put his plate on the table, as well as the goblet. It was only then that he realized he'd forgotten silverware. He retrieved it quickly, and when he returned to the table, he found that Smith had already filled his glass with wine.

"I hope you don't mind," Lakewood said as he took his seat, "but I had planned to have dinner with Gerome Berkshire this evening. He should be here any time."

"Good. That saves me from having you send for him." Smith continued eating as if he didn't know how many social rules he had broken by barging into Lakewood's house and making himself at home. The fact was, he didn't care about such formalities even though he'd been raised in society.

"You've probably already figured out that I gave the staff the evening off," Lakewood said.

Smith nodded. "I ran into the last of them as I arrived. I told them you were expecting me, and they allowed me access. You really should get better servants. I could have been anyone."

"True enough." Lakewood could hardly tell Smith that he was at the top of the list of people Lakewood wouldn't have wanted in the house.

A knock sounded on the front door, and then it opened. Gerome Berkshire announced himself.

"We're in the dining room, Gerome," Lakewood called. "Come join us."

He heard Gerome's boots cross the foyer and then come down the hall. He would no doubt be just as surprised to see Mr. Smith.

"What in the world is this all about?" Gerome questioned, coming into the room. He saw Mr. Smith and stopped. "I didn't know you'd be here."

"Neither did Mr. Lakewood," Smith replied. "Come in and have a chair. In fact, get some dinner. We aren't standing on formalities here tonight."

Gerome hesitated, then gave a nod. He went to the sideboard, throwing careful glances at Smith and Lakewood as he chose his meal. When he was finally settled in the seat across from Lakewood, Smith picked up the conversation.

"I was just telling Mr. Lakewood how glad I am that you were coming this evening. Otherwise I would have had to send someone to find you. This makes it much simpler."

"What can we do for you?" Lakewood asked. He hated the feeling Smith gave him. Smith was younger than he and Gerome were, yet he commanded a presence that dominated the room. He was in control of the entire plan. It was his family's wealth and power that had drawn Lakewood's attention, and Lakewood's resources that had drawn his. It seemed a good marriage of sorts.

Smith finished eating and even polished off his wine before saying another word. Lakewood didn't like having to wait for information, but there was nothing he could do. Smith was in charge and would do things his way.

"I understand," Smith said, pushing his plate back, "that we've had more than a little attention from the government. I'm curious why I haven't heard the details of this until now."

Lakewood wondered who was giving Smith information. When he found out, he would have that person eliminated, but for now he'd have to play his cards close to the vest.

"I didn't think it worth bothering you with," Lakewood replied. "I'm already dealing with it."

Smith gave a cold smile. "I don't pay you to do my thinking, Lakewood. I am the only one who will decide what is worth my trouble. It seems to me that a government investigation in which one of our close associates is forced to turn over evidence is reason enough for me to be involved."

Gerome coughed, spewing wine across the table and onto Lakewood's face and clothes. Lakewood slammed a fist on the table before thinking. Cursing, he grabbed his napkin and wiped his face. "Control yourself, Berkshire."

Smith watched the exchange with an expression of ennui. He picked up the wine and poured himself another glass. "What else haven't you told me, Lakewood?"

"Me? I, ah, I don't know what you're talking about. I haven't kept anything from you. I send the reports as requested, and all the shipments of guns have been stockpiled and are ready for your use. I sent you the complete inventory and location of everything."

"Yes, I have that, as well as the list of men who work for you. What about the situation with Seth Carpenter? I thought I told you last Christmas to kill him. Why is still alive?"

"He stopped being a part of the investigation, and I thought maybe he could be useful to us down the road," Lakewood replied, hoping the answer would show Smith that he was only thinking of the end results. "He has connections that we might be able to use."

"So once again you were doing my thinking for me. Is that

it?" Smith shook his head and got to his feet. He paced a moment, then took a stand directly behind Gerome. "I can't have that, Lakewood. I'm quite capable of doing my own thinking."

He drew a revolver, and Lakewood's eyes widened. His chest tightened. Smith needed him. He needed his help. He wouldn't kill him.

Gerome looked confused. "Samuel, you look as if you've just seen a ghost."

Lakewood had opened his mouth to assure Smith that he was completely useful to him when the gun went off. A bullet tore into his chest.

For a moment Lakewood felt searing pain. The bullet seemed to pin him to the chair. He tried to take a breath, but only a strange gasp sounded, and no air entered his lungs.

As he fought to stay alive, Lakewood watched Smith move to the side of the open-mouthed Gerome, put the revolver to his head, and pull the trigger. Gerome slumped forward and his head hit his plate of food. Blood poured out across the fine linen tablecloth.

It was the last thing Lakewood ever saw.

CHAPTER 24

Faith could think of nothing but the danger in which she'd put her family. Lakewood would be furious when he found out she was gone. She never should have left.

Andrew took pity on her and cut the trip short. "You won't be at ease until you see for yourself that everyone is all right," he told her as they raced back to Portland from Astoria.

They docked late afternoon on the twenty-fifth, and Faith wanted only to go to the hospital and check on Seth's condition. Andrew refused to let her go alone, so he put his men in charge of the *Morning Star* and accompanied her in a hired cab.

"I'm here to see Seth Carpenter," she told the nurse at the reception desk.

The woman looked at her for a moment. "Who are you?"

"I'm his . . . well, he's married to my cousin. Her name is Nancy, and she runs the boardinghouse where we all live." Faith knew she was rambling, but there was something in the woman's expression that worried her. "What room is he in? I know my way around the hospital from my classes here."

The nurse glanced over her shoulder as if making sure no

one could overhear her. "He's not here anymore," she replied, turning back to Faith.

Faith's heart dropped. "He died?"

The nurse again looked around the room and down the hall. She shook her head. "No. I don't know where they took him. They were worried about his safety."

Faith let out a sigh of relief. "Thank you." She turned and took hold of Andrew's arm. "Let's go."

At the boardinghouse, Faith was surprised to find two armed soldiers on the front porch. She knew Major Wells had promised protection, but it seemed strange to have uniformed men patrolling her place of residence. After answering the guard's questions and waiting for someone to verify who they were, Faith and Andrew were finally allowed to come inside.

"It's been chaos." Bedelia was the one who had identified them and seemed to feel it her duty to catch them up on all that had happened. "The soldiers arrived not long after you left. They had orders to guard us and to protect Mr. Carpenter at the hospital."

"But he's here now, as I understand it." Faith discarded her wrap and hat.

"Yes. Mrs. Armistead and Nancy thought it best to care for him here at the house. The doctor comes once a day unless there is a problem. We haven't had any real complications, however, since last week. He's doing much better, but it will be a long recovery."

"I'm sure." Faith looked over her shoulder at Andrew. "Why don't you wait for me in the front room while I check on Seth? Maybe you can sweet-talk Miss Bedelia into a cup of coffee." She smiled at the spinster. "I think we could both use one, if it isn't too much trouble."

"Of course not. There's always a pot on the stove, as you well know." Bedelia sounded gruff, but there was a softness in her expression that hadn't been there before. "I'm glad you've come back. We were quite concerned for your safety."

"Well, you needn't have worried. My fiancé was overseeing my protection."

Bedelia looked surprised. "You're engaged?"

"We are."

The spinster huffed and turned toward the kitchen. "I believe you drink your coffee black, Captain Gratton."

"I do, thank you."

Faith looked at Andrew and winked. When Bedelia was out of earshot, she leaned close. "I think she likes you."

"That's a relief." His tone was sarcastic, but Faith knew it meant a lot to him to be accepted.

Without further delay, Faith made her way to Nancy's bedroom. The door stood open, and to her amazement, the room had been transformed. At one time there had been a sitting area, but now that was taken over by a makeshift hospital room. There was a single iron-framed bed and several tables with various bottles and instruments, bandages, and other medical supplies.

Seth was asleep, but he did look better. His head still sported lacerations, bruises, and bandaging, but much of the swelling was gone. Faith moved closer and found Seth's arm splinted and wrapped tight. Otherwise, he seemed to be resting well. She glanced at the other end of the room where Nancy, great with child, slept on the bed she'd once shared with her husband.

A tap on her shoulder made Faith jump. She turned to find Grace motioning her away from the room. She followed Nancy's mother down the hall to the dining room.

"I just finally got Nancy to rest." Grace embraced Faith. "It's good to have you back, but I didn't expect you for a few days yet."

"Andrew knew I was miserable and cut the trip short. He broke all sorts of records speeding us home." She pulled back. "Now, tell me how Seth is doing. He looks better."

"He is much improved. It was a frightful ordeal, and we thought we'd lost him more than once, but he's a fighter, and Nancy wouldn't let him quit. Bringing him here was actually the major's idea. He knew it would be easier to protect all of us at the house rather than going back and forth to the hospital."

"That makes sense. What about Nancy?"

"She's doing well, but I think the baby is going to come early."

Faith nodded. "I thought so too. I'm sure the stress of all this has taken its toll. Hopefully the baby will be all right. If not, we'll see to it that he or she is well cared for."

"Indeed." Grace smiled. "I feel better just knowing you're here." She sobered. "There is something you need to know."

Faith shook her head. "Bad news?"

"Lakewood and Berkshire are dead."

It felt as if someone had forced all the air from her lungs. Faith reached for a dining room chair and gasped. "When?"

"The night you left. The police want to speak with you."

"Me?" Faith sat on the chair, shaking her head. "You'd better tell me everything."

Grace pulled out the chair beside her and sat. "They had supper together at a house in town. At first it looked like a murder and a suicide. They considered that Mr. Berkshire had shot Mr. Lakewood and then shot himself. However, there was a third place setting where someone had obviously eaten their meal, then departed. But the police have no idea if that person left before the shooting started or if they were perhaps responsible for it."

Faith couldn't comprehend that Samuel Lakewood was dead. The man who had sworn to hurt her and her family couldn't cause her any more pain.

"While searching for information, the officers found a letter in Lakewood's pocket addressed to you. In the letter he demanded you join him at the address where he and Berkshire were killed. The police came here, asking after you, and we explained that you had left that evening with Andrew. They wanted to know what your relationship was to Lakewood, and we told them we weren't entirely sure. Nancy remembered you'd spoken at Mrs. Lakewood's lady's tea.

"They told us about the contents of the letter and asked if you two were having some sort of affair. We assured them no, that couldn't be the case, but we didn't want to say how much we all despised Lakewood. Apparently, however, they later learned about Mr. Lakewood having a part in getting you expelled, so they came back, spouting how you had motive to want him dead."

"I did want him dead," Faith said, trying to understand what Grace was saying. "He planned to kill members of my family if I failed to agree to be his mistress and help him start an Indian war." She looked up, feeling a terrible sense of dread. "I can hardly admit to that, however, without causing problems for the government's investigation. Seth felt certain Lakewood had the cooperation of most of the police department and that many of them were probably involved in the plot to stir up a war. Oh, this is such a mess."

"Tomorrow we'll send a telegram to your father and ask him to come right away. He'll know how to advise us."

Grace sounded so calm that Faith couldn't help but feel her fears fade. Maybe it wasn't that big of a problem. After all, she had witnesses of where she was that night, and the details of why and what she'd said to Major Wells surely could remain untold.

"Mother? Oh, good, Faith. I'm so glad you're back," Nancy said, standing in the doorway to the dining room. She looked rather confused. "I think my water just broke."

"Are you sure everything is all right?" Nancy asked her mother. "I'm not having very strong contractions."

"No, but they're quite regular, and I assure you they will strengthen as the night wears on. First babies usually take their time in coming, so just go about your business."

Seth watched from his bed, where Faith was changing one of his bandages. "She worries about everything, doesn't she?" he murmured.

"She does." Faith finished what she was doing and smiled. "You're doing so much better. I'm sure part of the reason is prayer, but the other part is sheer determination on your part."

"I had to be here for my family."

"Still, it will take a while, and you must obey doctor's orders."

He smiled. "Seems I have so many doctors, I have little choice."

Faith squeezed his hand. "I can't help but feel like this is my fault. I managed to anger the wrong people."

"It's not your fault, Faith," Nancy said from where she sat by the fire. "No more than it's mine. After all, my dead husband started all of this."

"It is the fault of the evil men who are continuing this scheme," Grace declared.

Faith gathered the old bandages and her scissors. "I'll get these soaking, and then I'm going to go see Andrew off. He's been so patient to wait while I've gone back and forth to help here. When I spoke to him about sending Father a telegram, he reminded me that he was heading to Oregon City at first light. He plans to ask Father for my hand and give him a ride back."

"Wait. What did you just say?" Nancy fixed her cousin with an open-mouthed gaze.

Faith laughed. "Andrew knows everything about me, and not only that, he shares my circumstance. His father and mother were both mixed-race, and when he puts together all the parts of one tribe or another that came through his family, he figures himself to be at least half Indian. The old Indian man I told you about—the one he saved during the fight—that's his grandfather."

"That's wonderful," Grace said from where she was busy arranging Nancy's bed for the birth.

"How did you find all of this out and when?" Nancy asked.

"When Lakewood demanded that I help him or he'd kill all of you." Faith put her dirty things in a cleaning basin. "I was so upset, and before I knew it, I was at the river looking for the *Morning Star*. Once I found Andrew, I just told him every-thing. I knew if I became Lakewood's mistress it would be the talk of the town, and I wanted him to hear it from me. When I explained my heritage, he told me that there was nothing stop-ping us now. I had no idea what he meant, but then he kissed me and told me we could marry because he, too, was part Native. I was never happier than in that moment."

"How romantic," Nancy said with a sigh. "I'm just so happy for you. All these years you've believed you could never have a husband and family, and now you can. It's truly wonderful."

"It doesn't mean there won't ever be problems," Faith warned her. "We'll marry as two white people, but at least, should someone want to make trouble for us because of my Indian blood, he'll be able to point to his own and show there is no breaking of the law."

"When do you plan to wed?" Grace asked.

"Soon, I hope. I see no reason to wait."

Nancy grabbed her belly as another contraction hit. "You'll wait long enough for me to deliver this baby and be able to attend the wedding."

Faith laughed. "Of course we'll wait that long. After all, I want you to stand up with me. You're the closest friend I have."

Forgetting about the pain, Nancy got to her feet and came to Faith. She embraced her cousin and held her tight. "I would be honored to stand up with you. Oh, you don't know how much that means to me. You were always like a big sister to me."

Faith laughed. "As the oldest, I've been everyone's big sister, but now I'm going to be the bride and thoroughly enjoy myself."

Nancy let go of Faith and made her way to Seth's side. "That last contraction was much stronger. I think this baby is going to be here before we know it."

"So long as you both come through this strong and healthy, I will be happy," Seth said. He couldn't really embrace Nancy because of his injured arms, but she leaned down and placed a light kiss on his cheek.

"I feel the same way about you. I want you back strong and healthy." Nancy straightened and shook her head. "The man who did this to you deserves the same."

"He deserves it," Seth said, "but we have to forgive him. Otherwise we're no better, and we'll only end up bitter."

"I know you're right, but I don't think I could bear being a widow twice. So you must recover and never come this close to death again." She grinned. "And that's an order."

Seth smiled. "Yes, ma'am."

Faith made her way to the kitchen with the basin of old bandages. She found Andrew there talking to Bedelia, of all people, and they seemed quite chummy.

"What are you two discussing?"

Bedelia gathered a stack of linen napkins. "We were considering where the two of you might live after you marry."

"Oh, and what did you come up with?" Faith ladled hot water from the stove's receptacle into the basin to let the bandages and scissors soak.

"I thought it might work to have you remain here," Bedelia said. "The captain will be traveling up and down the river, and it would be awkward for the crew to have you with them all the time. Not only that, but you wish to practice medicine."

Faith frowned. She hadn't yet thought about their future living arrangements. She knew Andrew's crew would more than welcome her to join them on the *Morning Star*, but how could she spend her time just going up and down rivers?

Bedelia continued. "However, if you remained here and the captain joined you when he was in port, then you could live like a normal husband and wife."

"But that would put another man in the boardinghouse."

The spinster shrugged. "What's one more?"

Bedelia left them to figure it out, and Faith covered her mouth to keep from bursting into laughter. She could see the twinkle in Andrew's eyes and knew he was just as amused.

"That is a rather big dilemma," she said. "I'd never really thought about where we'd live."

Andrew got up and came to take her in his arms. "We'll

figure it out in time. First, I'm determined that you be allowed back in college to get your certificate."

"My class graduates tomorrow evening." Faith had been doing her best not to think of it.

"Would you like to be there, or would that be too painful?"

She considered it for a moment. "I'd like to go. I want to see my friends get their certificates." She smiled. "Would you go with me?"

"I will. Maybe your father would like to join us. We should be back by then."

Faith hugged him close. "Thank you for loving me. I love you so dearly, and if you didn't return that love . . . I think I would die."

He held her tight. "Then you should live forever, because I will never stop loving you."

John Alexander Carpenter was born at dawn the next morning. He was blessed, as Grace declared, with a headful of auburn hair and beautiful blue-green eyes.

"I'm pleased you named him after your fathers, but what will you call him? That's much too formal a name for such a little peanut," Grace said, holding her grandson close.

"I think you should call him Jack," Faith suggested. "A lot of men named John go by that nickname."

Grace held the baby up for Nancy and Seth to see. "What do you think? Jack?"

"I think it's a perfect name," Nancy said, then yawned.

"All right, you've both been up all night, and it's time for you to get some sleep." Faith pulled the quilt up over the sheet that covered Nancy. "Your mother needs some sleep as well."

"It's hard to even think about such things with this little guy finally here," Nancy said, glowing with happiness.

"Yes, but he needs to sleep as well." Faith took the baby from Grace. "I promise that if he needs anything I can't provide, I will put out a call for help. For now, and speaking as the only person who had several consecutive hours of sleep last night, I'm in charge, and you are ordered to rest."

She swept from the room with little Jack, looking forward to spending time with him, and dreaming of holding her own child one day. For so long she'd buried those dreams, but now there was nothing to stop them from coming true.

CHAPTER 25

The little blue booklet read, *Fifteenth Annual Commencement of the Medical Department of Willamette University*. Faith bolstered her heart to take courage. This was a happy evening for her friends, and she wanted very much to honor them. She'd even worn the dress her mother had made when they'd thought Faith would also graduate.

"You came," Malcolm declared, pushing through the crowded foyer of the First Methodist Church of Portland. "You look beautiful. I saved you seats with my family."

Faith smiled and looked to her father and Andrew. "Is that all right with the two of you?"

"Sounds perfect," her father replied.

"Good." Malcolm seemed pleased. "I'm hoping we'll be able to get together afterward. There's so much to talk about. I'm sure you've heard what happened with Mr. Lakewood and Mr. Berkshire."

"Yes, we know all about it," Faith admitted.

Malcolm nodded, seeming already to be thinking of something else. "I'll show you where my parents are seated."

Faith followed him, knowing her father and Andrew wouldn't allow her far from their sight. There were still so many unanswered questions, and instead of feeling safer, Faith now felt even more in danger. Someone had murdered Samuel Lakewood and Gerome Berkshire. And it was very possible that the threats made by Mr. Lakewood toward her and her family actually came from his superior—perhaps the very man who had ended his life.

"Mother, Father, I want to introduce my dear friend Faith Kenner."

Faith smiled at the couple. "It's very nice to meet you, Mr. and Mrs. Digby. Let me in turn introduce my father, Lance Kenner, and my fiancé, Captain Andrew Gratton."

Malcolm's expression momentarily flashed with pain. "You're engaged?"

"Just. We can talk about it later." Faith laid a gentle hand on his arm. "Is Violet here?"

"Yes. She's already seated down front. I wish you were graduating with us. It's not fair that you were expelled."

"No, it's not," a voice said behind Faith. She turned to find the college's president, Josiah Parrish. He smiled. "That's why we're allowing you to graduate with your class."

Faith thought her heart might have stopped beating. For a moment it seemed the entire room went silent. "What?"

"I had a meeting two hours ago with the Board of Trustees. I explained the situation, and we all agreed that as our top student, it was foolish to allow Lakewood to dictate your expulsion. You will, of course, have to submit your thesis and complete your final exams, but I've no doubt that you can accomplish those things with little difficulty. I apologize for putting you through this ordeal, and I hope you'll still be willing to accept a certificate from our institution."

"Mr. Parrish, I'm pleased to hear this," Faith's father said, extending his hand. "Thank you."

306

"This is wonderful news. Wait until I tell Violet," Malcolm declared before rushing off.

Only Faith remained sober. Even Andrew was grinning from ear to ear. "But . . ." She glanced around. There were so many people here, and she didn't want to reveal the details of her ancestry to the entire world. "There was that one issue Mr. Lakewood brought up." She prayed Parrish would understand what she was hinting at.

He nodded. "Lakewood told me it was a lie. He only said it to further discredit you in case your father wanted to sue the college."

Faith looked at her father. Should she allow Parrish to believe it was a lie? That seemed even more a sin than neglecting to tell the truth in the first place. She couldn't keep lying. Not in such an important situation. Her father gave her a reassuring smile.

Faith squared her shoulders. "Mr. Parrish, it wasn't a lie. I'm not sure why Mr. Lakewood would tell you that, but what he said was true. I can't accept your offer based on the restrictions of the college."

Parrish looked at her for a moment. "You fulfilled all that was expected of you, and frankly, that is all I find necessary in order to give you your certificate."

"But—"

Father put his hand on Faith's shoulder. "You did the required work. If Mr. Parrish, as president of the medical college, is satisfied, then we should accept his offer."

Faith began to tear up. "Thank you," she whispered.

"You'd better take your seat. We're about to begin the ceremony," Mr. Parrish declared. "Oh, and I will see you first thing in my office tomorrow morning to schedule your exams."

Andrew handed her a handkerchief, and she quickly dabbed her eyes. "I'll be there, Mr. Parrish. Bright and early."

Father kissed the top of her head. "I'm very proud of you. Now, go take your place with your friends. I will be here with Andrew to cheer you on."

She hugged her father, then turned to Andrew to give back his handkerchief.

"Keep it for now," he said. "I have a feeling there will be more tears."

"You're probably right."

"I usually am, Dr. Kenner."

She couldn't help but smile. "Soon to be Dr. Gratton."

"Your father said the police asked you questions about Mr. Lakewood and Mr. Berkshire." Faith sat alone with her mother.

"They did," Faith agreed, "but I told them there wasn't much to tell. They had heard about Lakewood getting me expelled and suggested I had a powerful reason to kill him."

"Oh dear. What did you say?"

"I told them it was a powerful reason to kill him—if I were a vengeful person. But I told them that I was a child of God, and they asked what that had to do with anything." Faith looked in the mirror to check the veil on her head. "This is crooked."

Hope reached for a hairpin. "I'm sure I can fix it. So what did you tell them when they asked that?"

"I shared the plan of salvation. I told them how we were all sinners and that the penalty of sin is death. But that it isn't a death one could deliver to another—it was eternal death that God alone would decide. I told them how Jesus knew that penalty and still came to earth to die in our place. I must have talked about that for fifteen or twenty minutes. I finally ended by saying that if God could forgive me and give me eternal life,

I could forgive Samuel Lakewood and allow him his earthly life. Father just sat there with a smile on his face."

Hope laughed and worked to straighten the veil. "I'll bet he did."

"Hopefully they'll leave me alone now and look elsewhere. Father told them he could raise at least a dozen witnesses to prove I was not even in town when those men were killed, and I think that impressed them—especially since one of the witnesses was Major Wells."

"There," Hope declared, "you are the perfect bride."

Since Clementine and Gabe were getting married on the thirtieth of May and family would be coming to Oregon City to join in the celebration, Clementine had suggested they share the day and have both weddings that morning. Gabe had heartily agreed.

Faith and Andrew figured they might as well have their wedding on the same day as her cousin. It had given them barely a month to plan it, but most of the work was already done, since Faith's family in Oregon City had been working with Clementine's family to arrange the event.

"If I am, then it's thanks to you," Faith said, taking another look in the mirror.

"I wish I could have been there to see you receive your certification." Her mother's words were barely a whisper.

"You were in spirit. I felt you there. When Mr. Parrish said he didn't care about my Indian heritage, I felt as if you were standing beside me." Faith turned and took her mother's hand. "Thank you for taking me back after Eletta died—for raising me. I know it must have been hard at times, having me here as a constant reminder of what happened to you."

Hope Kenner shook her head and cupped her daughter's face. "You've been a constant reminder of God's blessings and His mercy. What happened at the Whitman Mission haunted me for a long time, but when you came back to me, I was finally able to let go of the memory of evil and focus instead on the beautiful child God had given me. I was so sure nothing good could come out of what had happened, but you did. Your presence was healing. I don't think I'd be the joyful woman I am now had you not returned to me." She kissed Faith's cheek, mingling her tears with those of her daughter.

Faith hugged her mother close. "I love you so, Mama."

And then it was time to march down the aisle to Andrew. Faith was so nervous that she feared she'd faint, but her father gave her a wink.

"Before you know it, it will be over, and then you can watch Clementine and Gabe get married."

Faith nodded and drew a deep breath. "I'm ready."

Later, as she sat twisting the gold band on her finger and accepting the well-wishes of family and friends, a sense of peace settled over her. All of her dreams had come to fruition in such a short time. She looked across the sea of people and saw Gabe and Clementine. They were so happy. They had already purchased a small house in Portland, and Gabe had taken over managing the family sawmill there. Clementine promised she'd make regular visits to the boardinghouse since, as a married woman, she could no longer teach school.

"Did you get some of this? I made it special for you," Remli said, coming toward her with a piece of wedding cake and a fork.

"I didn't. I'm so delighted that all of you came to the wedding that I haven't yet sampled any of the food."

"Well, you can now." He handed her the cake.

Faith knew he wouldn't let her refuse and took a bite. It was one of the best fruitcakes she'd ever had. "This is delicious. Is it your recipe?"

He gave her a proud smile. "It is, Miss—Missus—Well, I'll be. Dr. Gratton."

She laughed and took another bite. "You shall have to teach me how to make it. Although I must warn you, I'm not very good in the kitchen."

"You don't need to be. You got me." He laughed and made his way through the crowd to join his shipmates.

"He's happy you're joining us. I'm happy too. You've made my spirit glad," Benjamin said in Nez Perce.

Faith replied in the same. "Thank you, Grandfather." She touched his hand. "You are my family now, and I am yours."

The old man smiled, knowing this was a pledge of her willingness to always care for him. "I'm gonna go eat Remli's cake. It also makes my spirit glad."

Faith laughed and sent him on his way. She looked forward to getting to know him and hearing the stories he could tell.

"You had a very lovely wedding," Bedelia Clifton said, taking a seat beside Faith. "The day is perfect for this outdoor reception."

"It is. I was so happy to see the rain clouds had disappeared." Faith looked around. "Where is Miss Cornelia?"

"Where else? She's with Nancy. She'll scarcely leave her side for fear of missing a chance to be useful with the baby."

"She's quite good with little Jack. He seems to prefer her over me."

Bedelia nodded. "And me."

"Everyone has a purpose in life, my mother always says." Faith could almost hear her saying it now. "Cornelia just had to wait a little longer for hers."

"Just like you had to wait for Captain Gratton."

"Yes."

"What are you two ladies discussing? Or do I even want to know?" Andrew asked, joining them.

"We were just saying how sometimes you must wait a very long time for blessings." Faith patted the bench beside her.

Instead of sitting, he reached down to pull her to her feet. "We're leaving."

"Leaving?" Faith gazed into his dark eyes. "And where are we going, Captain Gratton?"

"To the *Morning Star*, Dr. Gratton. The crew cleaned her from top to bottom, and Remli left us food in the galley. They're taking the night off, away from the boat, so we can be alone until tomorrow morning."

"But where will they stay?"

He laughed. "I said we can be alone until tomorrow, and you worry about where my crew will sleep?"

She smiled. "They're my family now."

"Well, it's appropriate you should say so, because your family is putting them up. Now, must I carry you off through this crowd, or will we manage it with a more civilized stroll?"

Laughing, Faith turned to Bedelia. "Apparently I must bid you farewell."

"I understand." Bedelia got to her feet and smoothed her dark gray skirt. "God's blessings on you, Faith." She looked at the man standing beside her. "And on you, Andrew."

Faith looped her arm through Andrew's as they walked across the churchyard. "Now you really are family, Captain, and in such a short time you have won over the heart of the sternest and most deliberate of us all."

He smiled and pulled her into his embrace. He lowered his mouth to kiss her and spoke just before their lips touched. "That, my dear, is the way of love."

312

Author's Note

The Storm King hit the Pacific Northwest on January 9, 1880. The accounts mentioned in the story are based on true reports of what happened that day and the resulting damage.

It is also true that Willamette University was the first college in the Pacific Northwest to have a medical college (1866) and to allow women students (1877). Though it was originally located in Salem, they moved the medical college to Portland in the winter of 1879–1880 and then back to Salem in 1895.

As for the laws regarding African-Americans, those are unfortunately true. Early in Oregon's history, exclusion laws were enacted that made it illegal for African-Americans to reside in Oregon Country. Wagon trainmasters signed agreements not to allow black settlers in their trains. In one of the museums I visited, a display told the story of former slave Rose Jackson hiding in a box built into the wagon bed so she could come west with her former owner and their family. She had to hide in this tiny space all day as they traveled and could only come out at night when the coast was clear. She was my inspiration for Alma's story.

There were three exclusion acts—Peter Burnett's Lash Law called for African-Americans to be expelled from Oregon Country, and if they refused to go, they were to be lashed. The law was rescinded in 1845, when it was determined lashing was too harsh a punishment. The next exclusion law was passed in 1849 and stated that it was unlawful for any person of color to enter or reside in Oregon Territory. It was rescinded in 1854. The third and final exclusion act was passed in 1857 and was actually written into Oregon's Bill of Rights. The clause prohibited African-Americans from being in the state, owning property, and creating contracts. Oregon became the only free state admitted to the Union with an exclusion clause in its constitution. It wasn't repealed by voters until 1926, with the final racist language not removed until 2002.

While the exclusion laws were generally not enforced, they hung over the heads of African-Americans who feared that at any given moment, new laws might be passed to strip away their possessions and force them from the state. It discouraged African-Americans from moving west to Oregon, as they were often told that it was illegal for them to be there, despite the laws not being heavily enforced. This was especially driven home when the Fourteenth Amendment was up for ratification.

The Fourteenth Amendment, which grants citizenship to all people born or naturalized in the United States, including former slaves, was ratified in 1866. Oregon ratified with a very narrow margin and then, fearing the power being given to African-Americans, rescinded that ratification in 1868. The Fourteenth Amendment in Oregon was not re-ratified until 1973. They also refused to ratify the Fifteenth Amendment, which gave African-American men the right to vote. That law wasn't ratified in Oregon until 1959.

For more information on these topics, visit the following websites:

climate.washington.edu/stormking/January1880.html

www.salemhistory.net/education/willamette_university.htm

oregonencyclopedia.org/articles/exclusion_laws/

oregonencyclopedia.org/articles/14th_amendment/

oregonencyclopedia.org/articles/15th_amendment/

Helen Hunt Jackson is a real character from history. She was so deeply moved by the plight of the Native Americans that she wrote a book called *A Century of Dishonor*, even going so far as to send a copy to every member of Congress. Sadly, it had little impact, but Mrs. Jackson continued to lecture and write. Her biography by Valerie Sherer Mathes, *Helen Hunt Jackson and Her Indian Reform Legacy*, is just one excellent way to learn more about this woman.

As for the laws against and conflicts with Native Americans, we should remember that despite being born in the United States, Native Americans weren't given full citizenship until 1924, when President Calvin Coolidge signed the Indian Citizenship Act, also known as the Snyder Act. However, even then, Native Americans were not guaranteed the right to vote in every state until 1962. The third book in this series, *Forever By Your Side*, which releases in the fall of 2020, will speak more to some of the various laws and conflicts the Native Americans experienced in Oregon.

I have worked to be accurate with the details of history, even though some of them are quite appalling. I think it's important to remember the past to keep those travesties from being repeated.

Jesus made it very clear in the Bible that we were to honor two commandments that can be basically summed up like this: Love God. Love others (Matt. 22:37–39). Yet we continue to treat one another with hate and prejudice. My prayer is that in seeing the conflicts of the past, we might find ways to eliminate those conflicts in our time so that in the future we will be able to hear from God, "Well done, good and faithful servant."

This isn't about politics.

It's about following Jesus. Loving God. Loving others.

—Tracie

Tracie Peterson is the bestselling, award-winning author of more than one hundred novels. Tracie also teaches writing workshops at a variety of conferences on subjects such as inspirational romance and historical research. She and her family live in Montana. Learn more at www.traciepeterson.com.

Sign Up for Tracie's Newsletter!

Keep up to date with Tracie's news on book releases and events by signing up for her email list at traciepeterson.com.

More from Tracie Peterson

When her grandfather's health begins to decline, Havyn is determined to keep her family together. But everyone has secrets—including John, the hired stranger who recently arrived on their farm. To help out, Havyn starts singing at a local roadhouse—but dangerous eyes grow jealous as she and John grow closer. Will they realize the peril before it is too late?

Forever Hidden
THE TREASURES OF NOME #1

You May Also Like . . .

From Montana to London, this series follows an all-women traveling Wild West show, with trick riders and sharpshooters who are on a mission to solve a perplexing mystery and find freedom in a world run by men. Will they all be able to overcome their pasts and trust God to guide their futures?

BROOKSTONE BRIDES: *When You Are Near, Wherever You Go, What Comes My Way* by Tracie Peterson
traciepeterson.com

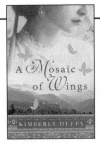

Determined to uphold her father's legacy, newly graduated Nora Shipley joins an entomology research expedition to India to prove herself in the field. In this spellbinding new land, Nora is faced with impossible choices—between saving a young Indian girl and saving her career, and between what she's always thought she wanted and the man she's come to love.

A Mosaic of Wings by Kimberly Duffy
kimberlyduffy.com

◊ BETHANYHOUSE

More from Bethany House

When Beatrix Waterbury's train is disrupted by a heist, scientist Norman Nesbit comes to her aid. After another encounter, he is swept up in the havoc she always seems to attract—including the attention of the men trying to steal his research—and they'll soon discover the curious way feelings can grow between two very different people in the midst of chaos.

Storing Up Trouble by Jen Turano
American Heiresses #3
jenturano.com

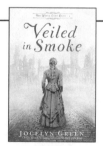

Ex-cavalry officer Matthew Hanger leads a band of mercenaries who defend the innocent, but when a rustler's bullet leaves one of them at death's door, they seek out help from Dr. Josephine Burkett. When Josephine's brother is abducted and she is caught in the crossfire, Matthew may have to sacrifice everything—even his team—to save her.

At Love's Command by Karen Witemeyer
Hanger's Horsemen #1
karenwitemeyer.com

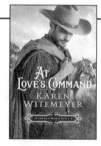

As Chicago's Great Fire destroys their bookshop, Meg and Sylvie Townsend make a harrowing escape from the flames with the help of reporter Nate Pierce. But the trouble doesn't end there—their father is committed to an asylum after being accused of murder, and they must prove his innocence before the asylum truly drives him mad.

Veiled in Smoke by Jocelyn Green
The Windy City Saga #1
jocelyngreen.com

BethanyHouse